Welcome to Montana—the home of bold men and daring women, where more than fifty tales of passion, adventure and intrigue unfold beneath the Big Sky. Don't miss a single one!

Montana ★ MAVERICKS™

JACKIE MERRITT

Sweet Talk

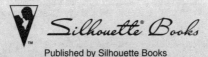

Silhouette Books

Published by Silhouette Books

America's Publisher of Contemporary Romance

Special thanks and acknowledgment to Jackie Merritt
for her contribution to the Montana Mavericks series.

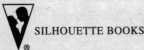 SILHOUETTE BOOKS

®

ISBN-13: 978-0-373-31073-9

PLEASE RECYCLE · THIS PRODUCT IS RECYCLABLE ·

Recycling programs
for this product may
not exist in your area.

SWEET TALK

Visit Silhouette Books at www.eHarlequin.com

Printed in U.S.A.

JACKIE MERRITT

is still writing, just not with the speed and constancy of years past. She and her husband are living in southern Nevada again, falling back on old habits of loving the long, warm or slightly cool winters and trying almost desperately to head north for the months of July and August, when the fiery sun bakes people and cacti alike.

Prologue

The Party, late May

She didn't normally go to parties, and she wondered what she was doing in Joe's Bar on a Saturday night with at least forty other people, the smell of booze and cigarette smoke assaulting her every breath and music she despised making her ears ring. She thought of her home, of her bed, of herself clad in soft pajamas and propped up with pillows against the headboard with the television on—sound turned down low— and a book on her lap. That was how she spent her evenings, not like this. It would be a cold day in hell before she let anyone—even her sister—talk her into attending another "birthday bash" at the local pub.

Val's gaze moved past the crowd at the bar to the jukebox in the corner. No one was listening to the teeth-jarring rhythms of the unidentifiable noise the machine produced, she thought resentfully, so why did they keep punching the same damn buttons?

"Enough," she muttered, and dug into her pocket for some coins. She might have to hang around this place a little longer, but she could at least do something about the awful music jangling her nerves. Armed with quarters, she left her table and wended her way through the crowd to the jukebox, where she studied the list of song titles for several minutes before finally spotting one she actually liked. She had just extended her hand to drop her quarters into the slot when someone jostled her from behind, causing her to drop the coins. She turned to give the person who had so rudely run into her a dirty look, but he or she had melted into the crowd.

Shaking her head in disgust, Val stooped down to look for the change. The floor was dark, she realized, much darker than the rest of the place. Hoping it wasn't too dirty, she got on her knees and began feeling around for the coins.

In mere moments she realized that a long, jeans-clad leg was very close to her head. She took in the costly cowboy boot below the hem of the jeans and let her eyes travel up the length of the leg, and then farther still, to an attractive white-on-white western shirt that was nicely filled out by an extremely good-looking man.

She knew who he was—Reed Kingsley—only because everyone in Rumor, Montana, recognized the town's fire chief, even if they weren't aware of his impressive family ties. There was nothing ordinary about Reed, especially his Romeo reputation. Val had heard that this guy went from woman to woman as most men changed shirts, which totally destroyed any interest she might have had in him—if she had been in the market for a man, which she wasn't, with very good reason. She no longer played silly games, thanks to that one awful day when her entire world had been torn apart. Reed was handsome and rich and involved in almost everything that went on in Rumor, but Val didn't care who the devil he was; he had usurped her place at the jukebox!

"Excuse me," she said coolly, and when he didn't immediately respond, added a highly sarcastic, "Hello?"

He looked around, saw her and grinned. "What're you doing on the floor?"

To hell with the quarters, Val thought, and got to her feet. "I dropped my coins. I *was* going to play H-32, but you took my turn, anyway, so to heck with the whole thing." She began walking away and was startled to feel his hand on her arm. She gave him a look that made him yank it back so fast it seemed to blur.

"Sorry," he said.

"Yes, you are," she retorted, and left him standing there with his mouth open. At her table again, she tossed out lies to the others seated there. She wasn't entirely sure of how she got out of Joe's so fast, but she was inside lying through her teeth one second and outside breathing fresh air the next.

Immensely relieved, she got in her vehicle and drove home.

Reed had rarely met a party he didn't like. Some were better than others, of course, depending on the people in attendance. But he enjoyed drinking a beer or two with friends, and there were very few people in Rumor that he didn't think of as a friend. Tonight's crowd at Joe's was a good bunch, he decided. Good friends, *old* friends, people he'd grown up with, for the most part.

But there were a few folks there he didn't know very well. One woman, in particular, Dr. Valerie Fairchild, Rumor's veterinarian, had been piquing his interest for some time now. They'd been introduced during a meeting of Rumor's business owners a while back, but she still acted as though she didn't know him when they ran into each other in a store or on the street. He was surprised to see her at Joe's tonight, and he watched for an opportunity to speak to her. Her trip to the jukebox seemed heaven sent. He ambled over slowly and got there just about the time she sank to her knees to pick up a dropped coin.

He pretended he didn't see her and began looking at the selections. When she said, "Excuse me," and then an extremely sarcastic, "Hello," he knew he'd irritated her in some way.

He put on his best grin and asked, "What are you doing on the floor?" He thought he had succeeded in sounding amicably amused but not patronizing, and looked for a smile on her strikingly beautiful face. He was sorely disappointed, for her parting remarks weren't friendly or even kind.

He rushed to apologize, and without thinking before acting, he put his hand on her arm. It was a huge mistake, for the look she laid on him made him feel as if he'd shriveled from his normal six feet to child-size.

"Sorry," he said quickly, hoping an immediate apology would alleviate her distress, which he didn't understand but felt responsible for.

Her reply, "Yes, you are," shocked him. He stood there like a ninny for a long moment, wondering what, exactly, she had meant with those three words.

But he knew. Deep down where it hurt, he knew. She had told him coldheartedly that she thought him to be a sorry specimen of humanity.

No one treated him that way, especially women. Doc Fairchild was a freezing-cold woman, one any man with a dram of good sense would give a wide berth, so why was he already trying—once again—to figure out a way to break through her icy exterior and reach her heart?

Chapter One

The wedding of Max Cantrell and Jinni Fairchild took place at the Rumor Community Church on Saturday, November 1, at 7:00 p.m. Valerie Fairchild was her sister's attendant and Michael, Max's son, all decked out in a gorgeous dark suit comparable to his father's, was best man. It was Michael's first experience with a wedding, Jinni had confided, and Val sensed strong emotion behind the youth's rather swaggering exterior. Obviously, Michael preferred that no one know how touched he was by this very adult affair.

Val understood exactly how the boy felt. She, too, was emotional. She had to bat her lashes every few moments to hold back tears. She didn't want to cry at Jinni's wedding, she wanted to be happy and joyful and smiling. Growing up, the Fairchild sisters had not been close at all, but when Jinni dropped everything in New York and came to Rumor to help out during Val's chemotherapy treatments, it had been the most pleasant surprise of Val's life.

Now the sisters were very close, and the frosting on the

cake was that Jinni had met Max Cantrell and they had fallen in love; Rumor, Montana, was now Jinni's home as much as it was Val's. It struck Val, while she stood there listening to Pastor Rayburn's kindly voice uniting her sister with the man she so dearly loved, that even when things looked darkest, there was often a ray of light on the horizon. Val's dark days had indeed been brightened by her sister's unexpected appearance. Jinni fairly glowed with her enjoyment of life, and she rarely had a negative word to say about anything. She had bolstered Val's spirits more times than Val could recall, and during their many conversations, hours spent talking and laughing, they had become true sisters.

"I now pronounce you man and wife," Pastor Rayburn said. Val sighed inwardly, feeling a spark of regret because the ceremony was over.

Max put his arms around his wife and kissed her. At that very moment, a wave of weakness—a backlash from her chemotherapy treatments—struck Valerie. No! she thought frantically. Not now! Given no choice in the matter, she sought someone to lean on. She took two shaky steps and grabbed Michael's arm. He looked at her as though she had sprouted horns.

"Bear with me," she whispered, comprehending his dismay. "I need to steal a bit of your strength…just for a moment or two."

"Uh, sure," he said, then remembered that Jinni's sister wasn't well. In fact, when he thought about it, there had been several instances of conversation about Dr. Fairchild doing battle with cancer. Just thinking the word sent icy fingers up Michael's spine, but he would crumble to dust right where he stood before letting this nice woman know that he was so easily rattled.

The guests in the small church left their seats to congratulate the newlyweds. Val managed to kiss her sister's cheek, then Max's, and to wish them every happiness before the crowd got to them.

"I'm fine now, Michael," she told him. "Thanks for the use of your arm."

"You can hang on to my arm anytime you, uh, need to."

Val saw the red stains on Michael's cheeks and adored the boy for his response. He always acted so tough and uncaring, but underneath his bored-with-it-all expression, his practiced glower, he was a sweet young man.

"You're a dear," she said with a soft smile. "I think you and I might be related now. Let me see. Jinni is now your stepmom and I'm her sister, so I think that makes me your stepaunt. What do you think?"

"Yeah, could be," Michael mumbled.

Val wanted to laugh, but for Michael's sake she didn't. The boy was well aware of Jinni's new status. He didn't have to call her Mom, but legally she was his stepmother. Val knew for a fact that Jinni was thrilled at gaining a son along with a truly marvelous husband, but Val could only guess at how Michael perceived the quite serious change in his life. Jinni was positive, and had said to her sister that she and Michael were developing a great relationship.

The church hadn't been full; only a dozen or so guests had been invited, as the Cantrell family wasn't exactly riding high these days. Max's mother was there, and Val noticed Michael gravitating toward her. Mrs. Cantrell was torn, Val could tell—happy for her eldest son, Max, and worried for her younger son, Guy, who was in jail, awaiting trial for the murder of his deceased wife, Wanda, and her lover, Morris Templeton.

There was not going to be a wedding reception, either. The Cantrells—with Jinni present—had discussed the event and decided that with Guy in such jeopardy they would eliminate any flamboyance. When the trial was over and Guy was freed—they were positive of the outcome, as they knew Guy could never harm, let alone murder, anyone—then they would throw a party that would knock the whole town's socks off. Jinni had ardently agreed with her future family.

While the newlyweds were kissed and congratulated by

everyone, Val dodged bodies, went to a pew and sat by herself. Watching the gaiety at the front of the church spill into the center aisle, she realized how much Jinni's family had expanded in the past few minutes. Val's family consisted of one person, Jinni, while her sister had Max, Michael, Mrs. Cantrell and Guy.

Val sighed quietly. She would never be a bride. She couldn't force herself to let a man get close no matter how clever his attempts. She'd been hit on many times since that horrible long-ago experience that still haunted her dreams. The extended therapy she had undergone after the incident had helped, of course, but she'd known from her first session that she would never regain her old confidence and be the carefree, flirtatious woman she'd been before that terrifying day. Absorbed wisdom from the best therapist money could hire had made her more or less whole again but it had also destroyed her affection for the opposite sex. She liked men, as long as they kept their distance.

It wasn't something she talked about; it was just who she was these days, a sexless being with a good career, a handful of friends and a sister that she had come to love very much.

But who wouldn't love Jinni? Val asked herself. She was so alive, so vibrant and beautiful. Jinni brought life into any room she entered. Was it any wonder that Max had fallen in love with her? The good citizens of Rumor had never met a sparkling dynamo like Jinni Fairchild, and she'd taken the place by storm. Now, of course, she was one of the townsfolk, and Val would bet anything that once Jinni and Max settled into their marriage, Jinni would become Rumor's leading hostess.

It was a pleasing thought, and Val was smiling when Jim and Estelle Worth approached her. These wonderful people had started out as employees, helping out when Val became ill, and had evolved very quickly into good friends. Both Jim and Estelle were retired, Jim from the U.S. Forest Service and Estelle from nursing. Jim was a big man with thick shoulders, a bit of a paunch and a full head of graying hair that would make many a younger man blanch in envy. Estelle was tall and thin—her dark hair also graying—and so full of cheerful energy that she appeared to bounce from one task to another. This great sixty-something couple still worked for Val, Jim in the Animal Hospital and Estelle in Val's home, and Val could talk with ease to each of them. Not about herself, of course, or her disturbing past, but Jim and Estelle had become parental figures to her. She truly loved them both.

"What a precious wedding," Estelle said with a nostalgic sigh, as though recalling her own wedding. Jim stood behind her and grinned. Maybe he, too, was remembering.

"Val, you look beautiful in that dress," Estelle said. "And Jinni's gown? Oh, my, I've never seen such lovely dresses in all my days. Where did you say they came from?"

"From New York City, Estelle. Jinni knows the designer. She called her, described what she would like shipped out, and we received the dresses two days later."

"And they fit perfectly." Her comment was a statement, not a question.

"With a nip and a tuck here and there, yes." Val could see that people were starting to leave the church. Max and Jinni were planning to fly to California and honeymoon at a fabulous resort, and it was time they headed out.

"I'm going to say goodbye, then I'll be ready to go," Val murmured while getting to her feet.

"We'll wait in the car," Jim called. "Take your time."

"Thanks, Jim." Val hurried to the happy newlyweds. Max was talking to a tall, well-dressed man, and Val barely noticed either of them while she took Jinni's hand and said with teary eyes and a catch in her voice, "You are the most stunning bride this little church has ever seen. Jinni, what can I say, except thank you for everything you've done for me. I don't need to tell you to be happy, because you always are."

Jinni blinked back her own tears. "You can be happy, too, sweetie. You just have to look at the bright side of life. We both know it's there, Val, but sometimes it isn't out in the open. You have to do a bit of searching to find it. Now, kiss me and say goodbye. We have to get a move on if we're going to make our flight.''

Smiling through her tears, Val kissed her sister's cheek, then turned to kiss Max. But instead of looking into Max's brilliant blue eyes she found herself looking into Reed Kingsley's brilliant *green* eyes. She was so startled that she let out a small gasp.

''Hello, Valerie,'' he said calmly.

''Hello,'' she answered, and twisted a bit to plant a quick kiss on Max's cheek. ''Have a wonderful honeymoon,'' she whispered, then backed away, turned and hurried down the aisle to the church's outer door. She was almost there, almost home free, when Reed caught up with her. He was a persistent cuss, obviously used to having his own way and unable to believe that a woman to whom he made overtures would not reciprocate. Val wasn't interested, and she wasn't about to explain to him or to any other man *why* she wasn't.

''Val, must you leave so quickly? Are you going straight home?'' Reed asked, while visions of getting to know this unusual woman, *really* getting to know her, danced in his head one more time. He didn't normally have to chase a woman for months and months to get a few words out of her. He could already tell that she wasn't going to be any nicer to him tonight than she usually was.

She slanted a glance at him over her right shoulder. ''Yes, I am. Good night.''

She had succeeded in putting him down once again, and it didn't help that he'd been right about her apparently irrevocable attitude toward him.

''Val,'' he said quietly, ''I only want to talk for a minute.'' He saw that his plea didn't move her, but he still held his breath until she spoke.

''I can't,'' she said coolly, politely. ''Sorry, but the Worths are waiting in their car for me.''

She left him standing there with a taken-aback look on his handsome face, which she dismissed with an annoyed toss of her head. He wasn't stupid, so why didn't he take the not-so-subtle hints she dropped every time they ran into each other? She hadn't known he would be at the wedding. Since he wasn't a close friend of Jinni's, he must be Max's business associate. Max, she knew from Jinni, had invited a few business buddies to the affair, the few who lived in the area.

Hell, maybe they played golf together. How would she know?

Val put Reed Kingsley out of her mind and walked to the Worths' car. As far as she was concerned, the evening was over. Jinni was married and her life with Max had already begun. It was a lovely thought, even if she didn't want the same thing for herself, Val conceded as she got into the car.

While Jim and Estelle took Val home, Reed, driving with a frown on his face, made a left on Main and considered stopping in at Joe's Bar, or maybe even pushing the envelope by going out to Beauties and the Beat strip joint. He nixed that idea almost at once; he would like some female company, but not with the gals who danced half-naked at the joint.

"Damn," he mumbled. This thing with Valerie Fairchild had crept up on him when he wasn't looking. He couldn't quite place the first time he'd seen her as a beautiful, sexy, desirable woman, but that seemingly irrevocable opinion had taken root without conscious direction from his brain. Now, it had grown into something that, considering Val's constant rejection, he'd be better off without.

The whole thing perplexed him. He had never been one to lose sleep over sex or romance or any other type of male-female relationship. He liked women—women of all ages, for that matter—and they liked him.

Except for Val. Why didn't she like him? Why, of all the women he knew, was she the one that had finally gotten under his skin? Was it because she played so hard to get?

"She's not playing at all," he muttered. "There's the problem." Rumor was a gossipy little town, and there was not one speck of gossip about Val and men, not old gossip, not new gossip. He'd wondered if her sexual preferences were with her own gender, but there wasn't any gossip about that, either. No, she was heterosexual, strikingly beautiful even if she did very little to enhance her looks, and simply didn't like him. She might be the one woman in his personal history who had truly gotten under his skin, but it was damn obvious that he hadn't gotten under hers.

Wasn't it time he called it quits? He'd had enough of Val's polite disregard of his very existence. There certainly was no shortage of available women in the area, and spinning his wheels over one who couldn't care less was utter nonsense. With that decision made, he told himself he already felt better.

But obviously he'd been driving on automatic pilot—his mind a million miles away—because he was long past The Getaway, a spa on the outskirts of town, before he realized that he'd left Rumor and Joe's Bar in the dust. Fine, he thought. He didn't want to drop into Joe's, anyway. Making a U-turn, he drove back down Main to Kingsley Avenue and swung a right.

He was going home, and the whole damn town would be old and gray before he turned himself inside out to get Val Fairchild's attention again.

Weatherwise, it was an incredible November. One perfect day rolled into another and another, each with brilliant sunshine and air so clear that whenever Val looked off into the distance, she felt the lovely, if unrealistic, sensation of limitless vision.

Bright, flaming colors had replaced the dark greens of the trees and bushes, and the unique smell of fall seemed to permeate Val's every cell. The residents of Rumor, Montana, had been enjoying the pleasures of a storybook, picture-perfect Indian summer for more than two months now.

People Val knew kept saying it wouldn't last, but they had started saying that in September and had repeated it almost constantly throughout October. Val took it a day at a time.

It couldn't last forever and no one with a lick of good sense really wanted it to. Last winter's drought had been the underlying cause of the summer's awful forest fire starting on Logan's Hill, and locals shuddered whenever someone mentioned that terrifying ordeal.

It was behind them now, but the barren, blackened hill, once so green and vibrant, was a strong reminder of the critical importance of a wet winter. It was really just a matter of time, people said with a nervous glance after praising the glorious weather of the day, as if to appease any bad-luck spirits that might be hovering in the immediate vicinity. After all, the long-range weather forecasters had predicted a hard winter, hadn't they? One of these mornings, someone would always say, the town would wake up to snow, or at least to a drenching rainfall.

It was neither snowing nor raining when Val awoke the morning of November 4; sunshine peeked through the slats of the vertical blinds at her bedroom windows, creating long, thin lines on the far wall. She opened her eyes and lay there thinking. Today was Election Day and she was going to vote if it killed her.

It wouldn't, of course, no more than her being part of Jinni's wedding had. Other than that one fleeting weak spell, she had come through it like a trooper. Still, she hadn't been really active since she was diagnosed with breast cancer. The whole thing had been a physically and emotionally draining ordeal, from the initial diagnosis to the day she'd heard her oncologist say, "There is no longer any sign of cancer, Valerie."

She had been trying very hard to believe it was true, trying almost desperately to trust in her doctor's prognosis, but she could not completely rid herself of doubt, fear and worry that it could come back. Every so often anxiety grabbed her in a viselike grip and wouldn't let go, sometimes for days. She hated when that happened, but she hadn't yet figured out a way to prevent the depressing occurrences. It was Jinni's opinion that Val's fear was a normal part of the healing process and would vanish in time. Val hoped so.

Lazily lying there, she found her thoughts drifting from her health concerns to the wonderful time Jinni and Max were undoubtedly having on their honeymoon, and then—for some unknown reason—to her parents. The Fairchilds hadn't been terrible parents, merely uninterested and self-absorbed. Wealthy and generous, they had sent their daughters to the best schools in the country, when neither had wanted to leave home.

It was one of the topics she and Jinni had discussed at great length. They'd finally decided that their parents, now deceased, had loved them in their own way; it simply wasn't the way kids needed to be loved.

"It's what turned you into an animal doc," Jinni had said matter-of-factly. "Pets love unconditionally. Neither of us got that from Mother and Dad."

"You could be right, but it didn't turn *you* into an animal doc," Val had wryly pointed out. She could have explained—or tried to explain—that veterinary school was the aftermath of the nightmarish episode that had nearly destroyed her at age twenty-two, followed by long-term psychiatric counseling. Working with animals, which she had always loved, had been her escape, Val had later realized. Her primary therapist had recognized that and pushed to get her headed in a productive direction. Veterinary school had given her a goal, a reason to go on, a nudge back to normalcy.

It had only worked to a certain point, however. Val saw herself as a divided personality now, with one part hiding behind the other. Her strong side could make friends with undemanding people—folks like Jim and Estelle—run her business, lovingly care for sick animals and put up a darn good front for anyone curious enough to wonder what made Dr. Fairchild tick. There really was only one person in Rumor with any genuine—or maybe unnatural—curiosity about her, Val knew, and there was no way she was going to let Reed

Kingsley get close enough to penetrate her facade of strength and get to her soft, vulnerable underbelly.

What she had to keep asking herself was why would a man who seemed to have it all bother with a woman like her? Had she ever given him more than a remote, polite smile? Or any reason to think she might be an easy mark? Never! He had to be flawed in some invisible way, which was one more reason to keep a safe distance between them. One of these days her disdain for his unwanted attentions would sink in. What in God's name had he thought she would do when he'd asked her at the church if she was going straight home—simper over the possibility of spending the rest of the evening with him? Maybe the rest of the night? What a jerk!

Snorting disgustedly, suddenly tired of dissecting life in general and herself specifically, she threw back the covers, got up and headed for the shower.

Twenty minutes later, dressed in jeans and a bright yellow cotton sweater, she walked into the kitchen and smiled at Estelle, who had arrived while Val was in the bathroom.

"Good morning. That coffee smells wonderful."

"I brought some homemade coffee cake for your breakfast. You're getting too skinny," Estelle said.

Val stuck her forefinger into the waistband of her jeans and pulled it away from her body. There was about a two-inch gap. "These used to be tight," she said.

"Well, you're not eating enough. Sit down and I'll fix you some eggs to go with that coffee cake."

Val let her. Sometimes she liked being fussed over, and Estelle was a natural-born mother, certainly one of the kindest women Val had ever met. It had been a lucky day, indeed, when Jim and Estelle Worth had knocked on her door with a copy of the *Rumor Mill,* in which Val had placed a help-wanted ad.

Holding her cup of coffee in both hands, with her elbows on the table, Val asked, "Did you ride in with Jim today, or did you drive your own car?"

"I rode with Jim. Now, don't you go worrying about a thing over at the clinic. I'm sure Jim has everything under control."

Val smiled. "I'm sure he does."

"We came in early to vote. Already did it."

"Well, that's where I'm going right after breakfast."

"Glad to hear it. Oh, are you feeling up to a bit of shopping? We need some things if I'm going to do any real cooking today. Jim can do it if you're not feeling well today."

"I'm feeling fine, Estelle. Write up a list. I'll take it with me and go to MonMart right after I vote."

"Wonderful. I like seeing you getting out and about."

"I like it, too," Val murmured.

She looked out the window while she ate Estelle's delicious scrambled eggs and homemade coffee cake. Her yard looked like fall. Mums and marigolds, the hardiest of plants, still bore scattered blooms, but there'd been enough heavy frosts at night to decimate everyone's flower gardens. Still, it was her yard and she loved it, just as she loved her house. Jinni had thought the ranch house quaint when she first saw it, but Val thought it perfect for Rumor.

After vet school she had looked for a place to move and set up a practice. She'd found an ad in a trade journal that piqued her interest—an established small-animal clinic in a small town in Montana. After calling the man who was selling and bombarding him with questions, she had made the trip to Rumor and looked everything over for herself. Indeed, the town was small. She had never lived in a town without stoplights and heavy traffic, and Rumor, along with its surrounding countryside boasting so much incredible scenery, had struck Val as utterly charming. Money was not one of her problems; her parents had left her and Jinni very well off. She had made an offer for the clinic, which the owner accepted, and the day she'd arrived in Rumor she had looked for a reputable building contractor. The rather run-down clinic had become the modern and attractive Animal Hospital, and while those renovations were going on, her house had been built on the vacant land that had been included in her purchase.

So she had never thought of her house as quaint; to her it was warm and cozy and comfortable. Jinni would be much happier living in Max Cantrell's fabulous mansion than she could ever be in a cozy little ranch house like this one, Val knew, but for her needs it was perfect.

Finished with breakfast, she got up and carried her dishes to the sink. Estelle immediately tut-tutted. "If you do the work around here, what do you need me for? Here's the grocery list. Go vote and have a good time shopping."

Laughing, Val took the list and went for her purse. Before leaving the house she told Estelle, "I'm going over to the clinic for a minute to check on those pups born yesterday. Then I'll be gone...probably for a couple hours."

"Take your time," Estelle advised. "Relax and enjoy the day. It's another beauty, and this weather won't last much longer."

Everyone said it, over and over again. Chuckling under her breath, Val left the house and walked toward her animal clinic. *Everything* might not be perfect in her world, but she was thankful for what was.

Chapter Two

Life was good for Reed Kingsley, and he knew it. He also knew that if some calamity should suddenly destroy his parents' great wealth, and his own, he would still have a good life. Reed believed that his greatest personal asset was a genuine fondness for the human race. In simple terms, he liked people.

Reed considered his having grown up on a ranch to be a stroke of luck, since he had loved country living from the time he was big enough to sit a horse. In his heart, though, he believed he would have derived a connection to the land if home had been a two-acre operation instead of the many thousands making up the Kingsley Ranch.

That attitude wasn't due to a lack of respect for his family's good fortune. Nothing had ever been handed to the Kingsleys free of charge. The family had worked hard to make their ranch successful, and the fact that it was the biggest and most productive in the area was merely a result of their efforts.

Now, of course, the elder Kingsleys were able to enjoy the fruits of their labor. At age sixty-five, Stratton, Reed's father, still mounted a horse and checked on the herds of healthy, hardy cattle in his fields, but not with the dedicated regularity of his early years. Stratton was becoming a gentleman rancher, a little more so each year. He had good men working for him, young cowboys full of vinegar, and the rides he took these days were more for enjoyment than necessity.

Then, too, he had MonMart on his mind. The immense discount store in Rumor was the flagship for what would soon become a national chain. Russell, Reed's older brother, was the driving force behind MonMart's inception and rapid expansion. Stratton was content to leave the kudos for MonMart's astounding success to Russell—and most of the enormous responsibility, as well. He showed up at the administrative offices just often enough to keep his fingers in the pot and let everyone know that he backed his eldest son one hundred percent.

Reed couldn't boast of anything as audacious as MonMart as a personal accomplishment, but then, he wasn't the spitting image of his father, either, as Russell was. Russell could talk cattle, horses, land, irrigation and anything else that went with ranching but it was all business to him. To Reed the land was so much more than a means to make money.

Reed had never envied Russell's business acumen or his younger brother Taggart's long-ago declared and seemingly permanent independence from the family coffers. Tag was happily married and made his living as a carpenter—an extremely competent carpenter, by all accounts. In his own way, Tag was as much of a success as Russell, their father and Reed himself.

Reed also had a sister, Maura, and he considered Jeff Forsythe, who'd been in the family since age six, as another brother. All the Kingsley kids were married or engaged, except for Reed. Not that it bothered him to be the only holdout. After all, his siblings had fallen in love and he hadn't. He sure wasn't going to get hitched just to join the pack.

Besides, he was happy as he was, content with his routines. For instance, he drove from his house—built awhile back on Kingsley land, same as Russell's house was—to his parents' home for early morning coffee. Carolyn, his mother, sometimes slept in, but usually she was up and active, planning her day and willing to talk about it. Stratton was always awake early, usually with plenty to say about the ranch, the MonMart chain, the family, the national and global news, or any other subject that might arise. It was a good way to start the day, and Reed rarely missed a morning.

Sometimes he did work at the ranch for his dad, and after that he drove to Rumor and put in a few hours at MonMart. Russell seemed to appreciate his input, and Reed enjoyed his time at the superstore.

Then he almost always went by the volunteer fire station. He was Rumor's fire chief and even when no one else was at the station, he liked checking equipment and making sure everything was in order. Last summer's fire had devastated the landscape for miles around and could have been worse; it could have turned and destroyed the town. It was a sobering thought, and Reed knew that while he'd always taken his job as fire chief seriously, the Rumor fire intensified his dedication to civic duty hugely.

This morning, Election Day, he drank coffee with his folks and discussed the candidates on the ballot. Around nine he drove to the Rumor courthouse, where voting booths had been set up in the lobby. He voted, then chatted with everyone he ran into, and finally turned his SUV back the way he'd come, toward MonMart. The superstore sat on twenty acres of lush, heavily treed land four miles from the center of town. Five acres were paved; the remaining acreage was gradually being turned into a park with bike paths and hiking trails. The store itself was Russell's baby, but the park was Reed's. Before the fire, his idea had been a good one. But after the conflagration that had blackened so much land south and southeast of town, it had mushroomed to greatness.

People already used the park, even though Reed didn't

consider it finished. Much of the underbrush had been cleared and some trails created, along with one bike path around the perimeter. But his plans included hiking trails crisscrossing the property, picnic areas, playgrounds for the younger set and a special area for youthful bikers and skateboarders. Also, he wanted to add plants and trees to spots of sparse vegetation. He had gone to the Billings office of the U.S. Forest Service and picked up several books and pamphlets about indigenous vegetation, so that along with what he already knew about the subject, he was able to lay out a sophisticated but sensible landscape blueprint.

His mother had become interested in the project and offered her services. Carolyn felt the town should be involved in both labor and finance. "People will feel a much stronger bond with the park if they help in some way to develop it, Reed," she had told him.

He couldn't disagree. His mother worked tirelessly for several fine charities, and he gladly turned over the financial end of the park's development to her. Rumor Park, as he thought of it—though he would really like someone to come up with a more meaningful name—was going to belong to the people of Rumor. Once completed, it would be ceremoniously presented to the town. In the meantime, Carolyn was seeking the approval and assistance of state and national environmental groups and, to arouse further local interest and enthusiasm for the project, was planning a Christmas ball. It would be a swank affair—the likes of which had never before been seen in Rumor—and would be held in enormous, heated tents set up on a good-size area of MonMart's parking lot. The decorations were going to be spectacular, and tickets were already sold out.

Reed grinned when he pulled into MonMart's busy parking lot and envisioned the glamorous event, which was scheduled for the second week of December. The bank account that had been opened for park funds contained a large sum of money, and by spring, Rumor Park would be finished. Just thinking about it delivered a thrill to his system. He loved being involved in community affairs, and he sometimes wondered if he shouldn't run for public office.

But then he would be tied to one job, and ever since high school he'd been happiest when juggling a dozen different duties and responsibilities.

After parking in the employees' lot to the right of the store, he went in, whistling between his teeth. He felt so good it had to be a crime, he thought, grinning at the first person he saw. The young woman smiled back and said, "Good morning, Mr. Kingsley."

"'Morning, Lois." He went upstairs to the administration offices and stopped in at the video room, where a security officer kept an eye on a dozen monitors, the output of the surveillance cameras placed around the store. It was too bad that retailers had to guard against theft, but shoplifting was a national scandal, and even in a nice little town like Rumor some people couldn't resist the temptation of sneaking goods into a pocket or handbag.

"How's it going this morning?" Reed jauntily asked Homer, the computer whiz manning the equipment today.

"Same as always," Homer replied with a big grin. "Busy downstairs. Looks like folks are getting an early start on Christmas shopping this year."

Reed glanced at the monitors and nodded. "It does, doesn't it? Goods have been pouring in and going out so fast it's a race to keep the shelves stocked."

"Well, you can't knock success," Homer drawled.

"Nope, sure can't." Reed made a move to leave, but then stopped short. He narrowed his eyes on a screen and bent closer to it. Was that woman in aisle twelve Valerie Fairchild? It was! His pulse quickened. Went a little bit wild, actually. Just the sight of her shopping made his blood run faster. He remembered his vow to leave her be, to never put himself in the position of being turned down by her again, but clinging to that oath while watching her with his own eyes wasn't easy.

"What's so interesting?" Homer asked, and took a look

at the monitor Reed couldn't seem to tug his eyes away from. "Did you spot something?"

"Just someone I know." Reed pulled himself together. "See you later, Homer." He hurried out and went to his office. But instead of sitting at his desk and doing something productive, he paced the floor and thought about Val. He'd felt so damn good not ten minutes ago. Now he ached all over, and he resented losing his fabulous mood over something so mundane as Valerie Fairchild doing her weekly grocery shopping.

By damn, he had every right to walk any aisle in the place! If he just happened to run into her—it had happened before— what could she do but be nice?

Groaning over Valerie's polished ability to be nice and ice-cold at the same time, Reed told himself to forget it. To forget her! Why couldn't he? He'd known women who were more beautiful, possibly women with more sex appeal, but she was the one he couldn't get out of his mind.

Leaving his office to get himself a cup of coffee at the snack bar down the hall, he passed the surveillance room and couldn't resist checking the monitors again to see where Val was now. Homer looked at him curiously, but Reed ignored him and searched each monitor screen until he found her. She was in the canned goods aisle, and she was... Bending over, he peered more closely at the image. What *was* she doing? It looked as if she was leaning against the shelves, but why would...

It hit Reed like a ton of bricks. Running from the room, he took the stairs two at a time, then rushed through the store like a madman. Everyone in town knew that Dr. Fairchild was recovering from breast cancer, and obviously she wasn't fully recovered yet or she wouldn't be propped against a damn shelf!

Reed hit the aisle running, saw Val still leaning there with her eyes shut, and hurried toward her. Bending low enough to anchor his left arm behind her knees, he scooped her in the air.

Val was so startled she just hung on while Reed Kingsley hurriedly strode to the front of the store, leaving her cart of groceries behind. Everyone they passed stopped dead in their tracks to stare, and her fury sprouted and grew. She was so furious by the time they went through the large automatic doors and outside that she could have cheerfully murdered the odious jerk intent on saving her from…from what? My God, she thought, with tears burning her eyes, this incident would be the talk of the town in five minutes!

"Put me down," she said in a lethally low and hoarse voice, afraid that if she spoke with greater volume she would screech loud enough to wake the dead in the Rumor cemetery. She could feel her shoulder bag bumping against his leg as he walked, and wished it were sharp and pointed and beating a hole in his thigh. Maybe it was a cruel thought, but she had never been so embarrassed in her life.

"In a second," Reed said. "You need some fresh air." He kept going, heading for Val's bright blue SUV. He recognized most of the vehicles around town, so it was no great feat to pick out Val's in the nearly full parking lot.

People who were transferring purchases from carts to their vehicles stopped to study the sight of Reed Kingsley carrying Valerie Fairchild through the organized maze of parked cars and trucks.

While they gawked, Val seriously—hysterically—considered slapping Reed Kingsley silly, which was exactly what he deserved. But that would only give friends, neighbors and complete strangers something else to stare at. She wasn't helpless; she knew she could wriggle and squirm and *force* him to put her down. But that would create another scene, and some of these shoppers were pet owners who brought their cats and dogs to the Animal Hospital. They knew her as the animal doc. Years from now they would still think of her in this debasing situation whenever they brought Snookums or Buffy or Killer in for a shot or some other procedure. She would never live this down—not ever!

Her only usable weapon was her voice and she went for

it. "I wish I could think of some way to hate you more than I do at this moment," she said in the same deadly tone she'd used before.

Reed was so shocked he nearly dropped her. He stopped walking and let her feet slide to the pavement. "I…I sure as hell didn't do this to make you hate me," he mumbled.

She wasn't quite steady on her feet and reached out to the closest car, grabbing it for support. She had enough strength to glare into this wannabe rescuer's eyes, though, with a look in her own that could have curdled milk. "What in hell did you think was going on in there?" she spat.

"You looked faint. You're still pale."

"I am not pale, and I wasn't going to faint. How dare you humiliate me in front of the whole town? What do you do— imagine yourself as some kind of knight in shining armor, running around saving damsels in distress? You should be locked up!"

Reed was so shaken by her fury he could barely think at all, let alone come up with a reply. He'd honestly thought she needed help; obviously he'd made a huge mistake. He felt sick about it.

"I—I'm sorry," he stammered. "I really thought—"

"Go to hell!" She let go of the strange car and walked the short distance to her own.

"Wait! What about your groceries?" Reed called.

"Put everything back on the shelf or shove them where the sun don't shine! I wouldn't go back in there if the damn stuff was free!" Val got behind the wheel of her SUV, started the engine and backed out of her parking space. Her eyes were burning like fire, but that Kingsley jerk was still watching her and she would rather drown in her own salty tears than let him see her wiping them away.

Reed realized the enormity of his act when he returned to the store and found that everyone he met asked him what had happened. The incident would be the talk of the town for days, and he had smeared Val's reputation by assuming something that wasn't true. She *hadn't* been feeling faint, she'd coldly told him; she'd been…what? She'd denied without explaining, but what would cause a woman to lean against shelving in a store?

Mumbling evasive answers to the curious, Reed hurried toward the stairs to the second floor. But when he remembered Val's cart, he made a U-turn. It was right where she had left it. Right where he had *caused* her to leave it.

"Damn," he muttered under his breath. The basket was loaded with meat, vegetables, dairy products, fruit and bakery goods. She'd done a lot of shopping, probably filling a weekly grocery list. And there it all sat. Would she calm down and come back for it?

"She won't have to," he said under his breath, pushing the cart toward the front of the store. At the first available checkout stand, he unloaded the pile of groceries and told the clerk to put the cost on his account, bag it and have it delivered to his office. He wasn't sure what to do with it but he figured he'd think of something.

He did. When a bag boy—Joe Harte, who was juggling high school classes and his job, trying to save money for college—pushed a cart with five stuffed bags of food into his office about fifteen minutes later, Reed had a slip of paper ready. "Hi, Joe. You have a car, don't you?" he asked the young man.

"I have a pickup."

"That'll do. I'd like this order delivered to this address." He handed over the piece of paper. "Tell the supervisor you're doing me a favor so you don't get hassled about your absence, all right?"

"I'll take care of it, Mr. Kingsley." Joe left with the cart, heading for the elevator. Reed left, too, but he used the stairs, as he usually did.

Once in his vehicle he drove to town and straight to Jilly's Lilies. Jilly, the owner and his cousin Jeff's wife, wasn't in, but her teenaged assistant, Blake Cameron was there. After a hello and how are you, Reed ordered flowers and wrote a message on a card, which he put in an envelope. Blake promised delivery within two hours, and Reed left.

His day was ruined, and he neither returned to MonMart nor stopped at the volunteer fire station. Instead he drove home, went inside, threw himself on the couch, stared at the vaulted ceiling overhead and tortured himself with the memory of Val saying that she wished there was a way to hate him more than she already did.

The day that had started out so great had turned sour—horrible, actually—and he wasn't completely sure it was his fault. After all, he'd only tried to help. It was his nature to help anyone in need. Didn't Val know him at all?

Val had fought flooded eyes and blurred vision all the way home. She was so upset that her whole body trembled. This had to have been the most humiliating experience of her life, or at least the most humiliating since her move to Montana. But strangely enough, when she finally pulled into her driveway, she wasn't just angry with Reed Kingsley, the sophomoric jerk, she was furious with herself. Why had she said such terrible things to him? She never lost her temper, and she didn't tell people she hated them just because they annoyed the hell out of her.

She turned off the engine and sat there staring into space while her stomach churned and her hands shook. Rumor was her home. Her business was here and there was no place else she wanted to live. But this was Reed Kingsley's home, too, and Rumor was too small a town to completely avoid someone, especially if that person was hot on her trail, as he seemed to be. The man's tenacity was amazing. She had never given him an ounce of encouragement, yet he kept showing up and making her notice him. Why, for God's sake?

Groaning, Val opened the door of her SUV and got out. Estelle came outside and walked toward her. "I'll help carry in the groceries," she called.

Val's spirits dropped another notch. "There aren't any."

Estelle had gotten close enough to see her face clearly. "Oh, my God, you're pale as a sheet. What happened? Did you have a bad spell in the store? Well, don't worry about the groceries. I'll send Jim shopping later on."

Was she really pale? Val frowned and brought her trembling hands to her face, as though she could detect the color of her skin with her fingertips.

"And you're shaking like a leaf," Estelle exclaimed. She took Val by the arm. "You are going straight to bed, my friend. Obviously you need to rest a bit."

Val rarely argued with Estelle when it came to matters of health. The woman was a trained nurse working in the field all her life until retirement a few years back. She adhered to the common-sense school of medical treatment, and bed rest was high on her list of preferred remedies.

Besides, hiding in bed for the rest of this unnerving day held a massive amount of appeal for Val. She let herself be led along to her bedroom, and obediently undressed when Estelle asked if she wanted pajamas or a nightgown.

"Pajamas."

Estelle went into the bathroom and returned with a thermometer, which she stuck in Val's mouth, and a blood-pressure cuff she placed around her upper arm. Val sat quietly for the procedures, wishing that Jinni was back from her honeymoon. Her sister would know what to say about that debasing incident—probably something funny that would make Val feel like laughing instead of crying.

Estelle said, "Your blood pressure is fine." She took the thermometer. "So is your temperature."

"I only had one of those weak spells," Val said. "I'm not ill, Estelle."

"Well, I still think a little nap is in order."

"I doubt if I'll do any sleeping." But she was getting into her pajamas, and her big, comfortable bed looked very inviting. Estelle folded back the bedding and Val obligingly climbed in.

"Do you still have that grocery list?" Estelle asked.

Val slid her gaze to the right, to the window, just to avoid meeting Estelle's sharp eyes. She would hear about the incident—it was highly unlikely that anyone living within a twenty-mile radius of town would *miss* hearing about it—but Val couldn't bring herself to talk about it. Not yet, at any rate. It was still too new, too painful to think about, let alone attempt to explain why she had left her groceries in one of MonMart's busy aisles.

"It's in the pocket of my jeans…I believe," she murmured.

Estelle picked up the jeans from the chair Val had laid them on and dug into the pockets. "Here it is. Good. I'll have Jim go to MonMart later on." She went over to the window and shut the blinds, which darkened the room considerably. "You rest for at least an hour, hon," she told Val. "Call if you need anything."

"Thank you, Estelle."

"You're very welcome." The front doorbell chimed. "Now who can that be?" Estelle exclaimed as she hurried from the room.

Val's heart sank. If Reed Kingsley had dared to ring her doorbell, she was going to get out of this bed and—and… Well, she wasn't sure what she would do, but it wouldn't be pleasant. She sat up and listened intently, heard voices and movement in the house, but nothing she could pick up was distinct enough to enlighten her nervous curiosity. If it *was* Reed at her door, she thought with a sickish sensation in her stomach, she would probably do no more than yank the covers over her head and play dead. He wouldn't really have the gall, would he?

Estelle finally returned and she was wearing a huge, excited smile. "Well, I never," she began. "That was one of MonMart's bag boys, Joe Harte, with all of your groceries. Doesn't that beat all? He said that Mr. Kingsley asked him to deliver the food right away. It's all in the kitchen. I have to get busy putting it away."

Val was so dumbfounded she couldn't even mumble a reply. After Estelle's hasty departure Val's mind went into overdrive, and she yelled, "What about payment?"

Estelle didn't hear her, and Val lay back on the pillows and said again, this time at normal pitch and with an agonized ache throughout her entire system, "What about payment?"

It didn't take very much thought to figure out how those groceries had gotten from a cart in MonMart's canned goods aisle to her front door. She groaned, turned to her side, reached for some tissues from the box on her nightstand and let the tears flow.

She knew—she *knew,* that she could beg Reed Kingsley from now until doomsday to tell her the total cost of that food so she could write a check for it, and he wouldn't do it.

"Damn that man," she whispered. She didn't need his charity, and she didn't want his friendship, even though she doubted that friendship was the only thing on his mind. She was thirty-five years old and saw a worn-out, used-up human being every time she looked in a mirror. She used to be vivacious and pretty, very much like Jinni still was, but these days she was barely a shadow of her former self. Why on earth would a vibrant, handsome, wealthy man—a Kingsley, no less—notice her, let alone do his ever-loving best to get *her* to notice *him?*

Chapter Three

Val dried her eyes, got out of bed with an angry flounce, yanked on her clothes and went into the bathroom to wash her face. Hiding in bed, even at Estelle's advice, was cowardly and disgusting. She was fine and she had a business to run. People would talk about the MonMart incident until something better came along, and there was nothing she could do about it, so she might as well hold her head high and pretend not to notice.

She dabbed on a little lipstick, then, because her face really was pale, brushed some blusher on her cheeks. Her light brown hair was short, about jaw-length, and nicely cut. At least *she* liked the cut; whether anyone else did wasn't something she worried about, although when she'd come home from The Getaway with the new style Estelle had complimented her on it.

It really didn't matter. Val felt fortunate that her chemo treatments hadn't taken her hair. It was still thick and glossy and now it was short and swingy and, Val thought, quite becoming.

She grimaced at her reflection. Her hairdo, or any other woman's, would never make the Life's Significant Priorities list. She'd learned what was important and what wasn't the hard way, and hairstyles were absolutely meaningless in the overall scheme of things.

Val was on her way to the kitchen to let Estelle know that she was feeling good and going over to the clinic when the doorbell chimed again.

She blinked in disbelief. Standing on her stoop was Reed Kingsley with a huge bouquet of flowers and an almost tragic, puppy dog expression on his face.

"Valerie," he said as he released a long breath, which, apparently, he'd been holding. "I ordered these at Jilly's to be delivered as soon as possible, drove home, worried myself sick over what happened at MonMart, then rushed back to town to deliver them myself." He held out the bouquet. "Will you accept these flowers *and* my heartfelt apology?"

She looked at the flowers, at Reed, at the flowers, at Reed, then turned her face away and wished she had stayed in bed.

"Could I come in for a minute?" he asked, startling her further.

The man was a barnacle, she thought drearily. He had, for some reason of his own, attached himself to her, and she was never going to be free of him. It was a depressing thought, and if there was anything Val didn't need these days, it was something else to lower her already down-in-the-dumps spirits.

But how could she say, "No, you cannot come in, and I don't want either your flowers *or* your apology. Please leave and never darken my door again." The bottom line was she couldn't. Reed Kingsley might be the most annoying human being she knew but he was a man to reckon with in Rumor. He was one of the town's movers and shakers, and she certainly didn't need enemies in the business community—especially now. Business had slowed during her illness, with people taking their pets to Whitehorn or Billings because their local vet wasn't available. Next on her to-do agenda was to rebuild her reputation and her client list by putting a back-to-work announcement in the *Rumor Mill*—and, whether or not she liked it, accepting Reed's apologetic gesture.

She stepped back and swung the door open; it was silent permission to enter, and she hoped he didn't take her concession as any form of surrender. She was giving him nothing but a minute or two of her time. She hoped he understood that without her spelling it out in succinct terms.

Reed's heart pounded. He couldn't remember the last time he'd been nervous about entering a woman's home. He'd always been confident in his innate ability to talk to people, both men and women, and his lack of confidence with Val Fairchild was damn disturbing.

"Uh, maybe you'd like to take these," he said after she had closed the door.

She *wouldn't* like to take them; she didn't want them, but she forced herself to accept the bouquet and say, "Thank you."

"You're welcome. Val, I'd like to explain what happened today…explain why I did what I did."

"You already did that. In MonMart's parking lot." She saw Estelle peering around the kitchen doorway and held out the flowers. "Estelle, would you please put these in a vase?"

Smiling broadly, the housekeeper walked over and took the flowers from Val. "Oh, they're lovely. Hello, Reed, how are you?"

"Fine, Estelle, and you?"

"I really can't complain."

"And how's Jim?"

"Well, he has that arthritis, you know. It flares up every so often, but he's been just fine this fall. Hasn't this weather been remarkable?"

"Remarkable and a little scary. We've experienced the result of a dry winter firsthand, and we sure don't want a repeat of last summer's fire."

"Heavens, no," Estelle agreed with a small shudder. "We nearly lost our town."

"We came very close, Estelle."

Val had to bite her tongue to keep from rudely interrupting this friendly little exchange. Of course Estelle knew Reed Kingsley—*everyone* knew Reed Kingsley! She was probably the only person within a hundred-mile radius who didn't *want* to know him!

Estelle smiled and began easing away. "I'll put these in water. Nice seeing you, Reed."

"Nice seeing you, Estelle." He waited until she was back in the kitchen before he looked at Val again. "They're a great couple, aren't they?" he said. "I'm talking about Estelle and Jim, of course."

"I grasped that all on my own," Val said dryly. "Imagine that."

Reed's face reddened. "I never quite say the right thing to you, do I?" He tried to smile and knew it came off weak. "I think you make me nervous."

"I doubt if anyone makes you nervous, Mr. Kingsley."

"*Mr.* Kingsley? Can't you bring yourself to call me Reed?"

"Well, I can, of course, but since we hardly know each other…"

"That's not my fault."

"Meaning it's mine? Well, fine. I can live with that."

"I wasn't placing blame. But you said we hardly know each other and that's something I've been trying to rectify. We're not getting very far, though, are we, not when you object to using my first name because we're not bosom buddies. Val, very few people around here stand on ceremony. There's very little formality in and around Rumor." Reed felt his face heating up again. "You already know that, don't you? You've lived here long enough to know everything I do.''

''I doubt if I could ever catch up with you on anything,'' she said coolly, hoping he realized that the word *anything,* in this instance, was a blatant reference to his reputation with women. ''Nor, I might add, do I care to try. But since small-town informality seems so crucial to you, I'll use your first name.''

How long was he going to stand around her foyer with that hopeful look in his eyes? She hadn't invited him into the living room, offered him a chair or refreshments. She hadn't done *any* of the things folks in Rumor did when someone dropped in. Reed didn't take hints, obviously, and she was trying to avoid overt rudeness, but she was getting very close to it, all the same.

He cleared his throat. ''Getting back to that explanation I mentioned…''

''Really, there's nothing that needs saying. You thought I required rescuing and I didn't. It was an unfortunate incident. I'm sure we'll both live it down…eventually.'' Reed's expression turned sickly before her eyes, but she pretended not to notice.

''You really can't accept my apology, can you?'' he said, sounding miserable.

''I could lie and say yes. Would that appease your conscience?'' Inwardly she winced, as that remark and question had *definitely* been rude. But why didn't he accept her lack of interest and leave?

Reed decided it was time to go. She was a hard, dispassionate woman, impossible to get to know. Why did he keep trying?

''Well, enjoy the flowers,'' he said, speaking in a much cooler tone himself. ''And you have my promise that if I ever see you looking pale and leaning against shelves of green beans again, I'll walk right on past.''

Val's eyes widened in surprise. That was the first thing

he'd ever said to her that warranted respect. Apparently her disdain had finally sunk in.

"I'll hold you to that," she said, and opened the door for him. He gave her one last look and then hurried out. She shut the door behind him, mumbled, "Finally," and turned the dead bolt.

The snap of the lock was heard by both of them. It gave Val a sense of security and made Reed wince. He walked to his SUV with his head down.

Val went into the kitchen and tried to ignore the flowers Estelle was arranging in Val's best crystal vase. "I'm going over to the clinic, Estelle," she said.

"Okay, honey." The housekeeper stepped back to study her handiwork. "Aren't these just beautiful?"

"Lovely," Val murmured, trying to sound as though she cared. "Estelle, I picked out a great prime rib at MonMart. Was it part of the delivery?" Her hand suddenly leaped to her lips. "Oh, hell," she moaned. "Why didn't I make that man tell me the cost of all that food? I never even thought of it."

"That man's name is Reed Kingsley," Estelle said dryly.

"I know his name. But I wish I didn't."

Estelle's eyes widened. "For heaven's sake, why not? Everyone likes Reed."

"Not everyone. Estelle, was that prime rib delivered?"

"Yes, it's in the refrigerator. I was going to ask if you wanted it in the freezer."

"I want it in the oven, if you don't mind cooking it, that is. And I'd like you and Jim to stay for dinner and help me eat it."

"Well, that would be nice. When you see Jim, ask him if he has other plans. I don't, but you never know what's on his mind."

"And you don't accept invitations without his say-so," Val said quietly.

Estelle smiled. "Of course not."

Val would never point out that Estelle often let Jim's plans come before hers, because they were truly the happiest married couple she'd ever known, and it certainly wasn't her place to point out what she considered to be a few small inequities in the relationship. She had wondered, since getting to know the Worths, how their marriage had survived for so long, when so many others did not. One thing she'd noticed repeatedly was that Estelle and Jim truly seemed to like each other. There were deeper affections between them—Val could sense that—but their liking was out in the open and pleasant to be around.

"I'll talk to Jim about it and let you know."

"Good." Estelle returned to her flower arranging and picked up a perfect pink rose. "Oh, my, this is lovely. Honey, are you sure you're feeling well enough to go over there today?" she asked with her back to Val.

"I'm sure. Talk to you later."

"You take care now, you hear?"

"Yes, Mother."

Estelle was chuckling when Val left the kitchen and then the house.

Reed felt at such loose ends that none of his normal activities held any appeal. He didn't want to return to MonMart and sit at a desk, he didn't want to go home and walk the floor again, nor did he want to stop in at the fire station. That really threw him. He always derived personal satisfaction and enjoyment from checking equipment and chin-wagging with any of the volunteers who happened to be there. Not today.

After leaving Val's home, he drove around town with a knot in his gut and tried to find some focus. All he could think about were her cutting remarks, the ice in her voice, the disdain in her beautiful aqua-blue eyes…all aimed at him. If he had fallen over dead in her foyer, she would have stepped around his lifeless body as though it weren't there.

He was nothing to her, less important than the dirt under her feet.

How could that be? He had never been anything but nice to her. Did she sense something sexual in his feelings for her, loath the idea and want to make darn sure that she didn't encourage it?

Trouble was, she encouraged feelings of that nature without realizing it. The chemistry between them was overwhelming and nearly swamped him every time he was within fifty feet of her, even though she obviously noticed none of it.

Reed ended up back at MonMart, but he didn't go into the superstore. Instead, he headed for the unfinished park behind it and took a long meandering hike.

It helped.

Val called the house from her office at the Animal Hospital. "Estelle, Jim said prime rib for dinner sounded great. We're on, okay?"

"Great. We'll eat around six. I'm going to make mashed potatoes and gravy. You need some fattening up."

"I happen to like being thinner."

"Your clothes are practically falling off. You either have to put on some weight or go shopping."

"Maybe I'll go shopping. See you later."

Jim came in just as Val was hanging up. "Did you call the paper yet? You said to remind you."

"All taken care of. The announcement will appear in tomorrow's newspaper and continue for a week. I think a week should do it, don't you?"

"It should," Jim agreed.

Michael Cantrell walked into the sheriff's office and up to the deputy on desk duty. "I want to see my uncle."

"Again? Don't you have better things to do than hang around a jailbird?"

"He's not a jailbird. He's innocent."

"Invisible, too, huh?" Several of the deputies loved kidding Michael about Guy's invisibility story. Guy had told the whole story at a community gathering held in MonMart's parking lot just before his arrest for the murders of his wife and her boyfriend. Guy had explained how the fire had started on Logan's Hill, and how he'd been knocked unconscious by his wife's lover, only to realize when he came to that he was invisible. He'd been splashed with his formula for the rapid healing of burn scars. Invisibility was an unforeseeable, temporary side effect of the formula, and he'd been as stunned by it as the townspeople, considering they had stared at him with their mouths open.

Michael flushed hotly. "He's not invisible now." He added defensively, "But he was."

"Yeah, me too. Helps keep the laundry down."

"You're not funny," Michael mumbled, red-faced.

The deputy chuckled. "Sure I am."

Sheriff Holt Tanner came in. "Hank, let the boy see his uncle!"

"I was just funnin' him, Holt."

"Well, stop funnin' him and move Guy from his cell to the visitor's room."

The deputy walked off, still chuckling, and Michael nervously shifted from foot to foot while waiting for word that he could go back to the visitor's room. When the deputy returned and escorted him there, Michael saw his uncle sitting on one side of a long table in handcuffs. He took a chair on the other side of the table and waited until the deputy left the room and locked the door.

Then he said, with tears in his eyes, "Hi, Unk. How you doing?" *Unk* was what he had called Guy since childhood, since realizing that his uncle was a brilliant scientist and so was he. Well, maybe not brilliant yet, but he would be. Someday.

Although Guy didn't feel in the least like smiling, he

smiled for his fifteen-year-old nephew, whom he loved like a son. "I don't want you worrying about me, Michael."

"I know, Unk."

"But I really appreciate your visits," Guy said quietly. He forced another smile. "Now, tell me what's happening in Rumor. Have you heard from your dad and his new wife? When are they due back from their honeymoon? And how's Ma taking all of this? You're still staying with your grandmother, aren't you? Until your dad gets home? Tell me everything, Michael."

"Mostly people are talking about your formula, even though no one understands it," Michael said.

"You know something, Michael? I don't understand it, either."

Dinner was delicious. Estelle was a good cook and the prime rib was roasted to tender, juicy perfection. The numerous side dishes were as tasty as food could be, and Val truly tried to do justice to the wonderful meal.

But after a few bites of the small portions she had taken, her appetite was fully satisfied. She took a swallow of the iced tea Estelle had also prepared.

"I made an applesauce cake for dessert," Estelle said. "I know you like that."

"Estelle, I liked the whole meal. I'm full."

"Well, I'm sure you can squeeze in a small piece of cake."

"Absolutely, but not right now. You two finish eating. Just because I can't get another bite down my gullet doesn't mean you can't enjoy the rest of your dinner. I'll sit here with my tea, all right?"

"Well, you're too thin and you're not eating enough, but I guess if you're full, you're full."

"Leave her be, sweetheart," Jim said. "She looks fine the way she is."

Val smiled. "Thanks, Jim."

"I think Reed Kingsley agrees with you," Estelle said rather pertly to her husband.

Val's smile vanished, a dead giveaway to her sudden discomfort. "Let's not talk about him," she said quickly.

"Is ol' Reed on your trail?" Jim asked in a teasing way. "When did that start?"

"He is *not* on my trail! For heaven's sake, he's the biggest pest this side of the Mississippi. And he embarrassed me to tears in MonMart today. If he has any silly ideas about me, he might as well get rid of them."

Estelle put down her fork. "What do you mean, he embarrassed you?"

Val sighed. "I might as well tell you about it. I'm sure it's the main topic of conversation at every dinner table in town." In as few words as possible, she related the still-embarrassing incident.

"Well!" Estelle exclaimed. "That certainly explains that grocery delivery. *And* that hundred dollar bouquet of flowers sitting over there."

They all looked at the vase of flowers on the dining room sideboard, where Estelle had placed it. "So we can enjoy these lovely flowers while we eat," she had said.

Estelle cocked her left eyebrow and met her husband's curious eyes. "Delivered by Reed himself, in case you're wondering."

Val felt resentment for the man again churning her insides. "I don't even like cut flowers in the house."

"Oh, you do, too," Estelle declared. "Jinni always had a vase of flowers in your room when you were feeling ill, and you loved looking at them. You said you did, anyway."

Val heaved a sigh. "Okay, fine, I *do* like flowers in the house, but I don't like Reed Kingsley's flowers."

"Now, that makes sense," Estelle said dryly. "Should I throw them out?"

"I'll do that myself. Let's talk about something else. Jim, I think those pups might be full-blooded Labs."

"Well, the mother sure is. Why in heck someone would desert a nice dog like her sure beats me."

The female Labrador had been hanging around the Animal Hospital for several days before Jim brought her inside. He'd been putting food out for her because she obviously had no home.

Val had then examined her and told Jim to put her in the Dog House to await the birth of her pups—the large area designed and constructed for the care and kenneling of dogs. The Animal Hospital also had a Cat House. That name often tickled Jim's funny bone, which it had done to Val, too, when she'd thought it up and had signs made for both of the kennel areas.

They all chatted about the animals presently under Val's care until the end of the meal. Jim and Estelle had a slice of cake with a dollop of whipped cream on it, but Val just sipped her tea and waited for them to finish.

"I'll take care of the dishes," she told Estelle. "You did enough today."

"Well…the pans I used are already washed and put away. I suppose putting the dishes into the dishwasher wouldn't be too strenuous for you. All right, we'll go on home. Come on, Jim, I'm just about ready for bed."

Val rose from her chair. "You worked hard all day. You always do much more than I pay you to do, Estelle."

The older woman waved her hand. "We'll have none of that now. I know my limits and I rarely overdo."

"This house was never kept as clean as it's been since you took over," Val said.

"Well, I do like things clean and smelling good."

Val followed Estelle and Jim around until they had collected their things and left through the back door. Immediately Val felt the silence of the house, but she didn't mind it. Sometimes she liked being alone, which had a lot to do with why she had bought her cabin in the mountains. Whenever she felt crushed under the weight of old memories or current problems, she drove the eighty miles to the cabin and absorbed the peace and quiet for a weekend.

She'd been thinking a lot about her rustic cabin lately, and she considered going to the mountains this coming weekend. She was well enough now to make the drive, wasn't she? If only those darn weak spells would stop. She'd discussed them with her doctor, and he'd told her they were normal and would gradually subside.

Okay, she decided, I'll go to the cabin this weekend if there are no more spells this week. If there are, then maybe I'll put it off for another week.

Val was in the kitchen, wiping down the counters and the front of the appliances, when something on the floor caught her eye. It was small and white and lying under the edge of a cabinet. Estelle had obviously missed seeing it or it wouldn't be there. Val bent over and picked it up. It was a small envelope with a Jilly's Lilies logo in the upper left corner, and it was sealed.

Obviously it had come with the flowers and fallen to the floor before Estelle had seen it. Frowning, because it of course contained a message from Reed Kingsley, Val thought about tossing it in the trash without opening it.

She couldn't quite do that, and grimacing over what could only be described as plain nosiness, she slit the tiny envelope open with a knife and extracted the card. Embossed at the very top of it were two words: *Sweet Talk.*

Val moved to a chair and sank down on it. Sweet Talk. For God's sake, why would Reed Kingsley pick out a card with that heading? Below it, of course, was some handwriting—his, obviously.

Val, I can sweet-talk with the best of them but, strangely, not with you. Still, I keep wishing you'd give me the chance to try sometime. Anytime. Forgive my transgressions, if you can, and let yourself see the real me. Reed K.

Groaning, Val put her arms on the table and her head on them. He wanted to "sweet-talk" her? Why? Damn it, why?

Chapter Four

Val's announcement appeared in the morning newspaper, and the phone at the Animal Hospital started ringing before she even opened the place for business. When she walked into her office there were messages on her answering machine, and she pushed the Play button to hear them.

"Dr. Fairchild, this is Ruth Machler. I'm so pleased you're feeling better. I'm sure you recall my little dog, Spotty. He's fine right now and doesn't need an appointment, but I just had to let you know how relieved I am to hear you're all right."

"Good morning, Valerie. This is Harry Lund. So glad you're in good health again. My family and I prayed for you all during your ordeal. Valerie, I was going to drive Pumpkin to Whitehorn to have her teeth cleaned, but I would much rather bring her to you. I'd like to make an appointment for tomorrow, if possible. Please let me know."

"Hello, Doc. My heavens but I was delighted to read that announcement in the paper this morning. I, and many of my friends, were so worried about you. I can't begin to describe how thrilled we all are that you beat that dreadful illness and are back to work full-time.''

The messages went on and on, almost every one of them conveying worry for her health and gladness that she was well again. The kindness and consideration of the community—some who left messages *weren't* customers—stunned Valerie. She sat at her desk in amazement while the messages played one after another.

Jim walked in and realized what was going on. He sat down and listened, and after the machine switched off, he smiled. ''Sounds like Rumor loves you, Doc.''

Before Val could reply to his remark, the telephone rang. She reached for it but didn't pick it up immediately. ''I…I'm truly touched, Jim,'' she said with a catch in her voice.

He nodded and got to his feet. ''The dogs and cats are fed. I'm going to clean out the kennels now. Is there anything special you want done this morning?''

''Not that I can think of. Thanks, Jim. Catch you later.'' She picked up the phone and said, ''Animal Hospital.''

It was a busy, stimulating day. People dropped in with their pets, some without a pet. Val felt very much as she had during those quite enjoyable years when she'd been as close to genuine happiness as she'd ever expected to get. She hadn't asked a lot out of life for a very long time; working with animals, and having her own home and veterinary practice, had been enough. And it had never occurred to her that something might be missing in her day-to-day existence.

Now she wondered about that, although she wasn't at all thrilled with the notion that a silly, certainly unsolicited message about sweet talk on a florist's card could actually make her rethink all that she'd made of her life. She did know, however, that an element she'd never expected to intrude upon her peace of mind was now doing exactly that. Behind conversations, tasks, almost every single thing that took place all day, lay the knowledge that instead of throwing that ridiculous little card in the trash last night, she had buried it under some filmy garments in a drawer of lingerie in her bedroom. Why hadn't she stuck the damn card in a drawer of sweaters?

Around three that afternoon her strength gave out. Exhausted, she asked Jim to please take over; she had to go to the house and lie down for a few minutes.

He agreed at once, of course, and Val told him to call the house should an emergency arise that required professional attention. Again he agreed, then he watched her leave with a concerned and caring frown on his weathered face. Val had become like a daughter to him and Estelle. The two of them had talked about their mutual affection for Valerie Fairchild many times. They liked Jinni, as well, but Jinni could take care of herself. There was something about Val that tugged at their heartstrings. She had never explained her past to them, but they felt certain something bad had happened to cause that bleak look to appear in her beautiful eyes every so often.

They had each seen it, discussed it, surmised all sorts of scenarios and worried themselves half to death over it. But they really knew nothing concrete about Val's past, and they didn't let themselves count on knowing more in the future, as their dear Val was a very private woman.

Heaving a sigh, Jim left to get some work done.

Val walked from the clinic to her house and went in through the back door. Estelle had left early; she had done so much in the house yesterday there'd been no reason for her to stay today. Val went directly to her bedroom, took off her shoes and fell across her bed. She was truly done in, and she closed her eyes and breathed a long sigh of relief just because it felt so good to be lying down.

Then she thought of Reed's card again, and her eyes flew open. Something told her that when he'd decided to deliver the flowers himself, he hadn't realized that the card he'd written earlier was attached to the bouquet. It hadn't been in plain sight, or Estelle would have seen it. Since her sharp eyes hadn't spotted it, it seemed sensible to conclude that neither had Reed's.

Val realized that she was thinking of that man by his first name. He had succeeded in burrowing into her psyche deeply enough to make himself a real person to her, a real *male* person!

She groaned, got off of the bed and went to her lingerie drawer, where she pulled out the card, stared daggers at it for a moment, then stuck it in the bottom drawer of the dresser, underneath some old sweatpants and tops. That damn card didn't belong next to her panties, bras or pretty night-gowns. She really should rip it to pieces and toss it in the trash.

But she didn't. She returned to the bed, lay down again and did her best not to think of that discomfiting card *or* of the man who had written it.

She wasn't very successful. It had been ages since she'd dwelled on a man's looks, but in her wild and woolly youth she had always been drawn to men with dark hair. Not too many of them had had green eyes, though. Black hair and green eyes…and a handsome face and a remarkable, trim body and long legs and a terrific smile and…

"Damn it, that's enough!" she shouted, glad that she was alone in the house so she *could* shout. She was *not* attracted to Reed Kingsley. She wasn't! He'd just better stay away from her or she was apt to lose her temper and embarrass both of them.

Besides, there had to be something wrong with a man who didn't comprehend blatant hints. How rude would she have to be before he finally figured out she wasn't interested and gave up for good?

On Friday afternoon Jinni came barreling into Val's office wearing a new designer outfit and a smile as big as all out-doors. Val got out of her chair and hurried around her desk. They hugged and Jinni delivered a big smooch to her sister's cheek.

"It's so good to see you. Mind you, I didn't miss you—much—while Max and I were in California. Hardly had time to think of anything but Max, and I guess I shouldn't apologize for that, should I? Poor Max had Guy on his mind a lot, but I expected that. The Cantrells are terribly torn up over Guy having been arrested for murder, and who can blame them? They all believe he's completely innocent, you know.

"Oh, Val, you really must give yourself a treat sometime and go to that resort Max took me to. It's truly fabulous...as posh as any resort I've ever visited. What a honeymoon! Every woman should be so lucky. Val, you look a bit peaked. Are you all right?"

"Heavens, you can talk fast when you want to. I'm fine, and I don't want you hovering and worrying because I look peaked, which I don't."

"Oh, really? I think I know if you look peaked or not, and you look peaked. What've you been doing, working day and night in this place?"

"I have not been overdoing it, Jinni. Ask Jim, if you don't believe me."

"All right, I believe you. But you could use a few pounds and some color in those cheeks. And I want a straight answer to one question. Are you still having those weak spells?"

"Only once in a while. They're going away, just as the doctor said they would. Sit down and tell me about your honeymoon."

"I can't today. I have a ton of luggage to unpack...we only got home an hour ago. But I promise to tell you everything—" Jinni grinned devilishly "—or *almost* everything next week. How about lunch on Monday?"

"Sounds wonderful. At the Rooftop Café? If this weather holds, we could eat outside."

"The Rooftop it is. I'll pick you up around one on Monday. Okay, I must be off. I just had to see you, if only for a minute."

The sisters hugged again and Jinni left in a flurry of chatter and expensive perfume. Smiling to herself, very glad that her sister was back in Rumor, Val returned to her desk. Before the wedding, Jinni had told her that the honeymoon was going to be short and sweet; Max was too concerned with Guy's situation to be away for very long. Val suspected that Jinni and Max were so much in love that their honeymoon would go on for a very long time right here in Rumor, and if there was any true happiness in her system these days, it was all for Jinni.

Val knew one thing for certain: Jinni could do all the talking during their lunch at the Rooftop Café on Monday. Val would enjoy hearing about California and Jinni's honeymoon, and she was *not* going to talk about Reed Kingsley or his peskiness or that silly note. Jinni already knew everything else going on in her life, except for all the phone calls she'd received. Reed was the only controversial subject Val had to talk about, if she was so inclined. Which she wasn't. She actually shuddered at the thought, as putting Jinni on that scent would only cause relentless torment. Jinni had stated clearly, more than once, that Val had lived a celibate existence for far too many years. Val didn't want to hear it again, or even worse, discover to her chagrin that her sister had decided to play matchmaker.

Heaven help her if that should happen, Val thought with another shudder. When Jinni got on the trail of a cause she deemed worthwhile, she moved full steam ahead and got the job done.

So, no, Val would not be mentioning Reed Kingsley to her sister. Not at lunch on Monday, not ever.

Reed drove to Billings to have dinner with Derek Moore, Attorney-at-Law, an old college buddy. Derek was in Billings on business and had called Reed early Friday morning.

"I flew in late last night. I'll be taking depositions all day and leaving tomorrow morning," Derek said. "I should be through today by four, possibly five. How about meeting at the Grove around six? We'll have a drink in the lounge, then dinner.''

Elated to hear from his old friend, Reed had agreed at once. "The Grove is a good choice. See you there.''

It would be great to see Derek. They would probably spend the entire evening laughing about old escapades.

When Reed walked into the Grove's lounge and spotted his friend among the crowd, Derek got up from the small table he had commandeered. Friday night Happy Hour was in full swing, and the place was packed.

"Derek!'' They shook hands, then gave each other a quick hug. "Man, it's good seeing you,'' Reed exclaimed as they sat down. "Other than a few phone calls, what's it been, ten years?''

"Just about.''

"Well, you're looking mighty prosperous,'' Reed said, eyeing Derek's custom-tailored suit.

"I was going to change, but I didn't have time.'' He waved a waiter over. "Name your poison, Reed.''

After the waiter had gone to get their drinks, Reed looked around. "I haven't been in here for a while, and I didn't think about it being Friday night. It's busy.'' He grinned. "And noisy.''

"We'll survive. So, how've you been? Are you married yet?''

"Nope. Are you?''

"For four years now.'' Derek pulled out his wallet and flipped it open. "The little girl is Merry, my six-month-old daughter, and the boy is Connor, my three-year-old son.'' He flipped to another snapshot. "That's my wife, Elaine.''

Something heavy invaded Reed's system. He spoke quietly, seriously. "You have a beautiful family, Derek.''

"I sure do.'' He looked at his wife's photo a moment, then closed his wallet and returned it to his inside jacket pocket. "How come you're still single? Wait, don't tell me. You're still changing girls like I change shirts.''

Reed cleared his throat. "I think I've heard something like that said about me before."

"But you know I was only kidding, don't you?"

"Yeah, so is everyone else. Derek, I think I might have finally met the right woman, but she won't give me the time of day. I've pretty much given up on her."

"Don't."

Their drinks were delivered, and after tapping their glasses together, they each took a swallow and set them down.

"Don't what?" Reed asked, picking up the thread of their conversation. "Don't notice that she can't seem to stand the sight of me?"

"If I'd given up on Elaine, I'd be the sorriest bag of bones practicing law in the whole darn country," Derek said. "She was a tough nut to crack, believe me. Independent as hell, full of idealistic notions about her public relations career, haughty as a queen looking down on her subjects and not one bit interested in a lovesick attorney. I came close to giving up on her two or three times, but she was just about all I could think of. I went to sleep at night thinking about her and woke up in the morning the same way. If this gal is anywhere close to that important to you, then don't even consider calling it quits. Dust off your sense of humor and make her laugh, if nothing else works. Women like guys who make them laugh."

"You're some kind of expert on the subject now?" Reed said dryly.

"Sort of," Derek answered with an amused glint in his dark eyes.

Their banter on the subject of women went back and forth, then it was time for dinner. That was when they discussed Derek's law practice and Reed's diverse interests. Derek was impressed that his old pal was Rumor's fire chief, and he listened intently while Reed related the details of the summer's destructive forest fire.

They lingered over coffee for hours and talked about everything that had happened to each of them from college graduation to the present. The dining room began closing at eleven, and Reed noticed Derek yawning.

"This has been great, Derek." He got to his feet. "Any chance of your coming back to Billings anytime soon?"

"Who knows? If I do, I'll let you know. Do you ever get to the East Coast?"

"Not for years."

"Well, if you ever do…"

"I'll let you know."

Derek walked Reed out to his SUV. They shook hands and said goodbye. Reed drove away feeling nostalgic and quietly content. The evening had been great. Derek had matured, as Reed had. They still enjoyed the same kind of humor and thought alike on a variety of subjects.

But Derek was happily married, and Reed wasn't even close. *Dust off your sense of humor and make her laugh.*

"Hmm," Reed murmured, his eyes on the highway ahead. Maybe it was worth a try, even though Val didn't strike him as a woman who laughed a lot. Of course, considering her recent health problems, she had damn good reason for not giggling at every little thing.

Truth was, though, Reed couldn't recall ever having seen or heard her giggling. Nor could he imagine Dr. Valerie Fairchild doing any giggling. She wasn't the giggling type. If and when she laughed, it would undoubtedly be a pleasant, throaty sound. He really would love to hear it.

And maybe he had an idea that would at least bring a smile to her beautiful lips.

Reed swallowed hard. He would rather kiss Val's luscious lips than see a smile on them.

But first things first. Smiles were immeasurably valuable in a hundred ways and certainly crucial to a close relationship. If he could get her to smile, to laugh, then things might fall into place for them.

It definitely *was* worth a try.

* * *

On Saturday morning Val and Jim were both busy. People and pets were coming and going, and Val was functioning as she used to, full speed ahead and enjoying her work. Things slowed down around noon, and she went to her office to eat the lunch that Estelle had brought over from the house.

Jim was dubious about his and Estelle's plans to leave early, but Val reassured him. "I'm certain the rush is over. Thanks for being here on a weekend. In fact, I'm going to lock the doors behind you and enjoy my lunch. If anyone comes along this afternoon, they'll have to ring the bell. It's time I got some of that stacked-up paperwork done."

After the Worths left, Val sat at her desk feeling relatively content. Lunch was good, and she looked through the pile of letters, trade journals and advertisements overflowing her In basket while she ate. Until the unknown cost of those delivered groceries from MonMart nagged at her. She pondered her options and grimaced at the idea of phoning MonMart and then talking to a dozen different people while they tried to pinpoint one particular grocery order and who had paid for it. If *anyone* had paid for it, actually. Maybe MonMart had some sort of slush fund for miscellaneous charitable expenses, she mused. It made a certain amount of sense, but she didn't want to be considered a charity case, especially not when one considered the ridiculous circumstances that had caused her to leave behind her cartful of food.

In fact, it was such a distasteful idea that she quickly got out her checkbook and began writing a check. But what amount should she send MonMart? Food didn't come cheap, and five large paper sacks had been delivered. Twenty dollars per sack? Twenty-five?

She decided on the higher figure, added on another twenty-five dollars to make sure, and wrote the check for $150.00. Intent on getting this done now that she'd made up her mind, she addressed an envelope, wrote a brief note explaining the check, and put both in the envelope. After stamping it, she took it and went outside to the mailbox on the curb in front of the Animal Hospital.

She was glad to have that behind her, and she'd just started up the walk to the clinic when a vehicle drove in and stopped in the customer parking area. It took only a second for her to recognize Reed Kingsley's SUV, and another second for her heart to start pounding in a ridiculously female fashion.

She gritted her teeth. Getting silly over a man was not on her agenda. It was never going to be on her agenda, and maybe today was the day to tell Mr. Kingsley to stop wasting his time in plain language...*very* plain language.

She hurried inside and cursed her bad timing. If she hadn't gone to the mailbox at the exact moment she had, then Kingsley would not have known she was on the premises. She could have ignored his arrival completely, for when someone rang the bell at either the dog or cat entrance, she could check on who was out there before letting him or her in.

Feeling strangely weak, she leaned against a wall and waited for one of the bells to ring. This weakness was nothing like those chemo-related spells, she realized, and she stood there in her white lab jacket and jeans and told herself that she was *not* weak in the knees because of a man.

But it was a lie, she knew, and she didn't like it one damn bit.

The cat doorbell rang, and even though Val had been expecting the sound, it made her jump.

"You damn fool," she muttered under her breath as she made her way to the door, unlocked and opened it. There, looking sober and serious, with nary a silly grin in sight, stood Reed Kingsley, dressed in great-looking jeans, boots, a royal-blue shirt and a dark leather vest. He was holding a cardboard box, from which came the unmistakable mews of very young kittens.

Val evolved from aggravated female to competent veterinarian. "Come in," she said, and swung the door wide for Reed to enter.

He lowered the box a little so she could see its cargo. Val

saw two tiny orange tabby kittens. "They're less than two months old," she said. "Whose are they? Where's the mother?"

"They belonged to one of the ranch hands. Their mother disappeared—she was a barn cat—along with a third kitten, about a week ago. Rafe thinks she was in the process of moving her kits, carrying one in her mouth, and got caught by a coyote. They are always a danger to cats and small dogs."

"Yes, they are. Well, what are you doing with them?"

"Rafe's been bottle-feeding these two, but he'd just as soon get rid of them, and he's adamant about not spending any money on shots or neutering or anything else that might cost a buck."

"Yes, well, some people feel that way, especially about barn cats. Why did you bring them to me?"

"Because I've adopted them, and I'm more than willing to pay for whatever you can do that will guarantee their good health."

"I can administer the recommended shots and procedures for young cats, but I can't guarantee their good health. No one can do that."

Reed thought of her personal fight for good health and felt a massive amount of admiration for her spunk. He was admiring her incredible eyes, as well, and her sensual mouth. She was an unusually pretty woman, and being this near to her was so pleasurable he wished he could take up residence right here in her animal clinic so he could see her all the time.

"You're right, of course," he said quietly, surprised that he could speak so softly when the sound of his heartbeat pumping blood through his veins was almost deafening. "But I would appreciate your examining them and making sure they're healthy now."

"Follow me." Val walked off at a brisk pace, deeply unnerved over something he couldn't have dreamed up. But maybe he had. Maybe he'd scoured the countryside for young kittens as an excuse to see her. Was his story about how he'd come by the two adorable kittens even remotely true? She didn't trust Reed Kingsley, she decided again as she led him into an examining room. Why on earth would she?

Then again, the man seemed perfectly trustworthy. She might even like him as a person if he hadn't been coming on so strong since…since— Good Lord, had all of this folderol started last spring at Joe's Bar, when she dropped her quarters?

She sighed inwardly, put on an expressionless face and picked up one of the kittens. It was so small it fit into the palm of one hand, and since she adored kittens to begin with, her entire demeanor became softer from holding this one's warm little body.

Still, she was a vet, and she began doing her job. "This one's a male," she said evenly, refusing to look directly at Kingsley, whose stare seemed to be boring holes through her skin. Could he be any more obvious?

"And this kitten is also male," she said, after examining the second one. She weighed them and looked into their mouths and ears. "They both appear to be healthy." She recited a list of the shots they should have to avoid illness. "And I highly recommend neutering. Adding to the unwanted pet population is terribly negligent. Also, if you intend for these babies to be house cats, then declawing is something you should consider. One guarantee I *can* give you is that they will rip curtains, furniture and anything else to shreds. Of course, if they're going to be barn cats, then they should keep their claws for protection."

"They're sure cute little things, aren't they?" Reed said.

Val sent him a quick glance. For once he wasn't staring at her. Rather, he was watching the adorable kittens exploring the examination table.

"They're precious," she agreed. She loved cats and dogs of all ages, but youngsters such as these were undeniably special. Thinking of that, she actually forgot about the predatory qualities of the man in the room. "Have you seen them playing yet?"

"Not really. I only picked them up this morning."

"Well, let's see how advanced they are." She got a piece of string from a counter drawer and held it in front of the nearest kitten. The darling thing lifted a tiny paw and tried to catch it, falling on his nose in the process.

Val laughed. "He's not quite steady on his feet yet."

Hearing her laugh—his goal today—was so thrilling for Reed that he laughed, as well. "Do you have more string?" he asked.

"Sure do." Val got him a piece and they both played with the kittens.

Val seemed genuinely enthralled with the baby cats, but Reed was a lot more enthralled with her, though he had to admit the kittens were exceptionally cute and a lot of fun. He honestly hadn't gone there to make a pass, but it was the first time that he'd ever seen Val so relaxed and friendly. And before he thought about it, he leaned over the examining table and pressed his lips to hers.

Too stunned to react, Val stood there and let him kiss her…for about five seconds. Then she backed up with her eyes blazing. "What in hell do you think you're doing?" she asked in a voice he would never mistakenly call friendly.

Reed felt so alive from that one brief kiss that he couldn't help grinning. "I think I was kissing you, and a fine kiss it was, if I do say so myself."

"A fine kiss? You…you *jerk!* Get your ass out of my building—*now!*"

"Why are you so hostile over one little kiss?"

"I'm not hostile over one little kiss, you cretin, I'm hostile over you, period! Aren't you ever going to get the message that I don't like you? That I want nothing to do with you?"

Reed held up his forefinger. "I have a theory. I don't think that the strong feelings a man has for a woman can all be one-sided. Let me take that another step. What I've been feeling because of you—"

"Don't you dare!" Val shouted, interrupting what she was positive was going to be something she didn't want to hear.

"You're not really as angry as you sound, are you?"

"I'm furious! I want you to leave, to take your two tiny excuses for coming here and get out of my life! Could I speak any plainer? Or maybe you just need repetition for something to fully register. Fine, I'll stand here and repeat it for an hour, if that's what it takes. Go! Leave! Box your kittens and get the hell out of my face!"

Reed shook his head almost sadly. "You're a hard woman. I thought we were getting along, but we really weren't, were we? You let down your guard because of the kittens. I had nothing to do with it."

Val's fury had drained her. Shrieking wasn't her style, never had been. He shouldn't have kissed her, and, my God, she shouldn't have liked the sensation of his mouth on hers. But it had happened, and now she just wanted it to go away, all of it—Kingsley and his kittens, plus a kiss she hadn't expected and wished passionately had never taken place.

"Leave when you want," she said, hearing the unsteadiness in her voice. She walked out of the examining room and left Reed to find his own way out of the building. About two minutes later, from her office, she heard the opening and closing of an outside door.

He was gone. "Good," she said out loud, then put her arms on the desk, her head on her arms and had a good cry.

She never did figure out the reason for her overwhelming need to weep buckets, except that it had something to do with a kiss that never should have happened.

Chapter Five

On Saturday night Reed sat in the bleachers at the high school with several hundred other football fans and watched the Rumor Rangers play the Whitehorn Wildcats. Last year the Rangers hadn't done very well, though no one could say they hadn't put their hearts into every game. This year was different. The Rangers were ahead in the league by three games, and the town was so behind them, so supportive and proud of its high school team, that turnouts for the games were huge.

Reed sat among dozens of boisterous friends. They drank cold sodas and hot cocoa, and filled up on hot dogs and popcorn. They laughed and teased and joked and shouted encouragement to their team of young players. They even applauded when the Wildcats made a good play, although there was little doubt as to which team was their favorite.

Of course, Whitehorn had a respectable fan attendance, too. A good one-third of the bleachers was filled with Wildcat supporters. It was a friendly rivalry and great fun.

Usually it was great fun. Reed's black mood—extremely unusual for a man who had grown up with a smile for almost every situation and person—made it hard for him to participate fully in the tomfoolery and laughter all around him. Driving away from Val's Animal Hospital that afternoon, he'd finally faced and admitted unconditional defeat. Sure, she'd kissed him back for about two seconds, and no, he'd probably never again kiss lips that sweet, but she had said straight out that she didn't like him, then she'd kicked him out of her building. She had obviously meant what she'd said, and he didn't intend to keep proving to Valerie Fairchild that he was a lovesick fool.

Today's confrontation had been the end for him. The vow seemed to be stuck in his mind, and he was glad it was, because if it slipped just an iota he started thinking of Val in ways that would get him another black eye…symbolically speaking, of course.

Still, he couldn't help wondering why a woman with Val's looks and intelligence didn't have a man. Surely he wasn't the only guy in Rumor who'd noticed her. There had to be others who had been shot down while trying to get past that iron-clad guard of hers. Of course, they might not have been quite as tenacious as he'd been, which could be the reason he'd never heard any gossip about Doc. But she was too unique for men besides himself not to have noticed.

"What the hell?" he muttered under his breath. *Leave it alone. Leave her alone! You're having fun tonight! Are you so far gone on a woman who loathes the sight of you that you can't even enjoy a football game? Or being with friends?*

Reed tried to look like one of the merry fans—deviant behavior for him because he was always part of the football crowd, and without having to try to be, to boot. Tonight he numbly watched the game. His mind was fuzzy, and he saw his teenage self on that field instead of the stocky young men who were actually running plays. He had loved the game, loved being on the team, loved being part of something that moved the whole town. In high school, he had been in the middle of everything, and he'd lived the same way ever since—actively involved.

Bottom line: he had always loved life. Now he had reason to believe that he'd missed the boat somewhere along the line. Almost everyone he knew was married, or at least paired with someone special. He could have a dozen dates with a dozen different women by making a dozen phone calls, and the only woman he *wanted* to spend time with couldn't stand the sight of him. Something was terribly wrong with that picture.

At the Fairchild house, Val was already settled in for the night. Her bedroom was equipped with a large television set, positioned for perfect viewing from her bed. She almost always went to bed early and turned on the TV. There were a few weekly shows that she actually watched—she avoided the popular news programs as reports about worldwide misery always depressed her—and an occasional movie caught her eye. But mostly, she kept the volume down and read. Her evenings were quiet and calming. She did a lot of her best thinking while staring blankly at the TV screen or at the pages of a book.

Tonight she was deeply troubled, and neither the current television program nor the book on her lap offered any comfort. She had behaved badly today with Reed Kingsley, and while she was still upset with him, she was even more upset with herself. The same thing had happened at MonMart when he'd pulled that big rescue scene with her. Maybe she had a right to tell him to back off, but this yelling business had to stop. Her temper was developing a hair trigger, and she was embarrassing herself—far more than anyone else ever could.

Val heaved a long sigh and then let the memory of Reed's brash kiss shove other thoughts from her mind. She hadn't been kissed for…how many years?

"Too many to count," she said in a whisper. Not that she wanted to be kissed. If she'd been longing for that sort of deviance from her rather staid lifestyle, she could have stood still today and let Kingsley take his best shot.

In all honesty, it hadn't been altogether unpleasant. His lips had felt rather nice on hers…for a few moments. Until she'd gotten past the shock of a pass she hadn't been at all prepared to deal with. Once she'd realized the extent of Kingsley's brass, she had pretty much gone ballistic.

And she wasn't proud of it. In fact, she was darned unhappy about it. He should never have put a hand on her…or a lip, damn him.

A giggle suddenly welled in Val's throat. Cursing him for putting a lip on her tickled her funny bone, apparently, because she was suddenly rolling around the bed, almost hysterical. It was one of those silly giggling attacks that had often occurred during her teens, as they did with most teenagers, but she hadn't been so overcome in years and years.

She laughed and laughed, and then she cried and cried.

Obviously her emotions were out of control.

And it was all Reed Kingsley's fault, the big jerk!

Reed went to his folks' ranch for Sunday brunch. Russell, Susannah, and their adopted one-year-old daughter, Mei, were there, as well, and Carolyn wished out loud that Tag, Linda, Maura and Ash had joined them. A full house would have included Jeff Forsythe and his wife, Jilly, too, but Stratton and Carolyn both loved having any family at their table.

"We're expecting *everyone* to come for Thanksgiving," Carolyn said firmly.

Those at the table already knew where they would be spending Thanksgiving Day, and none of them could doubt that the rest of the family hadn't already been put on notice, as well.

The food today, as always, was delicious and plentiful, and the conversation was pleasant and easygoing, as it usually was when the family got together.

Russell talked about the seasonal decorations at MonMart. "We took down the Halloween witches and goblins the day after the holiday and began putting up Thanksgiving turkeys and colorful cardboard Pilgrims. We're also starting on the Christmas decorations, just to remind customers that December 25 is not that far off. We'll go all-out on Christmas merchandise and decorations during the week of Thanksgiving, because as everyone knows, the day after the holiday is traditionally the best shopping day of the year. Right now the Rumor store is looking quite festive. I'm constantly in touch with the managers of our other outlets, and they're all in sync.''

They all chitchatted about that for a while, then Reed changed the subject. ''I've been considering about holding a contest to name the park.'' Off and on, in between long spells of thinking about very little besides Valerie Fairchild, he'd thought about the park project. ''What's everyone's opinion on that idea?'' he asked, his gaze wandering over the group.

Carolyn's eyes lit up. ''I think it's a wonderful plan!''

Everyone agreed, and they began tossing suggestions around. There should be a prize, or perhaps more than one, something for the best name submitted and lesser prizes for two or three honorable mentions. And they must have impartial judges, people who truly cared about the park and would do their very best to choose the most appropriate name.

''The winning name could be announced at the Christmas ball,'' Carolyn said excitedly. ''Reed, I really love your idea. Now, who would make good judges?''

''None of us,'' Stratton said firmly. ''None of the Kingsleys.''

''Well, of course not. Reed, how about Pastor Rayburn, for one? I think he would agree, don't you?''

By the time brunch was over the rules for the contest were settled upon and written down, and they had five names from which, hopefully, they would find three judges. They still had to decide on the prizes, but Reed was leaning toward gift certificates from MonMart.

It had been a good morning, he thought to himself while

driving back to his own house after everyone had said good-bye. *See? You can get along, enjoy yourself and even be happy without Valerie Fairchild!*

He wholeheartedly hoped that was true. Hoped? Actually, what he was thinking felt more like a prayer.

Val spent most of Sunday at the Animal Hospital. Jim and Estelle didn't work on Sunday anymore, so all of the necessary chores, such as putting out food and fresh water for any pets in residence, had to be done by Val.

But that took only a few minutes. The rest of her time was spent at her desk, where she finally reached the bottom of that daunting pile of unopened mail, bills to be paid, advertisements to throw out and trade journals to set aside for later perusal. She even gave the top of her desk a good polishing, and it looked great all clean and shining.

After checking on the kenneled animals again, she locked up and went to the house. She'd been thinking of a shower, but she decided that a leisurely bath would do her a world of good. Even though she had accomplished a lot today, her mood was still down around her ankles, and she didn't like herself very much. She was so looking forward to lunch with Jinni tomorrow. Maybe she would find the courage to unload the burden of her tasteless behavior with Reed on her sister, although talking about herself with anyone, even Jinni, still wasn't easy for her. But Jinni was so much smarter about men than Val was, and would know what to say to make her feel better. In truth, Val had to forcibly stop herself from calling her sister on the phone today and yelling "Help!"

That would be much too selfish. Jinni and Max were still honeymooning. Yes, Max's son was undoubtedly in the house with them, but it was a huge house with plenty of breathing room for three people. Besides, it was almost as urgent for Jinni to bond with Michael as it was for her to strengthen the bond with her new husband.

Resigned to waiting until tomorrow to talk to her sister, Val ran water in the tub and added bubbling bath beads. She quickly undressed and got into the tub when the water was only ankle deep. It crept up her body, hot and silky. She laid her head back and felt the kinks caused by unpleasant memories gradually relaxing their hold on her.

She would never be as happy as Jinni was, but she could derive enjoyment from the little things—things like a clean, freshly polished desk and a hot bath.

Val felt that way until she got out of the tub twenty minutes later and dried off. Catching her reflection in the bathroom mirrors, she lowered the towel and looked at her breasts. They appeared normal, but were they? She looked healthy—in spite of Estelle's opinion that she was too thin. Was she destined to live with the fear of recurring cancer for the rest of her life?

And also a fear of men because of that one terrifying incident and the painful aftermath of long-term therapy?

For that was it, wasn't it—the reason she couldn't let herself like a man? Plain old fear? Combined with terrible memories?

Trembling suddenly, she finished drying off and hurriedly pulled on a robe. She didn't like looking at her body and very seldom did it. Gazing at herself without clothes always made her worry about that awful word, *cancer,* and then that worry opened her mental wounds. It had been drummed into her by the best clinical psychologists money could buy that she had faced her demons, that she was as healed as anyone could be after such a frightening experience and she should get on with a normal life.

Well, she'd gotten on, all right, but was her life normal? The question was almost laughable. Val knew she *wasn't* normal, not in the way Jinni was, for example.

But maybe that was okay; for the most part Val put up a damn good front, giving everyone she knew the impression that she was a strong, organized and happily independent woman.

Or she had until Reed Kingsley had decided to invade her safe little world.

*   *   *

Jinni entered Val's house at a quarter to one on Monday as she always entered any home or room—talking a mile a minute and hugging everyone in sight, which happened to be just one person today, Estelle Worth.

Laughing, always happy to see Jinni, Estelle hugged her back and then complimented her on the stunning sweater dress she was wearing, along with her jewelry, stylish pumps and handbag. They were discussing famous clothing designers when Val walked in.

Jinni hugged her sister, who was wearing a three-year-old pant suit. "That thing is not only years out of style," Jinni said after giving Val's outfit a quick once-over, "it's way too big. You really have lost weight. How many pounds?"

Val shrugged. "I have no idea."

"You don't weigh yourself?" Jinni was clearly astonished. "I step on the scale every morning to make darn sure that great globs of fat didn't sneak up on me during the night. Well, you look terrific, Val, but we *have* to do something about your wardrobe."

Val laughed and shook her head. "Jinni, you never fail to cheer me up."

"During lunch we'll plan a shopping excursion. Ready to go?"

"Ready," Val confirmed. "We'll see you later, Estelle."

"Have a good time," she said, walking to the door with the sisters.

It was a beautiful day but not quite warm enough to eat in the Rooftop Café's outdoor dining area. They were greeted warmly when they entered the establishment, and Val recognized the hostess.

"Mrs. Clayton, it's good seeing you," she said. "How is your little poodle, Buffy?"

The woman looked enormously pleased. "Buffy is just fine. My goodness, do you remember all of the pets you see?"

Val smiled. "Not all of them, but Buffy is...quite special."

Mrs. Clayton positively beamed. "She certainly is to me. Table for two, ladies?" She led them through the dining room, and different groups of diners said hello to Val—most calling her Dr. Fairchild—as they walked past.

Seated at an excellent table, they scanned their menus. Then Jinni said, "It appears that most of the people in here recognize you. By any chance, are you becoming known as Rumor's beloved animal doc? I'm not sure thirty-five is old enough to qualify you for that title." She lifted her gaze from the menu and grinned teasingly.

Val couldn't help laughing. Jinni was such good medicine, always coming up with some off-the-wall remark. "What happened is that I put an announcement in the paper about my being back to work full-time. Everyone's been really nice ever since."

"Well, that's great," Jinni said. She leaned forward and whispered, "Do you really remember Buffy?"

Val whispered, too. "Buffy tries to take a bite out of me every time I see her, so yes, I definitely remember her."

"Saying so certainly made Mrs. Clayton's day," Jinni said wryly. "Doesn't she know her sweet little poodle is a biter?"

"People are practically blind to any faults their pets might have." Checking the menu again, Val asked, "What looks good to you?"

They finally made their lunch choices, and after ordering their food and a small bottle of wine they both liked, Jinni sat back and asked, "So, how was your weekend?"

"It was just great," Val said, hoping the lie didn't show on her face.

Jinni stared, then scoffed. "You never were a good liar. I thought of running over to see you at least a dozen times, but Max kept me busy, and when he didn't require my time, Michael did. I'm not making excuses for neglecting you, Val, but—"

"My God, I am not your responsibility. Jinni, if I started thanking you today and kept repeating the words until I had covered everything you did for me during my illness, I would still be mumbling 'Thanks' as I drew my dying breath.''

"Oh, come on. It wasn't *that* big a deal.''

"It was to me, and you are to live your own life now and not concern yourself with mine. You have a husband and a stepson now, and they need you far more than I do.''

The waitress appeared with the bottle of wine, which she opened at the table. "Would you like to try it before I fill your glasses?'' she asked, her gaze moving back and forth between Val and Jinni.

"Just pour it,'' Jinni said. "I'm sure it's fine. We both know this brand very well, and that particular year is especially good.''

The wine *was* very good, and after a few sips Jinni returned to the conversation the waitress had interrupted.

"Tell me all about your great weekend,'' she said with one eyebrow raised dubiously.

"You don't believe me.''

"Of course I believe you. I only want to hear what was so great about it. I'll be happy to talk about mine after I hear about yours.''

Val knew that she'd been neatly cornered, and she thought of devising a dramatic tale of exciting events just to throw Jinni off track. In truth, telling her high-stepping sister that she had derived a great deal of satisfaction from polishing the bare surface of her office desk wasn't going to appease Jinni's judgmental curiosity in the least.

"Okay, the truth,'' she said quietly. "I worked this weekend.''

"All weekend?''

"Well, yes. Practically. What else would I have done? What do you think I did every weekend before you moved to Rumor?''

"I hope to God you did more than work!''

"Well, I didn't. Not much more, anyhow. Jinni, we've talked about this before. You know I live a quiet life.''

"You live a boring life, and there's no reason for it.''

"Well, maybe I'll put on a bikini top, a pair of short shorts and some glittery high heels and spend my weekends dancing at the Beauties and the Beat strip joint," Val said dryly. "Would that make you happy?"

"It would be better than dying on the vine in that pet hospital. Or dodging Buffy-bites."

"Dodging Buffy-bites?" Val started giggling. She covered her mouth with her hand and still couldn't stop. This was her second fit of the giggles in two days, and she was embarrassed by it. Jinni merely smiled and watched her.

She finally wound down and was able to gasp, "My gosh, what is wrong with me? I lost it yesterday, too."

Jinni sipped from her glass. "What set you off yesterday? Don't get me wrong. I love seeing you laugh like that, but I'd also love to hear about yesterday's big joke."

"I'm not sure it was a big joke," Val murmured. She had to think a moment, and when she remembered why she'd fallen over on the bed giggling yesterday, her face got red.

"Uh-oh, something's up," Jinni drawled. "Your face doesn't get red for nothing. Now you have to tell me about yesterday for sure."

"It—it was really nothing," Val stammered.

Their food was delivered, and Val took it as divine intervention, pretended to be hugely hungry and started eating at once. But it wasn't a minute before Jinni said casually, "I noticed the bouquet of flowers wilting on your dining room table. Who sent them?"

Val had totally forgotten those flowers, which probably were very wilted by now. But there would be no fooling Jinni into thinking that bouquet hadn't been very expensive and something she had whimsically bought for herself. So she couldn't lie about it. Nor could she tell Jinni that it was none of her business. After everything her sister had done for her? Besides, Val had thought of talking to her witty, wonderful sister about Reed's unwanted interest. If anyone could help her out with some advice on how to deal with a never-give-up guy, it was Jinni.

Val drew a deep breath. "No one sent them. I mean, they weren't delivered by the florist." She took another breath, this one sounding nervous even to her own ears. "Reed Kingsley brought them to the house."

Looking utterly astonished, Jinni lowered her fork and stared. "Reed Kingsley?" she finally repeated questioningly. "He suddenly decided to bring you flowers for no good reason?"

Val cleared her throat. "It...wasn't that sudden. I mean, he never gave me flowers before but he's been trying to...trying to..."

"To what?" Jinni prompted, excitement building in her beautiful blue eyes.

"Well, he came by the clinic yesterday with two adorable kittens and kissed me, so that might clarify what he's trying to accomplish."

"He *kissed* you?" Jinni sat back, looking positively floored. "And exactly how long has this been going on?"

"Uh, since last spring," Val mumbled.

"Last spring! And you're just now telling me about it? My God, girl, do you realize what a catch Reed Kingsley is? If he's been trying to accomplish...well, whatever he's been hoping to accomplish with you for that long a time, he's serious!"

"Yeah, right. What's he serious about? Getting me into bed? I'm not interested!"

"Well, you should be. I can't believe this. What else has he done?"

Val related the MonMart incident, which sent Jinni into spasms of laughter. "Oh, that is too rich."

"I'm surprised someone didn't already tell you about it. I'm sure the whole town heard within ten minutes of it happening."

"Oh, what do they care? What do *you* care? Val, if I sat around and worried about other people's opinions of the things I do and the way I live, I'd be dying on the vine, too. And, honey, that's just not something I'm ever going to do."

And neither are you, if I have anything to say about it. Jinni
smiled serenely at her sister, giving away none of the myriad
ideas racing through her mind, or even that she *was* devising
scenarios that would most certainly give Val something to
do on weekends. "Isn't this fun?" she said. "Let's make a
pact right now to lunch together every Monday. What do you
say?"

"I'd like that," Val said quietly.

"Great! Now, let's talk about your wardrobe. Where
should we go for our shopping spree?"

Val smiled weakly. Jinni's energy was sometimes overwhelming. She liked her clothes just fine. So what if they
were too big now? She would probably gain some of that
weight back, and then any new clothes she bought would be
too tight.

Besides, it was hard to think of anything but the fact that
she had bared her soul on such a private matter. Jinni now
knew everything that Val did about Reed Kingsley and his
arrogant attitude.

Rather, Jinni now knew everything with one exception.
Val hadn't mentioned that Sweet Talk florist's card with
Reed's handwriting on it, and she wasn't going to, either.

How would she explain keeping it when she was so adamantly opposed to Reed's attentions?

Chapter Six

Throughout lunch Jinni talked about Max, their marvelous marriage and their incredible week in California. She mentioned Michael several times, so Val knew that Max wasn't the only Cantrell male making her sister's eyes glow. It was all about family, Val thought, trying hard not to be envious of the starry-eyed happiness Jinni conveyed. Never one to hide her feelings in any case, Jinni simply couldn't stop herself from bubbling over with love for her husband and stepson.

It was over coffee that Jinni's ebullient mood changed. She spoke in a quieter tone of voice as she related how closely Max was working with the lawyers he had hired to defend his brother.

"Max is completely convinced of Guy's innocence, Val. He said that Guy was always a big softy and had never hurt anyone or anything in his life. When they were kids themselves, other kids teased Guy unmercifully because his head was always in the clouds, pondering some off-the-wall question. Questions like why is the sky blue? Or the grass green…or why am I tall and you're short? He was born a scientist, Val, and that's all he ever wanted to be. Max wonders how Wanda ever got her hooks into Guy, but I told him that even a scientist needs affection. Actually, what I said was that even a scientist needs sex. I mean, when it comes right down to it humans are still only animals. We just have bigger brains, vocal cords, straight backs and opposable thumbs. Am I right or am I right?''

Val nearly choked on a swallow of coffee. ''You are very close to being right, but how in the world are you able to summarize the human condition in one brief sentence?''

Jinni took her sister's question in stride, with barely a pause. ''My writer's imagination, I guess. Anyhow, scientific brain or not, Guy Cantrell had—*has*—physical needs, just like the rest of us, so if he hadn't let Wanda get her hooks into him, as Max defines the relationship, he would have let some other female latch on to him.''

Just like the rest of us. The phrase repeated in Val's mind as Jinni continued to talk. Not everyone has physical needs, Val thought, putting herself in that picture. A sudden sadness gripped her and she forced a smile to her lips while she listened to her sister.

Finally Jinni wound down and picked up the check. ''I'm paying, and I don't want an argument.''

''Go ahead and pay. I'll pay next Monday.''

''Well, we'll see about that.''

Val shook her head. ''I'm not going to let you pay for everything we do together, so you might as well face the fact that I can be as stubborn as you can.''

''Me, stubborn?'' Jinni smiled. ''The Fairchild sisters, together again.''

''When were we ever together before this? That five-year difference in our ages seemed more like a hundred when I was fifteen and you were twenty.''

''Bite your tongue!'' Jinni exclaimed. ''And by the way,

I've told no one, except Max, my exact age. Keep 'em guessing is my motto.''

"Sister dearest, you are something else," Val drawled in amusement.

"I certainly hope so. There are two things that are no one else's business, my age and my weight." Jinni laid money on the check and looked around for their waitress.

"I've been thinking about taking a trip to my cabin in the mountains for a few days," Val said rather matter-of-factly, never dreaming that Jinni would object.

She was wrong. Jinni's head jerked around and there was nothing *but* objection on her face. "Alone? All by yourself?"

"Of course alone. Jinni, for heaven's sakes, I've been going there alone since the day I bought the place."

"Yes, but you were strong and healthy then."

"Supposedly, according to my doctors, I'm strong and healthy now," Val said quietly, then drew a breath and changed her tone. "Jinni, I've been longing for a few days in the mountains. Someday I'd love you to go with me. Not now, of course... I know how busy you are with Max and Michael and the rest of your new family, but sometime." Val paused, then smiled. "On second thought, tranquillity really doesn't ring your bell, does it?"

"And it shouldn't be ringing yours, either. You're thirty-five, in the prime of life and looking like a model with that svelte new figure." Jinni leaned forward and spoke excitedly. "Let's go to Billings tomorrow and do some shopping. I'm dying to see you in some new clothes. The hot new styles are feminine and sexy, great for a woman with a perfect figure...like yours."

Val was taken aback. Jinni had never been stingy with compliments, but categorizing her figure as "perfect" was really too much to swallow. Val nearly said out loud what was on her mind—the word *ridiculous* featuring prominently—but she decided not to bait Jinni into an argument over something so silly, and shut her mouth instead.

In the next breath she opened it again. "We'll shop next

week, or the week after, if you still want to. I'm going to be getting ready for a trip to the mountains this week, when I'm not working. Actually, I may stay at the cabin longer than the weekend, which means stocking up on food and supplies, and packing more than an overnight bag. The length of my stay will depend on Jim and Estelle, of course. If they have plans of their own and can't take over during my absence, then I'll have to vacation around their schedule.''

Jinni frowned at her. "Val, I wish you wouldn't do this. Darn it, you don't even have a cell phone!''

Val rolled her eyes, but she was smiling. "I suppose if I carried a cell phone while I hiked around the mountain and a grizzly came at me, I could dial your number and let you listen while he gobbled me up.''

"Val, that's not funny! There really are grizzlies in those mountains!''

"There are also black bears, moose, elk, deer and…and chipmunks,'' Val said, laughing with genuine relish. "Don't let your *writer's imagination* carry you away, Jinni. I've yet to see even a small bear on my property, although I've watched many deer and elk grazing around the cabin, and the sight of those beautiful, graceful creatures is always deeply moving.'' At the concern on Jinni's face, Val said, "Please don't worry about me, not when I'm here in Rumor and not when I'm at the cabin.''

"I wouldn't worry quite so much if you took a cell phone with you.''

"It probably wouldn't even work in the mountains.''

"It would if it was one of those satellite phones.''

"Jinni, I don't need or want a phone out there. That's one of the reasons the place is tranquil, one of the reasons I love the cabin. The only sounds are made by Mother Nature, and they're lovely…and restful. Oh, there's our waitress coming over.''

In a few minutes the Fairchild sisters were outside, walking toward Jinni's car. "This weather is unbelievable,'' Val said. The sun was so bright she pulled her sunglasses out of her purse and put them on.

"The weather is great," Jinni agreed, "but don't think you can get me to stop worrying about your little jaunt into the nether regions of Montana by changing the subject."

"Oh, don't sound so gloomy. You're *never* gloomy, and if you go home with worry lines on your face, Max will think I cried on your shoulder all during lunch."

"Worry lines? Where?" Jinni stopped and pulled a compact out of her purse, which she immediately opened and used. "Oh my God, I *am* getting worry lines!"

"You are not! Put that thing away. This sunshine is so bright you're squinting into that mirror, and those little squint lines are the only ones you're seeing. Your skin is as smooth as Pete's head."

They looked at each other and burst out laughing. Pete had been a neighbor when they'd been very young, and they had giggled then about his shiny bald head. It had been years since either of them had thought of Pete, which made Val's comment even funnier.

In a good mood again, Jinni drove Val home, but when they got there she turned off the engine and got out when Val did.

"You're coming in?" Val asked.

"If it's okay with you."

"You *know* it's okay! What is with you today?"

"Lunch was fun and I feel good. Hi again," she said to Estelle as they walked into the house through the kitchen door.

"Well, you two look well-fed and happy," Estelle said with a smile of her own.

"*I'm* well-fed," Jinni quipped. "Skinny here ate about three bites of her Chinese chicken salad." She walked off toward the dining room, leaving Val and Estelle staring in surprise.

Then Val caught on and hurried after her sister, who was checking out the wilting blossoms on the sideboard.

"This was not an inexpensive bouquet," Jinni announced with a smug glance at Val. "Men do not spend two hundred dollars on flowers without very good reason."

"That's a terrible exaggeration," Val scoffed. "That bouquet probably cost around fifty dollars. Maybe seventy-five."

"No way. It cost a bundle."

"Well, you stand there and admire it to your heart's content. I need to call Jim." Val left the dining room and a minute later Estelle walked in. Jinni sent her a glance. "Did you see what was written on the card, by any chance?"

"What card?"

"The card that came with these flowers."

"Reed brought them himself. There wasn't a card."

"Hmm." Jinni thought that over, then, because she wasn't quite convinced, asked, "Are you positive?"

"I put them in that vase, Jinni. If there had been a card, I would've seen it."

Jinni gave up. "Okay. Guess I'll be off. Oh, one thing. Not that I'm asking you to give away any secrets lurking around this house, but was Val nice to Reed when he delivered the flowers?"

"I'm sure she was. Val's nice to anyone who comes to her door, isn't she? But if you're asking me if I heard or saw something pass between them that could be described as titillating, or even slightly, dare I use the word, *romantic* that day, I didn't. I spoke to Reed briefly and then took the flowers to the kitchen. That was the extent of my participation."

"Gotcha," Jinni said dryly, resigned to the fact that she would never hear one word of gossip about Val from Estelle. "Well, it's time I went home. If I don't see Val on my way out, tell her goodbye for me and that I'll be calling later today or tomorrow." Jinni was almost through the door when she stopped. "Did she tell you that she's going to that cabin of hers in the mountains?"

"Not specifically, but it doesn't surprise me because she's been mentioning it in a general way since...since your wedding, actually. She truly loves going up there, Jinni."

"Well, it worries the hell out of me. I hate her going out there alone. Have you been there?"

"No, dear. Jim and I only became acquainted with Val after she became ill. Remember?"

"Yes, that's right. Well…'bye." With a frown of concern between her eyes, Jinni departed.

Reed parked his SUV next to the fire station and got out. Stopping by the place to make sure everything was ready for the next emergency call was habit and a generally satisfying task for him. He usually strode in purposefully, busied himself inside for fifteen minutes to an hour, depending on whether or not another volunteer was there, then locked up and went on to whatever else was on his agenda for the day.

Today, however, he stopped short of unlocking the door and walking into the building, turning his head to look across the intersection of Logan and Main Streets to the Animal Hospital, situated on the corner, and Val's house, next door to that. Was she there now, either at the hospital or in her house? he wondered. It angered him that he cared *where* she might be, and it angered him that he couldn't put her out of his mind however determined he was to do so.

Was she really that special, that unique?

He was still pondering that question when he drove away from the fire station about twenty minutes later. What made Val special? What was the big draw—her beauty? Reed snorted. Val was pretty, no one could doubt it, but there was no shortage of pretty women in Montana. Val's attractive face and tall, lean body did not make her unique.

"Then what the hell is it?" Reed muttered. Chemistry? Okay, so he was knocked out by the chemistry, but if she didn't feel it and it was all one-sided, then there was something wrong with his reception.

More than likely, though, it was Val's that was on the fritz. Maybe she was naturally a cold fish and wouldn't recognize chemistry with a man if it took the shape of a flying dragon and hovered over her head.

Reed grimaced. His thoughts were getting ridiculous. But that woman was driving him crazy, or rather *he* was driving himself crazy because of that woman.

"Aw, hell," he mumbled. He still didn't understand why he couldn't eliminate Valerie Fairchild from his mind, his life, his everything, and what was really tough to accept was the knowledge that he might not *ever* understand it.

Along with the book she was currently reading, Val took a pad and pen to bed with her that night. She was wearing soft pajamas, the television's volume was set on low, her bedside lamp was on and her back was comfortably supported with pillows. Half sitting, half lying down, she picked up the pen to begin a list of things that she needed to take with her this coming weekend. It had been months since her last visit to the cabin and she never left perishable food there, so she would need to shop for groceries.

Just the thought of entering MonMart made her shudder, though. There was no place in Rumor where she was more apt to run into Reed again, and she didn't want to have to say hello and then stand there tongue-tied, trying to think of conversation that wouldn't give him weird ideas about her. He already had enough weird ideas about her, and where he'd gotten them from she would never know. She had never done or said anything in his presence to make him think she was interested in him. She didn't even remember *how* a woman flirted and did silly things to spark a man's interest. Of course, she didn't try very hard to remember those things. She'd been good at batting her eyes, smiling flirtatiously, saying clever things and wagging her butt in a sensual way at one time, but that was a different life. She'd been a different woman.

Val sighed and laid her head back against a pillow. She'd been so carefree back then, so full of light and life…very much like Jinni still was. And then…

No, she wasn't going to think of that day. Raising her head, she again turned her thoughts to her list. This time she wrote the words *paper products* on the pad, and with that first line filled in, necessary items to take with her flooded her mind and she wrote rapidly.

An exciting aspect of this trip to the mountains was that Jim and Estelle had both agreed to stay in her house and take care of the dogs and cats in the Dog and Cat Houses for as along as she was gone. She could stay at the cabin for a week, if she so decided.

It also meant arranging any appointments requested by pet owners around next week, but that wasn't difficult to do.

It was all doable, and it was lovely to contemplate. The cabin had always been good medicine for her, the *best* medicine.

She could hardly wait for the moment when her SUV was packed and ready to go. She was ready now—emotionally ready, at any rate—and she'd told Jim and Estelle that she would like to leave on Friday morning. She hadn't yet told Jinni that she was leaving on Friday instead of Saturday but she would, of course. Val wouldn't go anywhere for a week without telling Jinni about it. But since she'd already heard her sister's negative feelings on the topic, she saw no good reason to impart her exact plans right away. She would tell Jinni later in the week and she would not let her sister talk her out of going a day early or at any other time, for that matter, however adamantly opposed to the trip Jinni was.

Val let her head fall back to the pillow again. She had always found such marvelous peace at the cabin, and just thinking about it gave her comfort. On Saturday she would attain that incredible sense of everything being right with her world once again.

And it was an appropriate time to go up there, in any case, because this perfect weather couldn't possibly last for much longer. She had to make sure the cabin was ready for a long, hard winter.

In the Cantrell mansion, Max and Jinni were settling in for the night. Michael's room was far enough away from the master suite that they couldn't hear him and he couldn't hear them. Not that Jinni would have minded him overhearing what she was about to discuss with her beloved husband.

In a drowsy, totally relaxed voice she said, "Reed Kingsley was at our wedding. Did you invite him?"

"Mom did, I think."

"Are they friends?"

"I think she admires him because of his contributions to the town."

"Contributions…in the way of money?"

"No, sweetheart, in the way of time and energy. Reed's always been very involved in civic affairs. And he played a big role in saving the town from the summer's big fire."

"Are you and he friends?"

"Oh, sure. Everyone is Reed's friend." Max turned over to face his wife. "Why all these questions about Reed? Am I already losing my beautiful wife to another man?"

"That'll never happen, sport." Jinni moved closer and kissed him. "No more teasing, okay?. This is serious business, or it might be. I'm not altogether sure of what exactly is going on, but Reed brought flowers to Val, and it wasn't a cheap bouquet, either. What do you think it means?"

"Maybe he likes her."

"Yes, maybe he does."

"Well, does she like him?"

"I don't know. She acts like she doesn't, but—" Jinni cut that sentence short and lay there pondering the situation. "Has he ever been married?"

"No."

"But he likes women."

Max chuckled. "Yes, darling, he likes women. Something's cooking in that nimble brain of yours. What're you planning to do, sneak up on Reed when he's not looking and rope him into the family?"

Jinni thought for a moment. "Val is going to that cabin of hers in the mountains this weekend. Leaving Saturday morning. Wouldn't it be great if I could figure a way to get Reed out there, too?''

''Playing matchmaker when the people involved aren't interested can get you in big trouble, sweetheart.''

''But that's the point, isn't it? To find out if they are interested in each other? Reed is or he wouldn't be buying Val flowers. It's *her* attitude that has me guessing. But I don't think she would be rude if he should suddenly appear on her doorstep, and they would be so nicely alone out there. Anything could happen.''

Max dropped a kiss on her lips. ''You worry all night about it if you wish, sweetheart. But I'm going to let Reed take care of his own love life, and go to sleep now. All I know is this—if Reed is only half as successful as I was in the romance department, he'll end up a happy man. Good night, wife.''

Jinni smiled. ''Good night, husband.''

She lay awake for a long time before a plan came to her. ''Yes!'' she whispered ecstatically. She hadn't come up with a way to get Reed out to that mountain cabin, but Val would still be in town—and at home—on Friday evening. It was a darn good place to start, and Jinni had complete faith in her plan. There was only one thing that could make her happier than she already was, and that was to see her sister deeply in love and in a permanent relationship. Reed Kingsley seemed made to order, and if Jinni had to practice a little sleight-of-hand to get Val and him together, so be it.

On Thursday Jinni walked to Jilly's Lilies and chose the most elegant bouquet the quaint little floral shop provided. After writing a message on one of the small cards that went with deliveries, she told the young man at the desk to please deliver the flowers to Reed Kingsley.

''I believe he lives out of town, at the Kingsley Ranch? It seems more logical to make your delivery to MonMart, wouldn't you agree?''

Another idea struck Jinni. ''Wait, I believe you can see

the fire station from here, can't you?'' Jinni stepped to the shop's front window and peered out. "Yes, there it is. I can see it quite clearly. Listen, I've been told that Reed stops by the station every day. Do you think you could arrange to have these delivered tomorrow when he's over there?''

The young man said yes, that he would keep an eye on the fire station and take the flowers over himself when he saw Reed.

Jinni left the shop with a satisfied light in her big blue eyes. Smiling to herself, she got into her car. She had gotten the ball rolling. The next step would be Reed's, if he wanted to take it, and Jinni suspected he would after he read the message she'd written on that card. After that it would be up to Val.

Humming happily, enjoying her sense of accomplishment, Jinni drove home.

On Friday morning, Val loaded her SUV. There was enough food for a week, among clean linens in boxes and her clothes in suitcases. The back of her unit was full and she was about to tell Estelle goodbye when Jim came running over from the Animal Hospital.

"Val! Val, there's an emergency! Come quickly!''

Val took off running with him right behind her. "Small dog…hit by a car,'' Jim explained between breaths as he ran. "In examination room two.''

Val hit the door at full speed and rushed to the examining room. There, on the table, was a small black-and-white dog, and his owner, an elderly lady, standing next to the table, weeping quietly into a handful of tissues.

An hour later the little dog had been tended—he was going to be fine—and Val, with a sinking sensation, realized that she could not be gone all next week. She had only recently announced in the newspaper that she was back to work full-time. Jim was great with the kenneled animals and tending to minor problems, but emergencies such as this one required a doctor's expertise. She could not go off for a week on a whim. The community counted on her, and she wouldn't have it any other way. She loved her work, after all.

But no one expected her to be on the job seven days a week, so a weekend away was perfectly acceptable.

Disappointed, but telling herself that a weekend at the cabin was better than no time there, she told Jim goodbye and walked back to the house. Jinni was waiting with an anxious expression on her face and a small box in her hands.

"Val, what in heaven's name is going on? Why is your car already packed?" her sister asked.

"I told you I was going to the cabin," Val replied.

"But you said Saturday."

"Did I? I might have, but as you can see, I'm going this morning."

Jinni frowned and fought an awful urge to tell Val to stay in town where she belonged. She managed to stifle it, and held out the box she was holding. "In that case, I'm glad I decided to bring this over this morning. Here, take this cell phone and charger with you. Max has dozens of the things and he said I could give you any or all of them. Michael helped me choose this one. He said it has good power and a fairly long range."

Val heaved a sigh and reluctantly accepted the small box of electronic components. "I'll only be gone the weekend," she told her sister.

"Well, that's good news, at least," Jinni said with a totally sour expression. What about this evening? she asked herself. What about Reed? Damn it, all of her plotting and planning was going to come to naught. "How come? I thought you were staying out there for a week."

"I can't be gone that long without letting the town know about it ahead of time." Val quickly explained the emergency she had just taken care of. "Even two days will be pleasant, though. Well, I'd best be off. I'll see you next week."

"I have the number of that phone, so expect to get some

calls,'' Jinni said. ''And if anything goes wrong, anything at all, you are to call me at once.''

''Jinni, if this phone works in the mountains, I'll report in morning, noon and night. How does that strike you?''

Jinni ignored her sister's sweetly sarcastic voice and barely managed to smile. ''It strikes me as sane and sensible,'' she said a bit sharply. Then she changed her tone. ''Have a good time, although for the life of me I can't figure out how you could possibly have a good time in a tiny little cabin in the woods all by yourself.'' *Now what? I guess I should cancel that flower delivery. Or should I just go back to the shop and change the message? Hmm, that might have possibilities.* Jinni smiled at the thought, only the second smile she'd shown her wayward sister that morning. ''Kiss me good-bye.''

Val kissed her on the cheek, and Jinni advised her to drive safely. Estelle came out to say goodbye, and she and Jinni stood and waved as Val finally drove away.

''Damn, I hate her going off alone like this,'' Jinni said passionately.

''I'm sure she'll be fine,'' Estelle said, and went back into the house.

A short time later, in the Cantrell mansion, Max went into the library where Jinni was standing at a window, worriedly looking outside and wondering if she should cancel the flower order, change the message or simply forget the whole thing.

Max announced, ''Sweetheart, we could be in for our first blizzard of the year. I was checking the weather forecasts for the entire country on the Internet, and Montana could be hit big time. Our weather's been so great that two feet of snow could be a jolt to the town.'' He saw the horrified expression on his wife's face and quickly added, ''Maybe it will miss us, though—never can tell.''

Jinni stood there frozen for a minute, then ran for the telephone. Frantically she dialed the number of the cell phone she had given Val.

But there was no answer. Obviously Val hadn't turned it on. Jinni cursed herself for not making sure it was turned on before she even gave it to her.

"Damn it, Max, the sun is shining," Jinni cried. "Are you sure of that forecast?"

"Hey, don't panic. That storm could pass us by completely."

Jinni's thundering heartbeat began to slow down. "Really? Val is on her way to the mountains right now."

Max shrugged. "Life doesn't come to a standstill around here because of bad weather, Jin. Honey, even if we do get some of that storm, Valerie knows what to do. She's lived here for years, and I'll bet that she's gone to that cabin during past winters as often as she has during good weather. Don't get yourself all worked up over nothing."

It took a minute but Jinni finally nodded. "I'll try not to worry, but I still wish she would turn on that damn phone!"

Chapter Seven

Val was thoroughly enjoying the drive. The sun was bright, the scenery spectacular, and there was so little traffic on the back roads she traveled that she was comfortable about letting her mind wander.

One thought *wasn't* all that comforting but she couldn't quite sidestep it. To avoid MonMart and another possible meeting with Reed Kingsley, she had asked Jim to do her shopping. He was such an agreeable man, Val thought gratefully. She was incredibly fortunate to have him and Estelle not only in her employ but also as friends.

That aside, she had taken the coward's way out and didn't like thinking she had limited her own sense of freedom in Rumor. There had to be another way to deal with Reed; unceasing avoidance simply wasn't possible in such a small town, and she hated the idea of peering around corners and looking over her shoulder for the rest of her life, or until he tired of the game.

In truth, thinking about the whole traumatic mess made

her squirm uncomfortably. Why the man would bother pursuing her continued to escape her, and she was going to have to figure out a way to communicate her disinterest to his apparently egotistical, big-man-in-town, hard head.

But not this weekend. She had lots of good food with her and the weekend was going to be wonderful. Actually, when she stopped annoying herself with thoughts of Reed Kingsley, Val felt as though her cabin might already be working its magic, even though the mountains were still miles in the distance.

Smiling, she inhaled a long, slow, serene breath. It was going to be just her and Mother Nature for two perfect days.

She felt good about that, *very* good. Indeed, some sort of magic was at work; how could she doubt it?

Reed heard about the approaching storm from various sources: the newspapers, a morning television newscast and his folks when he went to their place for coffee and conversation. The ambiguous forecast didn't alarm him in the least. The low front *could* drop as far south as central Montana or it could sweep across Canada and only cause low temperatures below the border. Even if Rumor did feel the full impact of a fierce winter storm, it was past due.

People talked about it, though. Even with the sun bright and beaming warmth to the earth, everyone was a bit more watchful of the sky, with some of them "feeling snow in their bones." Reed didn't doubt "feelings" of that nature; it was his experience that some older people were pretty good weather forecasters. Oddly, the possibility of seeing the end of Indian Summer and facing a full-blown blizzard put pep in a lot of folks' steps. Reed got a kick out of the hustle and bustle he observed around MonMart that morning. People bought snow shovels—and motorized snow blowers—and stocked up on bottled water, flashlights, batteries, candles and groceries, with many relating survival stories of blizzards that had lasted for weeks.

Reed was still working on the contest for naming the park,

and he stayed busy most of the morning on the project. Shortly after lunch he drove to the fire station and went inside. Two other volunteers—Bob Harrison and Lyle Malesky—were there, kicking around, and the three of them were talking and kidding each other when someone rapped at the side door of the building.

Everyone called, "Come on in. It's not locked," and the door opened. A teenager carrying a huge bouquet of flowers walked in.

"Hello," he said. "I'm Blake Cameron. I work part-time at Jilly's Lilies. I was sent over here to deliver these to Reed Kingsley." He finished by saying, "Which one of you is Mr. Kingsley?"

Reed grinned, and Bob and Lyle guffawed. "I'm Kingsley," Reed stated with a smug look at his pals. "No one would send flowers to these two dunderheads." He took the paper-wrapped bouquet and saw the card. "Thank you," he said to Blake.

"All right, who sent 'em?" Lyle demanded the second he was gone.

"As if you're ever going to know," Reed drawled, stuffing the small envelope into the back pocket of his jeans. He was burning with curiosity himself, but he wasn't about to let these jokers in on the name of the lady who had sent him flowers. It never entered his mind that a man might have sent them, a business associate, or an organization. No, a woman had sent this massive bouquet and he was dying to find out *which* woman.

"Well, so long," he said with another grin for his nosy friends. He walked out of the building to his SUV, carrying the flowers. While getting into the vehicle he noticed dark, threatening clouds moving in from the north. "Oh, yeah," he said with a nod of his head. "It's definitely coming." He laid the bouquet on the passenger seat and then dug into his back pocket for that tiny envelope. He pulled out the card and read it.

Reed,
Tit for tat, right? You brought me flowers, I send you flowers. Shall we consider these beautiful blooms as our own private way of communicating? I've been regretting every rude word I've said to you and I hope we can try again, this time getting off to a better start. If you come by my house this evening I promise to apologize in person.
Val

Reed stared in disbelief and read the card again. His heart was thundering in his chest, his pulse rate absolutely wild. Val had asked him over tonight to apologize in person. What had changed her mind about him? This was fantastic, unbelievable, the most exciting thing that had happened in ages.

He drove back to MonMart feeling fifty pounds lighter, with a song in his heart.

Jinni was on pins and needles. She kept calling the cell phone she'd given Val and getting no response. The blizzard was on its way. Doubt that it would reach central Montana was fading fast. She walked the floor and then, suddenly, grabbed a jacket and yelled to Max that she was leaving for a few minutes, whereupon she ran from the house, jumped into her car and drove to the Animal Hospital.

Rushing around her sister's place of business, she found Jim and, all out of breath, started talking a mile a minute. "Where's Val's cabin? Have you been there? I need directions to find it. She can't be out there alone when that killer blizzard hits. Talk to me, Jim. Help me out with this."

The poor man looked befuddled. "If you'd give me a chance to get in a word," he finally said, "I could set you straight in one short sentence. I've never been to the cabin and Val never told me how to get to it."

Jinni threw up her hands. "My God, what should we do? Call the highway patrol?"

"Jinni, calm down. I'm sure when Val realizes that a storm is on its way, she'll come back to town without any of us calling in the law. She's an intelligent woman. Give her some credit, okay?"

Jinni weakly leaned against a cupboard. "Jim, I'm worried sick about her and everyone keeps telling me I shouldn't worry at all. If it was Estelle out there, alone in a blizzard, wouldn't you be worried?"

"Not if she was in a cozy little cabin, I wouldn't. Jinni, Val is not going to be wandering those mountains on foot during a storm. And she's got plenty of grub and warm clothes with her. Even the worst blizzards usually blow themselves out in a day or two."

"Really? I seem to remember some fierce storms in New York that lasted longer than two days."

"Well, that happens, of course. But I just don't enjoy thinking the worst. Plus, I have infinite trust in Val's good sense."

"Oh." Jinni pushed away from the cupboard. "I guess I do, too," she said, then sighed. "I'm making too much of this, aren't I?"

"Yes, ma'am, you are."

As Jinni walked out she stated, "Even so, I'm going to keep on calling that cell phone I gave her."

Jim shook his head and chuckled. Not that a blizzard wasn't a dangerous animal. People around Rumor respected storms and used good sense to survive in the most comfortable way possible. A warm home, well-stocked pantries and emergency supplies to use in case the power was knocked out were things that relieved the stress of an impending storm. Val had those things with her. She would be just fine.

With a sinking heart slowing her normal full-speed-ahead-and-damn-the-torpedoes approach to life, Jinni roamed the Cantrell mansion and waited for the storm to hit. She didn't actually wring her hands, but she came close.

At one point she remembered the flowers and the note

she'd sent to Reed Kingsley in Val's name, but it was such a trivial concern compared to her worry for her sister's safety that the prospect of Reed going to Val's home with romantic intentions hardly even registered. Jinni was a city woman, through and through. She had never deliberately spent time in the country, except for places like the Hamptons, which was nothing at all like the wilds of Montana. All she'd known about country life before moving to Montana were lovely forests with gorgeous homes and lots of people throwing posh parties and playing with their expensive toys.

She loved Rumor, but, damn it, she had not bargained for this kind of worry when she decided to move here, and she couldn't even whine to Max about it because he was once again locked up in the library with a flock of lawyers, plotting Guy's defense.

She had a notion to call the police, even if Jim didn't approve.

And maybe she would do that. Maybe, damn it to hell, she *really* just might do that!

Val saw the three deer nibbling on the grass at the back of her property the second she drove into the crude cut in the terrain that passed as her driveway. She turned off the engine and watched them. They had raised their beautiful heads and were watching her just as intently. After a few minutes of supreme pleasure, Val opened the door of her SUV and the deer bounded away into the trees.

"Such lovely creatures," she said quietly as she got out. Taking a huge breath of the clean mountain air, she reached back into her vehicle for her jacket. The temperature was always at least ten degrees lower in the mountains than it was in town, but today it seemed even cooler. It was then, while she was still looking around, that she noticed dark clouds in the sky.

She was pretty sure that the clouds were moving in from the north, but she certainly wasn't afraid of a little rain or even of snow. In fact, she loved when it rained at night up here, as the cabin had a metal roof and the sound of rain when she was snug and warm in bed was positively delicious.

Val didn't immediately unload the SUV. First, she went to the electrical box on the side of the cabin and switched on the power. Then she went inside and made sure the refrigerator was running. She could hear the electric water pump working and bringing water from the well into the cabin, and she turned on the faucets in the kitchen and in the bathroom to clean out the pipes.

There was a small storage shed behind the cabin, filled with all sorts of things—junk mostly, although she had added a few items to those already there when she'd bought the place. The cabin itself was one large room, except for the small bathroom in one corner. It had a decent little kitchen— electric stove, refrigerator, sink, a few cupboards, table and chairs—and a huge fireplace—the only way to heat the place, should she need heat. The bedroom, as she laughingly called the bed and dresser, was situated near the bathroom. The living room—a sofa and two chairs—was close to the fireplace.

She loved it. It was old and used, chipped and worn, but it had the necessities—a shower stall in the tiny bathroom being one of them—and she truly loved it.

With the utilities up and running, she began hauling in her things.

Reed couldn't concentrate on anything but the card in his pocket, and forcing himself to sit at his desk felt like a prison sentence. He endured the torture for about an hour, then got up, let everyone know that he was leaving for the day, and left the building.

Outside and heading for his vehicle, he faced a strong wind—a strong, *cold* wind—and felt some flyaway raindrops on his face. The sun was completely obliterated by a heavy cloud cover; the first severe storm of the winter was underway. For the first time since receiving Val's message he thought of something else—his horses. The four beautiful, valuable Thoroughbreds were outside and should be in the barn. He would see to it.

He drove home with the windshield wipers on intermittent because the rain came in spurts, and then parked in the garage. After bringing the bouquet of flowers in and laying it in the kitchen sink, he went to his bedroom and changed clothes, donning much warmer pants, shirt and jacket. He settled a favorite old cowboy hat low on his head and, carrying a pair of lined leather gloves that he worked onto his hands as he walked, he left the house and strode out to the horse pasture.

Three of his horses were huddled together, but he couldn't see the fourth—Sheva, a young mare. With the pasture being completely fenced, she couldn't be far. He brought the other three into the barn, leading two of them into their stalls. He saddled the third and rode out into the gusting wind and rain to bring in Sheva.

He was riding for about five minutes when he realized that the raindrops were slushy; it was starting to snow.

Val was nearly knocked off her feet by a fierce gust of wind as she hauled the last of her things into the cabin. She managed to stay upright and hurried in, wondering how bad this storm would get. Rain she liked. Snow was fine, too, but high winds had no redeeming qualities whatsoever. They were, in fact, scary.

But they would be just as scary in town, and besides, she decided, driving in wind this strong was more dangerous than staying right where she was. The cabin was chilly now, though, so out she went again to haul in some firewood. She had a standing arrangement with a local man to keep her woodshed full of cut, split wood, so she had plenty of fuel.

She made about a dozen trips and filled the wood box tucked up against the left side of the rock fireplace. Then she looked around. Her one-room cabin was a mess, with boxes and suitcases everywhere, taking up what little space wasn't used by furniture. She hated clutter, especially in a small place like this, and she was itching to put everything away.

But first things first. She built a fire in the fireplace, and when it was burning nicely and even throwing a little heat, she began the chore of putting away more groceries than she could possibly eat in two days, and, finally, her clothes.

When she got to the small box Jinni had given her, the one with the cell phone and battery charger, she turned it on, knowing in her bones that it wouldn't work in these heavily forested mountains. She got a message—no available service—accepted what Jinni had refused to consider, and put the phone back in the box. Val set the box and its contents on top of the refrigerator, and then gave in to the hunger pangs that had badgered her while she was hauling in wood.

It was while she was eating hot soup at her tiny kitchen table that the rain turned to snow, almost before her eyes.

The storm seemed to be getting worse by the minute. Val finished her soup and watched out the window. She debated the wisdom of staying put versus braving the storm to get back to town.

But visibility was already poor, and she didn't doubt that the blizzard would get worse before it got better. The sensible thing was for her to stay right where she was. Even if the power went off she still had more than enough food, the fireplace, plenty of wood and…and water?

Jumping up, she began filling the large bottles she kept at the cabin for just such an emergency.

She was fine. She was *going* to be fine. The blizzard didn't frighten her, but one did need to keep a cool head during this kind of storm.

With water pouring into a bottle, Val went over to stoke the fire. She added two more large chunks of wood, then hurried back to the sink to turn off the faucet. Lifting the full bottle to the floor took all of her strength, but she quickly replaced it with an empty one, turned on the faucet again, then grabbed her jacket and hurried outside for more wood.

The wind clawed at her clothes and hair, and icy snow

pelted her face. She fought her way to the woodshed and loaded her arms. She made three trips and finally decided she had sufficient fuel to last throughout the night. She would deal with tomorrow when it came. The storm, after all, could have completely died down by then.

Rumor was turning white and so was the Kingsley Ranch. Reed finally located Sheva and brought her in. When she and the horse Reed had ridden were safe and secure in their stalls, he made sure all four horses had water, forked hay into their feed troughs and put out small helpings of oats. He left the barn and bucked the storm on his way back to the house.

After a hot shower, he pulled on clean jeans and a shirt, then went to the phone and dialed Val's home number. He wanted her to know that the storm could get ten times worse and he would still knock on her door this evening. In fact, it seemed crucial that she know this.

Estelle answered. "Dr. Fairchild's residence."

"Estelle, hello. This is Reed Kingsley. Are you all faring all right in this weather?"

"Jim and I are faring just fine, but we've been wondering how Val is doing. We decided to stay in town so Jim could tend the animals and—"

Reed had been sitting more or less relaxed in a chair, and he suddenly jerked erect. "What did you say about Val?"

"Well, she's out at that cabin of hers, and—"

"What cabin?"

"Goodness, Reed, I'm trying to tell you. You needn't shout."

"I'm sorry. What cabin, Estelle?"

"She went to her cabin today, around noon, and of course the sun was still shining. While people were talking about a storm maybe coming this way, I guess it didn't worry her none. Didn't really worry Jim and me, either, to be honest about it, but then I don't think we were anticipating something this bad."

Reed tried to clear his head. Why had Val invited him over

tonight, then gone off to the mountains? She'd probably expected to be back before this evening. Yeah, that was it.

"So, what time are you expecting Val to be back?" he asked, trying to sound normal and as though his heart weren't making every effort to beat a hole through the wall of his chest.

"Late Sunday, but—"

"Estelle! Where's that cabin?"

"It's in the mountains, but—"

"Can you give me explicit instructions on how to find it? She should not be anywhere alone in a storm of this magnitude, and I really don't understand why she went at all when... Never mind, that's not the point. How do I get there?"

"I have no idea. Neither does Jim. Jinni asked the same question. She's never been there, either, and she's worried."

"Estelle, *someone* must know the location of that cabin!"

"Someone does know. Val knows," Estelle said curtly. She liked Reed, but he wasn't being very nice about something that certainly wasn't her fault.

"But...but—" Reed was having trouble talking and breathing at the same time. Val was in the mountains. *Which* mountains? The whole damn valley was surrounded by mountains!

And the question remained and beat in his head like a tom-tom: why would Val invite him over in such a provocative way and then go to some cabin in the mountains that no one knew the location of, and tell Estelle she wouldn't be back until Sunday? It made no sense at all.

"Reed? Are you still there?" Estelle said.

"Uh, yeah. Listen, if Val shows up, would you ask her to call me?"

"Yes, I could do that," Estelle said slowly, conveying distinct curiosity. Reed might have some questions about Val's whereabouts, but Estelle had a few of her own. Not about the precise location of Val's cabin, but about Reed calling like this and conveying panic. Yes, panic was what she was hearing in his voice. It was possible, of course, that he was merely concerned for a fellow citizen's well-being, but when Estelle thought of that wilting bouquet in the dining room, she couldn't quite believe neighborly concern was the only thing driving his bus.

"Thanks, Estelle," Reed mumbled. He put down the phone while she was still saying goodbye, then he got up and paced his house like a caged animal. *What in hell is going on?* He stopped and looked at the bouquet still in the sink. He grabbed a vase from a cabinet, put some water in it and then the flowers.

But it was the card, which he read again, that reached deep down inside of him and wrung him out. Val had finally decided to like him, then... No, that couldn't be right. Nothing added up. People didn't invite someone to their home, then take a damn two-day jaunt!

So what did it mean? Were this card and the flowers a bad joke? Was this Val's way of saying "Get the hell out of my life?"

Reed felt broken. No one had ever done something so hurtful to him before.

Then, in the next second, a memory flashed through his mind. His brother, Tag, owned property in the Spring Mountains, and when Tag bought the land—some years back— he'd mentioned other people in town buying property right next to his. And hadn't Tag mentioned Dr. Fairchild? It was a vague memory, and Reed wasn't sure it was accurate. But what if it was?

He ran to the phone. With his heart in his throat he dialed Tag's number. And while he waited for someone to pick up there, he wondered why in hell he was going to such lengths to make sure that a woman who had done what she'd done to him today was all right.

There was only one logical answer to that question and it hurt like hell to even think that he might be in love with Valerie Fairchild.

What hurt even more was the knowledge that she couldn't care less.

"Tag? Look, am I remembering something correctly? When you bought your land in the Spring Mountains, did you say something about Dr. Fairchild buying a piece of property near yours?"

Chapter Eight

The wind blew snow in a swirling, circular pattern, wrapping it around and around Reed's SUV as though ingesting the vehicle. He squinted to see through the mass of moving white in his headlights and was grateful for side-of-the-road reflectors that hadn't yet been buried in snow. If the storm maintained this ferocity all night, there would be little to see in the morning beyond the bleakness of storm-stripped trees in a solid white world.

None of it frightened Reed. He'd grown up with winter storms like this one, he knew how to drive in near-blinding conditions, and he had packed his vehicle with food, water, blankets and everything else he thought he might need, should he lose his way or become stuck in a snowbank.

He didn't plan on getting stuck, though, nor did he anticipate losing his way. Tag had given him explicit instructions on how to find Val's cabin. "It's only about a mile from my property, Reed. She bought her land in the Spring Mountains about the same time I bought mine."

Darkness had fallen about the time he'd started the drive from Rumor to the Spring Mountains, and there was something eerie about being a part of a black-and-white landscape. Tag had also said, "If you're worried about Dr. Fairchild, maybe we should call Montana Search and Rescue."

Reed had immediately nixed that suggestion. "I don't think so," he had responded, thinking Val would lay both of them low if they made a public issue out of his daring to think she might need rescuing. Besides, Reed had participated in several serious search and rescue operations, and making sure Val was safe really didn't qualify as an emergency situation.

"No, I'm sure she's fine," he'd told his brother. "I just don't like the idea of her being out there alone."

And then, of course, Tag had asked questions about Reed's connection to Dr. Fairchild, and Reed had given him the minimum information and gotten off the phone. Telling anyone, even one of his brothers, that he was smitten by a woman who wanted nothing to do with him was an embarrassing prospect, especially when he was still asking himself *why* he was so smitten.

He was crazy as a loon to rush to the rescue of a woman who was probably doing just fine on her own, but there was always the chance that she *wasn't* doing fine. Reed didn't like thinking the worst about any situation, but doubting the danger of a powerful blizzard wasn't smart. He had to wonder if Val had heard a weather report before leaving Rumor.

And, of course, nothing else he thought about, not the storm or Val needing help, had the power to overwhelm the painful uneasiness that hit him when he asked himself why she would send him a provocative message and then leave town.

"Damn," he muttered, and made fun of himself by adding in a voice heavy with sarcasm, "Reed to the rescue of a woman who can't stand the sight of him. You're a damn fool, do you realize that?"

* * *

Val was snug as a bug in her tiny cabin. She'd been keeping the flames hot and high in the fireplace. She sat with a blanket snuggled around her in a comfortable old chair in front of the fire, sipping tea and listening to the storm. As always when she was at her cabin, rain or shine, she felt a marvelous sense of peace.

The electricity was still on, but she had placed candles and matches on almost every flat surface in case the power went out. She truly wasn't worried. She had plenty of wood to keep the cabin heated and three huge bottles of water for bathing and cooking, as well as the bottled water she'd brought for drinking. She also had a two-burner propane stove—it had come with the cabin—and extra propane canisters, so if the electricity went, she would still be able to heat soup or cook something.

She was all set for anything the blizzard might throw at her, and she enjoyed knowing she was completely alone on the mountain. The wind blasted the north side of the cabin every few minutes, but Val merely nestled a little bit deeper into her blanket, took a swallow from her mug of hot tea and sighed contentedly.

But then she thought of Jinni, who was probably worried about her. Val really hated worrying her sister. She had absolutely no faith in that cellular telephone working in this blizzard, but she pushed aside the blanket, got up and took the phone down from the top of the refrigerator, setting it on the small counter.

She had left the phone on, and she quickly punched in Jinni's number. All she got was another message that she was out of the service area. Val plugged in the charger and put the phone into the slot, but it was useless in these mountains, among so many trees and in a storm.

She was returning to her chair by the fire when she heard a discordant sound, one that didn't fit with the storm's normal growls. Was it a car? Some kind of motor? My God, was someone lost out there, driving unfamiliar, snow-covered roads, trying to find the way out of the mountains? There were so many little roads running this way and that, and it would be very easy for a stranger to get turned around and lose his sense of direction.

Val hurried over to her front window and pushed aside the heavy curtain that kept out an enormous amount of cold. Peering into the storm, she saw a flash of light. Someone *was* out there! It was a vehicle of some kind, possibly with a panicked driver. She kept watching and realized that the intermittent flashes she saw were headlights.

Val switched on the light next to the front door of the cabin. She would, of course, assist a bewildered traveler in any way she could. That could be a family out there, lost and frightened, a family with small children.

"Oh, Lord," she whispered, and opened the curtains so that as much light as she could provide would shine through the window and lead the driver to the safety of her cabin.

In mere moments Val realized the vehicle had turned into her driveway. The driver had spotted her lights, and, undoubtedly relieved, would appear at her door seeking information, if not a place to wait out the worst of the blizzard.

Her gaze swept the interior of her cabin. If there were children, she would let them use her one bed. Grown-ups could stretch out on the floor near the fireplace. She had plenty of blankets and food. Yes, she would definitely help out whoever came to her door, whether it be man, woman or child.

Then she heard a voice. "Val? Val?"

Startled at hearing her own name shouted loudly enough to compete with the wind, she stiffened defensively. Who was out there? In the next heartbeat Val relaxed. Jinni had sent someone to check on her. Maybe it was Jim, badgered by Jinni and possibly Estelle to brave the storm and make sure Val was safe and sound.

She went to the door before the person had time to knock, with words such as, "My God, Jim, you didn't have to come way out here just because Jinni's a worrywart,'' on the tip of her tongue.

Only once the door was opened wide enough for her to see the man bent into the wind and making his way to her cabin, Val's heart nearly stopped. She was looking at Reed Kingsley….

She almost slammed the door in his face. She was so angry she truly couldn't speak. In fact, the only thing she *could* do was walk over to the fireplace and stand with her back to it while she stared daggers at this intrusive busybody of a man who believed so much in his own macho charm that he *couldn't* believe in her disinterest.

Reed stepped in, shut the door behind him and stood there not quite knowing where to put himself. Val was all right. Her cabin was small, but it appeared comfortable and adequately equipped. In fact, it was a cozy little place. One room.

"I—I guess I was, uh, worried for nothing,'' he stammered. "About, uh, you, I mean.'' This was embarrassing. He *never* stammered.

Val opened her mouth and started to say, "And why would you worry about me, in any case?'' She got to the word *worry* and nearly choked on it because of the explosive crash that came from outside and actually shook the cabin.

Reed was as stunned as Val. It took a second for him to get his bearings and sprint for the door. Val rushed outside right behind him, and only because of the light by the door could they make out the behemoth of a tree that was lying across the front half of Reed's SUV.

"What the hell…?'' Reed mumbled, only because he didn't know what to say. His SUV was barely recognizable. The huge pine tree had smashed the vehicle's hood and windshield, lying at a peculiar angle. True, the back end of his rig wasn't crumpled, but it wasn't much good without the motor.

Val's SUV was in front of his. He had parked in her narrow little driveway right behind her rig, and there was no way to maneuver her vehicle around his, or the tree. They were—both he and Val—stuck.

How long they would be stuck on the snowy mountain depended on the duration of the storm. Maybe after six or seven days Tag would decide his brother had been in the mountains long enough and call in a Montana Search and Rescue team.

For some strange reason, that thought made Reed laugh. The sound carried to Val, who was shivering in the cold and staring at the mess that had once been a proud and stately tree and an SUV that had probably cost three times what she had paid for her much smaller car. And Reed thought it was funny?

Shuddering because she might be out here with a madman, although he'd never seemed *that* odd before, she turned and ran back inside the cabin. They had left the door open and the place was now almost as cold inside as the storm outside. She slammed the door and hurried over to the fireplace to stoke and poke and add more wood.

Reed walked in and he, too, slammed the door shut. Then, without an invitation to make himself comfortable, or even a sympathetic look from Val because his SUV was wrecked, he took off his heavy jacket and asked, "Where should I put this?"

Oh, what an opening that was, she thought, with the answer she would love to express burning her tongue.

But, considering the situation, crudity or bald-faced rudeness wasn't her best course of action. He was here, intruding once again, but this time, furious or not, she couldn't kick him out.

While she was making up her mind on how best to speak to this overbearing person, he got back into his jacket. She stared. He *was* crazy!

"I'm going to haul in some things," Reed said, as though he had every right to crowd her little cabin with God knew what.

She watched him go, then went over to her chair and got

her blanket, which she drew around herself. But she didn't sit down, because that would put her back to the door, and she wanted to see what sort of "things" he hauled in. Instead, she stood as close to the fire as was safe—it had a sturdy screen to block flying embers—and watched the door.

It opened and Reed came in carrying a huge box. "This is food."

Val finally found her voice, and she totally forgot about it being best to avoid rudeness. Sounding downright hateful, she said, "And you brought food up here because...? Do you think I'm brainless enough to come out here for a weekend without something to eat?"

Her sarcasm, her displeasure, her dis*like,* gave Reed a start. He took a breath and told himself to get over it. She didn't like him, she never had liked him and she probably never would.

So he'd made another mistake, hadn't he? Rescuing Valerie Fairchild, or *attempting* to rescue her, was, in her eyes, a hanging offense. She wanted no man's help. She was a self-sufficient, independent woman and...

But wait! If all that were true, and it sure seemed to be true, why had she sent him those flowers? And invited him to her house tonight? It didn't add up...none of it.

"I've never thought of you as brainless, quite the opposite, in fact. I'll just set this box over by the refrigerator for now." Reed put the box down and went back outside.

Val felt hopeless...and helpless. Apparently she wasn't smart enough to make Reed Kingsley understand that she didn't want him poking around in her life. She didn't want *any* man hanging around, telling her lies about her beauty and intelligence just to get into her panties.

She glanced at the bed. One bed, two people. Well, if he had come up here under the guise of saving her from the storm to try one more time to pierce her protective armor and get her into bed—and what else could he want from her?— he was in for one very big surprise.

Val returned to her chair and a second later Reed came in again, this time loaded with blankets and a big canvas bag.

She took one look, then turned away and stared into the fire.

"Bedding and a few personal things," Reed said. "I can see you don't have a lot of extra space in here, and I know you're pissed off at me because I dared to invade your privacy once again, but would you please stop sulking long enough to give me an inkling of where you would prefer I put these things?"

"Sulking? I'm sulking?" Val got to her feet. "I can't believe your gall, even though you keep proving it over and over again. What I'd really like to know is who delegated you my keeper?"

Reed strode to the bed, let the blankets drop from his arms onto it, then set his bag on the floor. He took off his jacket and laid it on top of the bag.

"You have no answer for that, do you?" Val said with a sneer.

"I don't waste my breath answering ridiculous questions." Reed walked over to the box of food and opened the door of the refrigerator. It was almost full, but he'd brought items that should be refrigerated, so he moved Val's food around to make room for his.

She was steaming. What was he doing, taking over the place? "My question was not ridiculous, but you are!"

Leaving the kitchen area, Reed cocked an eyebrow and eyed her with a withering look. "And you, apparently, are something I never would have guessed before today's fiasco." He was thinking of the dirty flower trick she'd pulled on him. "You, Dr. Fairchild, are immature."

Val's jaw dropped. "And just how mature do you think a man determined to get a disinterested woman into bed is?"

He snorted out a sarcastic laugh. "Is that what you've been thinking—that the only reason I've tried to get to know you was to get you into bed? Now that is beyond immature. What do you think we are, a couple of teenagers? Can't you conceive of a male-female relationship without taking it into the bedroom?''

Val's brain stalled, but just for a moment. No way was she going to let him get away with that line of hooey.

"You are so full of crap it's a wonder it's not coming out of your ears," she scoffed.

"Sure I am. That's why I came out here during the worst storm of the decade to make sure you were all right, and why my SUV is crushed under one of your trees!''

"So it's my fault a tree was blown over and fell on your stupid SUV?" she shrieked.

"I don't know if it's anyone's fault, but think about this, Doc. If my SUV hadn't been parked exactly where it was, when that tree fell it would have landed on this cabin!''

Val backed up a step and thought of the odd angle of that fallen pine, pictured the scene outside in her mind. It stunned her. This overbearing jerk was right. My God, he was right! A very strange fate—a capricious fate?—had timed Reed's arrival with the deadly gust of wind that had sent that tree crashing toward her cabin.

Suddenly weak-kneed, she plopped into her chair and laid one hand over her eyes.

"Hey, are you okay?" Reed asked as he hurried over to her.

She sensed him standing there, and she dropped her hand to glare at him. "Don't you dare!''

"Dare what?''

"You know exactly what I'm talking about.''

Reed shook his head in disgust and backed up, which put him closer to the fire. It felt great and he stepped aside just a little so some of that wonderful warmth would also reach Val. He doubted she would notice his consideration. And even if she did notice, she wouldn't mention it or thank him.

He was right. She sat there with a distant, unreadable expression on her face and stared into the flames.

"I'm hungry," Reed said. "Would you like something to eat?''

"No. But you go ahead and make yourself at home."

Her tone was so patronizing, so scathing, that Reed actually winced. But he hadn't eaten since noon and really was hungry, so he simply walked away and opened the refrigerator to take out things for a sandwich.

Val wouldn't look at him. It was still hard to believe he was here, destroying her contentment, acting as though he owned the place, totally ruining her previous enjoyment of simple pleasures. But then she thought of that big pine and how Reed's SUV had taken the brunt instead of the north side of her little cabin. Her nice metal roof could have had a huge hole in it; huge branches of pine could be crowding her into a far corner, where she would be stunned, cold—a hole in her roof would turn the cabin into an icebox in minutes—and scared out of her wits.

"Would you like a sandwich? I brought some very good turkey with me," Reed called.

She slowly turned her head and finally looked directly at him. "I don't want a sandwich."

Reed stood with his backside to the fire and ate his sandwich. "I'm glad you're well again," he said quietly.

Val's eyes jerked up. "The state of my health is not a subject open for discussion," she snapped.

Reed sighed inwardly and took another bite. She was the hardest person to talk to he'd ever known. Had she always been so distant, so guarded? What made Valerie Fairchild tick? And why did he care? Why, after the many cold shoulders she'd shown him and all of the downright nasty things she'd said to him, did he still want to know her? Why did he like looking at her? Her short hair was disarranged, she wore no makeup and her clothing was bulky and without any sex appeal at all, and still, just looking at her raised his blood pressure and created exotic images in his brain. And he'd denied having ideas about sweet-talking her into bed? She'd read him like a book. If only he could do the same with her.

Reed tore his gaze from Val to try to get his thoughts

headed in another direction, and took his time in looking around, finishing his sandwich while he did so.

Val saw his scrutiny as patronization. After all, he was as rich as Croesus and this tiny cabin probably looked like a hovel to him. "I happen to love it," she said coldly.

"Pardon?" Reed brought his eyes back to her. "You happen to love what?"

"What you were checking out so closely."

He tried to pinpoint her meaning. What had he been closely checking out? All he'd done was look around the cozy interior of her comfy cabin. Why would that annoy her?

"Look," he said calmly. "Let's at least pretend to get along. In case it hasn't yet sunk in, we are going to have to put up with each other until the weather clears up."

"And then some superhero is going to fly in, remove that big pine from the roof of your car, move it out of the way so I can drive mine to the road and—"

"Oh, please!" Reed was tired of her sarcasm. "Don't you even know how to be civil? Weren't you taught anything about hospitality or civility?"

Val threw aside the blanket and jumped up. "I doubt that your education was any better than mine! Civility is wasted on unaware people."

"And I fit that category?"

"Like a glove." Val stormed around the room, wishing ardently for the peace that had permeated the air before this man's arrival.

Of course, if he *hadn't* arrived, she'd be shivering in a corner with a hole in her roof.

Valerie Fairchild, would you stop being a brat! It was her mother's voice in her head. She was twelve and throwing a tantrum because she didn't want to go to yet another private school after being politely kicked out of the last one.

Val stopped racing around the room and inhaled a long breath. "Would you like some tea?"

Reed started as though struck by an invisible fist. She had

actually sounded civil. Dare he trust his own ears? "Yes, I would thoroughly enjoy some tea," he said cautiously.

Val walked over to the pot. "This has cooled down. I'll make more."

Afraid to count on Val's surprising civility to last for very long, Reed left her to her own devices. His inquisitive gaze landed on the blankets he'd dropped in a heap on the bed. Nodding because he'd come up with a positive plan of action, he got the blankets and began spreading them out on the rug in front of the fireplace. He had them smoothed out when Val walked over with a fresh pot of tea and another mug.

She stopped at the edge of the blankets and glared at Reed. He *was* unaware; he'd just proved it again by spreading his damn blankets without seeking her opinion or invitation.

But she was trying to be thankful that her roof didn't have a gaping hole in it. And thankful that she wasn't shivering in a corner as snow fell into the cabin and froze her into a large icicle, so she gritted her teeth and said—civilly, of course—"The tea is ready."

Chapter Nine

It was getting colder. The wind-driven snow hit the windows and outside walls of the cabin like sharp, tiny needles. Val wrapped her blanket more tightly around her and Reed, seated on *his* blankets on the floor, added more wood to the fire.

"This cabin wasn't intended for winter use," Reed commented.

"I've used it many times during winter months."

"In this kind of storm?"

"Well...no."

"You know, you could have some electric heaters installed. I'm talking about professionally installed electrical panels, for safety's sake."

"Which would be enormously helpful if the power went out," Val drawled.

"The power's not out now, is it?"

"I've been expecting it to happen since the blizzard began."

Reed had noticed the candles and matches she'd put out, and, of course, she was right about electric heaters being useless should the power go out. But while a blizzard, or even a strong electrical storm, could wreak havoc with the utilities of an area, it hadn't yet happened in this case. And she would have been more comfortable with heaters blowing warm air.

Reed tried not to judge but it was obvious she would rather argue than agree with anything he said, which was why he didn't voice his next suggestion: propane heaters. Instead, he stared into the flames and thought about what might have caused Val to erect such an unbreachable wall around herself. Why was she protecting herself? Jinni was so different, so open and outgoing with friends and strangers alike, that Reed could only conclude that Val's past contained some element that Jinni's did not. He'd seen Val at work with the animals, and it was obvious she loved life at the Animal Hospital. But then, cats and dogs weren't an emotional threat, were they?

But something was. Men, possibly? Startled by the sudden clarity of his analysis—it seemed pretty darn logical—Reed decided to leave that subject alone for the time being. He got to his feet and threw another chunk of wood on the fire.

"Do you have a flashlight?" he asked. "Mine, if they're still usable, are in my rig."

Val looked up. "Yes, I have a flashlight...several, in fact. Why?"

"I want to take another look outside."

"Your SUV is totaled, if that's what you're thinking about."

"It's badly damaged, but I doubt that it's totaled. Where's that flashlight?"

"There's one by the bed, one in the bathroom, one in the cupboard next to the window in the kitchen and one right here." Val snaked her arm out from the warmth of her down-filled comforter and picked up the flashlight she'd tucked under the edge of her chair.

"I see you're prepared for the worst," Reed said.

"And hoping for the best."

He gave her a long look. "You know, that's a very intriguing remark. What, in your book, would be the best that could happen, sweetheart?"

Val's eyes widened in sudden shock. Sweetheart? *Sweetheart?* "Here," she said stiffly, holding out the flashlight. "If you want it, take it."

Reed stepped closer to take it from her hand and noticed how fast she pulled back so no part of her would touch any part of him. He thought again of the conclusion he'd reached about Val's wariness, and said quietly, "I'll give you this, Doc. You're exceptionally adroit at elusion."

"At *illusion?* What's that supposed to mean?"

Reed caught on and snorted out a fragment of a laugh. "I was talking about the fine art of eluding my efforts to be friends with you."

"Oh, right. Friends," she said coolly. "From what I've heard about you in Rumor, you have all the *friends* you can handle."

He wondered if he should respond to that remark, which certainly couldn't be construed as kindly. But it could be further proof of her intentions to keep him off balance, and he wasn't going to let her get away with it.

He decided to take it lightly, and grinned to indicate amusement. "There you go again, putting a friendly attitude between a man and a woman in the same category as bed partners. I'll be outside for a few minutes, but whatever you do, don't sit there and worry about my braving the blizzard all by my lonesome."

Val refused to talk about such nonsense with him for one more minute. He already had silly ideas about her and God only knew what else, and where he'd gotten them she would never know. She wasn't going to further her own execution, for Pete's sake. She said not another word while he pulled on his jacket, woolen stocking cap and gloves, took up the flashlight again and finally went through the door.

"Give me strength," she moaned when he was out of ear-

shot, incredibly glad to be rid of him, if only for a short
breather. But as irritating as he was, she found herself listening hard for sounds of him hiking around outside. She heard
nothing but the ferocity of the blizzard, and she began to
worry. "You damn fool," she mumbled, angry with herself
for being such a wimpy turncoat. Why should she worry
about a man who couldn't mind his own business to save his
soul? He'd taken it upon himself to come to her rescue, again,
and what in God's name made him think that she was constantly in need of deliverance? Her demons were private,
locked in the deepest, darkest cells of her soul, and there they
would stay. But Reed's seemingly dedicated concern was
odd, as though he sensed what she never talked about. Not
that he had a right to sense *anything* about her.

His annoying concern was his reason for being here; it had
to be. But how had he learned where she was? What had put
him on her trail in the first place? Had he talked to Jinni? To
Jim or Estelle? Most mystifying was what had prompted him
to talk to *anyone* about her today.

She was still frowning and puzzling when he came back
in and stamped the snow from his boots.

"This is one dilly of a storm," he declared, taking off his
jacket. This time he hung it on one of the wall hooks he'd
noticed before. "You don't mind my using one of these
hooks, do you? My jacket is damp."

"Heavens no," she said in a voice that said just the opposite. "I told you to make yourself at home, didn't I?"

"And I know you really meant it." Reed returned to the
blankets in front of the fireplace and held his hands out to
the flames. "The temperature's going to drop below zero
before morning. We're lucky you have so much wood. We're
going to need it."

"So, is your rig totaled or merely damaged?"

"It's damaged pretty badly. I don't know what the insurance adjuster will say about it."

"If he ever gets a chance to see it, that is."

"Val, are you thinking we might not survive the night?"

He tried to sound upbeat and amused, but without the fireplace going full blast, they might *not* survive. No, that was an exaggeration. They were under cover, they had lots of clothes and blankets, and more food and water than they would need. If they ran out of fuel for the fireplace, they would still survive. Maybe not comfortably, but there would be little chance of even a mild case of frostbite if they stayed put.

He turned sideways to look at her. "You're cold right now. Why don't you sit down here closer to the fire? I'll get out of your way, if you're afraid to sit next to me."

"Afraid? Hardly," she scoffed. "This is my place, you know, and I'll sit wherever I please!"

"Sorry, bad choice of words. But let me say this. Sometimes it's better to get warm from the inside out than from the outside in."

"What *are* you talking about?" she asked grumpily.

"Brandy, my sweet, brandy. And coffee." Reed scrambled to his feet, thinking that one thing Val Fairchild was not was *sweet*. But he sure would like a chance to eradicate that cloud of despair she seemed to live under. He would love to get her talking—*relaxed* and talking—and while candy was dandy as an offer of friendship, liquor was quicker. He smiled slightly and tried to remember the name of the person who had originated that gem. Ogden Nash? Yes, he was sure of it.

"I'll make a pot of coffee, if you tell me where you keep the equipment," he said to Val.

The tea that remained in the pot Val had made at least an hour ago had long since cooled to room temperature, which wasn't very high. Hot coffee and brandy sounded wonderful to her, and she didn't put on a phony face and pretend otherwise.

"The coffeepot is in the bottom cabinet next to the sink, right side. You'll find a can of coffee on the same shelf."

This particular response greatly pleased Reed; she had actually sounded like a normal person conversing with another normal person instead of biting his head off. Wouldn't it be great if she dropped her guard long enough to let them really get to know each other?

Even greater would be a night of lovemaking. She obviously didn't feel the chemistry between them, but he did. Of course, the mere thought of anything sexual between them was almost ludicrous. Or maybe *he* was ludicrous. After all, she had said only a few civil words to him and his imagination already had them in bed, staying warm by getting naked....

Yeah, right. Chuckling under his breath, Reed found the pot and the coffee. When it was brewing he went to his canvas bag and took out the bottle of brandy he'd brought along for medicinal purposes. After all, he'd been heading into a blizzard not knowing what to expect.

And hadn't the worst happened? That tree lying on his crunched SUV was damn disturbing. He and Val were stranded until the storm died out and someone came along. And someone would, he was certain. Too many people knew where one or both of them had gone.

Noticing the cellular phone and charger on the counter, he picked it up and listened for a dial tone. There was nothing but static in his ear, which didn't surprise him. Ordinary cells didn't work well in the mountains on good days; they sure weren't going to pick up signals in this kind of weather.

Val left her warm blanket to go into the bathroom, which was freezing cold because she hadn't left the door open. Not that any part of the cabin, except directly in front of the fireplace, was truly warm. Fireplaces were great for atmosphere and slightly chilly evenings, but most of the heat went up the chimney.

She still didn't regret coming to the cabin, though. If that nosy Nellie brewing up coffee hadn't decided to intrude on her life one more time, she would already have dragged her mattress to the floor near the fire, loaded it with blankets and gotten into her warmest pajamas. She would be lying down, snug as a bug, instead of shivering in that chair. God, what a nuisance the man was.

Val frowned then. Would that tree really have hit the cabin if Reed's SUV hadn't been parked where it was?

She returned to her chair and blanket, and Reed handed her a mug. "It's really hot, so be careful," he cautioned her.

"Hello," she said with drawled disdain. "I doubt that your coffee is any hotter than my tea was."

"Uh, right." Damned if he was going to argue over the temperature of beverages. Holding his own mug, he lowered himself back to the blankets on the floor.

"Maybe you noticed, maybe you didn't, but I left the bathroom door open," Val said curtly. "It was freezing in there. Hopefully a bit of warmth from the fire will drift that far and take some of the chill off."

"How's the hot water?" Reed asked after taking a sip of his brandy-laced coffee. "Do you have a hot water tank?"

"Well, of course I have a hot water tank. This place might look like a shack to you, but it has all of the conveniences I want."

"Except for some kind of heater. Look, I like your cabin, but you couldn't possibly be against a few improvements."

Val arched her eyebrow. "Improvements, as in plural? Besides 'some kind of heater,' what other improvements does your highness recommend?"

Reed studied her for a long moment. "You wait for opportunities to put me down, don't you? Why is that, Val? What is there about me that makes you not only back off, but get set in the next instant for a fight?"

"You're imagining things." She lifted her mug for another swallow. He had added a little sugar or some kind of sweetener to the coffee and brandy, and the drink was delicious. She felt its heat in her mouth, her throat and her stomach, and she was definitely feeling warmer all over because of it.

"I'm not imagining a damn thing, and you know it. Only you'd rather argue about it, just like everything else I say." After a moment he added, "Maybe you just don't like men."

She barely managed to keep from gasping. He was figuring her out, and she didn't want him knowing her that well.

"Don't bother," she said coldly.

"Pardon?"

"I said, don't waste your time trying to dissect and understand me. Just so you don't come up with some ridiculous notion about my sexual preferences, I used to like men just fine. I've merely outgrown the need to have one or more of them underfoot. I realize many women believe they cannot exist without a man, but I don't happen to be one of them. I would appreciate it if you would accept that without question and drop the subject. At least," she added rather sarcastically, "for as long as we're confined together in this small space."

Reed put on a big show of thinking it over. Then he sighed dramatically and said, "Sorry, but I can't do that. You're an intriguing woman, even more so after that bunch of hooey you just laid on me. There is nothing I would like better than to get into your head."

"Liar. It's not my head you want to get into, it's my bed. Well, sport, that's not going to happen."

"Hey, I didn't mean to get you all steamed up."

"But you do it so well."

Reed grinned. "That's 'cause you like me and you don't *want* to like me."

"You are amazing, do you know that? Absolutely amazing. It's your ego, of course. Since yours is the size of this mountain, you're not even insulted that I don't want to like you."

"Then I'm right? You do like me, even though you're trying not to?"

"Drop dead." Val finished off her drink and held out her cup. "Make yourself useful and fix me another coffee and brandy."

"Say please." The change in her personality was subtle but encouraging. He would gladly feed her brandy-laced drinks all night if they loosened her tongue and put a crack in that shell she hid behind.

"Never mind, I'll do it myself!" She started to get up, and Reed quickly reached out and grabbed the mug from her hand.

"Would it have killed you to say please?" he asked.

She looked him straight in the eye. "Would it have killed you not to be so damn childish?"

He shook his head. "You're a tough nut, babe."

"I'll accept the tough nut label, but not the other one! I am *not* a babe!"

He uncoiled his long, lean body from the floor and got to his feet. "You keep telling yourself that and you'll get exactly what you want out of life, which, from where I stand, appears to be nothing. You know, I have to ask myself why a woman as pretty and smart as you are is terrified of letting a man get close enough to know her." Carrying both mugs, he walked away.

Val sat there, stiff and—surprising to her—on the verge of tears. How dare he dig and prod and poke through her psyche and form his own conclusions about the kind of woman she was and what she would get out of life if she didn't change her attitude? If she wanted a life without some man mucking everything up, it was none of Reed Kingsley's business, damn him.

But at least he hadn't said "beautiful" while singing her praises. She could handle pretty, but not beautiful, which would have been too absurd to let pass. Actually, he shouldn't be complimenting her at all, if he even meant what he'd said. More than likely those particular words were nothing but flattery.

"Oh, who cares?" Val muttered. He wasn't going to get anywhere with her no matter what he said, so why needlessly upset herself by looking for hidden meanings in anything he might do or say?

Reed brought in two fresh drinks and settled himself on the blankets again. He sipped and stared into the fire; Val sipped and did the same. Neither spoke for what seemed an eternity. She didn't trust Reed. He might not be talking, but he was thinking, plotting something that she probably wouldn't like.

Then she sighed quietly. Her own imagination was as bad as Reed's. He shouldn't be here, in her cabin, but he was, and she could sit and resent every breath he took, which was pretty much what she'd been doing, or she could give him a break and treat him like a guest. An unwanted, an uninvited guest, but a guest nonetheless.

But damn, it was hard to shed the tons of reluctance she'd weighted herself down with years ago, and give *any* man a break. Breaks were dangerous. Give a man an inch and he'd take a mile. Reed would probably take *ten* miles!

"What puzzles me is why you refuse to give up," she said.

"What?" Reed had heard what she'd said, but it had come without warning and totally taken him by surprise.

"I...I guess I was, uh, thinking out loud," she mumbled, embarrassed that she'd said something that might make him think she cared about anything he did.

"Interesting thoughts," Reed said, and brought his mug to his lips with a twinkle in his eyes. "You know, you've puzzled me since the day we met. That was quite a while ago. Do you remember it?"

"No."

He laughed softly. "I didn't think you did. But I do. Everyone was glad that you had finally attended a meeting of the town's business owners and managers, and you and I shook hands."

Val cleared her throat. "I probably shook hands with everyone there."

"Could be, but when you put your hand in mine I felt a jolt of electricity that nearly knocked my socks off."

"I didn't notice a thing."

"I always wondered if you did, so I'm glad you cleared up that question."

"Yes, I'll just bet you are."

"Sarcasm again? Oh, well, so be it. Anyhow, then there was that party at Joe's Bar. It was somebody's birthday, I think. I saw you walk over to the jukebox, and then you dropped your coins and you got down on the floor to find them and—"

"I happen to remember *that* particular incident, so I do not need to hear a blow-by-blow narration of it."

"I was sure hoping for a dance, but one minute you were there and the next you were gone. You didn't stay for long."

"I knew that some guy on the prowl would ask me to dance if I hung around, so I made my excuses to the birthday girl and left."

"And that's the reason you don't go out very much, isn't it? You're afraid of some guy on the prowl trying to get too friendly. Or maybe just a little bit friendly. Maybe smiling at you, or saying a casual, 'Hi, how are you?'" Reed looked into his mug. "Empty again. I'm going to have another. How about you?"

"Yes, I'll have another." While Reed was making the hot drinks in the kitchen area behind her, Val sat in her chair with her head spinning and realized she didn't have a tense muscle in her body. It was the brandy, of course. She wasn't used to drinking hard liquor, or even beer, for that matter, although she did enjoy a glass of wine with some meals.

By the time Reed put another full mug in her hand, she was wondering how many times he'd done that. Three? Four? Was this really her fifth drink?

No, it couldn't be. She would be tipsy if it were, wouldn't she?

"Thanks," she said, and held the hot mug with both hands, enjoying its heat on her palms. "Would you please put another log on the fire?"

"Glad to." Reed was astounded. Not only had she said thanks and please, she had sounded relaxed and comfortable enough to ask him to do something for her. *Oh, yeah, a definite breakthrough,* he thought, with great gobs of affection for her heating his system far better than the blazing fire ever could. He liked her way more than any woman he'd known before, and the reasons for liking her just weren't important anymore. He had analyzed his feelings for Val dozens of times since their first meeting and he still had no logical explanation. The whole thing was out of his hands, beyond his control. It was…fate.

After fueling the fire he said, "Hey, let's change places. I'll take the chair and you get down here closer to the heat."

Val thought it over for a moment, then nodded. "Thanks. I'll leave this blanket for you. You'll need it." She got up with her mug and sat as close to the fireplace screen as she could get. The blaze immediately warmed her face and she breathed a sigh of pure pleasure.

Reed folded the blanket she'd been using around himself after he sat down and realized that the warmth he felt was Val's warmth. It was an incredibly arousing thought. His imagination went wild again and put them over there in her bed, nude, entwined and making passionate love.

"Wow," he whispered, suddenly *over*heated. Didn't she feel any of the torture he did every time he looked at that bed? It wasn't fair if all the suffering in this relationship was heaped on his head.

But then, they really didn't have a relationship, did they?

Not yet, they didn't, but his hopes were higher than ever. If this storm held for one more day, he could get very lucky, and he didn't mean in bed. If Val ever smiled at him with genuine fondness, or kissed him just once, he might die a happy man.

He smiled. He was *already* a happy man from being in this rustic cabin with her. From being alone with her. From possessing the gift of sight and having her sitting a few short feet away from him so he could look at her to his heart's content.

He'd wondered before, but the question had never been quite as defined as it was now: was he in love with Valerie Fairchild?

Chapter Ten

Val's inner clock told her it was nearing midnight. More awake than not, only slightly drowsy, she felt lazy and loose, almost boneless, without any of the muscular kinks and tension that had tied her in knots for so many years. The sensation of total relaxation, at least in her body, was amazing, and she wished she could capture the feeling and take it back to Rumor with her.

The cabin always had been pure magic for her, but tonight it was especially noticeable. It was the brandy, of course. She wasn't so tipsy that she didn't know the reason for her uncommon insouciance. Why, she was actually talking to a *man*, and doing it without watching every word. She had even been nice to him. First, she'd felt guilty about hogging the heat by the fire. Then she'd gotten up to tote her bed pillows over to the blankets, and, finally, she'd said it was all right for him to sit next to her—if he was chilly where he was, of course.

Reed had transferred himself from the chair to the blanket-covered floor so fast he got a bit dizzy, but he wasn't going to hem and haw and miss this golden opportunity.

Thus, they were sprawled on the blankets and pillows—heads at opposite ends of the makeshift bed—and absorbing the warmth Reed kept alive and thriving by feeding the flames from the wood box.

"I'll probably stay awake all night," Val murmured.

Reed loved the sound of her voice at this late hour. It had a dreamy quality he'd never heard before tonight. He liked thinking the dreaminess might have something to do with him, though his rational mind told him to be grateful he'd brought the brandy with him.

"I'll stay awake for certain," he said quietly. "It wouldn't be good to let the fire die out."

"I love listening to the storm." Val smiled softly, looking into the fire, barely aware of Reed's eyes on her. "Even though it sounds as though it's throwing all of its weight against the cabin."

The storm was raging with such strength that the cabin actually shook from the onslaught.

"Maybe it's huffing and puffing and blowing my house down," Val mused. She sent a glance to Reed. "Do you suppose?"

He smiled. Each time he'd gotten up to refresh their drinks he had turned off one more light. None were burning now. Val hadn't noticed—or hadn't cared—as the bonfire in the fireplace threw an enormous amount of light. Reed loved watching her in the dancing firelight, loved that they had removed their shoes and her stocking-clad feet were close enough to touch, should he extend his hand a mere few inches. Her clothing was loose—dark fleece pants and a sweater. Hardly garments to raise a man's libido, but they did. The way she ran her fingers through her hair every so often did an incredible amount of damage to his decision to keep his hands to himself until he knew in his soul that she would not object to a kiss or a caress.

But he was so aware of her lying next to him that it was

an effort for him to think of anything else. Telling himself to stay cool, to be thankful for the gains he'd already made tonight, was getting harder to do.

"Christmas is just around the corner," Val said in that slow, dreamy tone. "Your family probably goes all out for Christmas."

"Always," he replied. "You have Jinni this year, and the Cantrells. You could have a big family affair, if you all choose to."

"None of us have talked about it, but it would be nice if we all got together. If Guy is convicted, though, the Cantrells aren't apt to be in a festive mood." She wiped away a tear, alarming Reed.

He quickly got away from that subject by asking, "What do you usually do for Christmas?"

A dozen lonely Christmases passed through Val's mind. "One year I...went on a cruise," she said in a wispy little voice.

"A Christmas cruise? That was probably fun."

It had been horrible. She'd been the only person without a partner, or at least the only solo traveler she'd been able to spot. Everyone else on the ship had been with a spouse, a friend or a *group* of friends. She'd been glad when it was over.

"It was...okay. Tell me about your Christmases."

Reed described Christmas at the Kingsley Ranch, a day that had been traditionally and emotionally similar year after year for as far back as his memory reached.

"You had a wonderful life," Val said when he'd finished.

"I *have* a wonderful life, Val." *And you could be part of it, a very* big *part of it.* "I'm getting the impression that... Maybe I'd better not say that."

She turned her face from the fire and looked at him. "I know what you were going to say. You're getting the impression that my life wasn't nearly as great as yours, and you know something? You're right. But do you want to hear about it? Do you *really* want to know me that well? How depressing for you.'' She looked at the fire again.

''Knowing you is *all* I want right now, Val. I would consider knowing everything about you as the greatest Christmas gift anyone could give me.''

''How sad.''

She *sounded* sad. Reed sat up. ''It can't be that bad,'' he said quietly.

''Oh, but it is. Believe me, you *don't* want to know the sordid details.''

Reed felt as though his heart skipped a beat. He'd suspected some deep, dark secret from the past haunting and hounding Val, but it was still a shock to hear from her own lips that he'd been right. He almost backed away from the topic, because hearing about something that was still causing her pain would cause *him* pain.

And yet, whatever it was should be talked about. He would never really know her until he knew *all* of her, the good with the bad, the bad with the good.

''Tell me about it, Val.''

She sent him a glance. ''No, I don't think so. Let's talk about something else. How come a man with your background is Rumor's fire chief?''

''Val, I don't want to talk about me. I want to talk about you.'' Reed inched closer to her, moving across the blanket until he was almost sitting next to her. He couldn't stop himself, and he raised his hand and gently brushed her fire-warmed cheek with his fingertips. He was astonished that she didn't back off, or tell him in no uncertain terms to get away from her.

Instead she looked at him with that dreamy cast in her beautiful aqua-blue eyes and he wondered if *he* weren't dreaming. He moved very slowly until he was leaning over her, then he lowered his head to brush her lips with his.

She sighed, a soft little sound that touched the core of him. ''Val,'' he whispered, and then kissed her the way he'd been aching to do.

Being kissed like that did things to Val that she had forgotten existed. She knew he had her on some kind of pedestal, a symbol of purity and feminine perfection, and she didn't belong there. Breathless when he finally broke the kiss, she whispered, "There were men…quite a few men…when I was a young woman."

Reed nuzzled her ear and the curve of her throat. "You're *still* a young woman."

"I guess," she conceded. "But I'm not a *wild* young woman…and I was, Reed, I was."

He raised his head to look at her. "There's been nothing wild about you since you've lived in Rumor, Val. I would have heard about it and so would everyone else."

"It all took place ages ago." Memories paraded through Val's mind. Not all were discomfiting or regrettable, but many were. Far too many, to be honest, and then there was that one awful day.

"I was a silly girl," she said in a husky whisper. She knew she should stop talking, but she couldn't seem to shut up. She felt something brewing within her, caused by only God knew what. The storm? This man's steadfast persistence? His kiss, his nearness? The brandy? She didn't believe she was intoxicated, but she couldn't deny an unusual and not unpleasant light-headedness.

But why should that cause her to feel an urgency to reveal old tales, some of which she hadn't even told Jinni?

"Look at me," she whispered, and Reed gladly complied. He was handsome, she realized as she studied his face—sensuously handsome. His eyes in particular conveyed both masculinity and sensitivity. Why wouldn't he have a truckload of women on his heels? And he wanted her? My Lord, why? And for how long?

She would not accept a one-night stand, and maybe that was the driving force behind her need to talk about herself. If he was still interested when he knew it all, maybe there was a chance that she wouldn't grow old all by herself.

"Doesn't what I said about other men bother you?" she asked.

"Do you want it to bother me?" Reed probed the depths of her eyes in the shadowy firelight. He'd rather make love than talk, but Val was undergoing some sort of transition tonight, and while she had let him kiss her once—albeit a thorough and extremely arousing kiss—she seemed to want conversation more than kisses.

And maybe conversation would open the door to a real relationship for them. He couldn't risk losing the gains he'd made on this stormy night by persuading her through touch and passion to kiss now and talk later.

"Not in a bad way, but doesn't a remark like that arouse your curiosity?"

It aroused something, Reed acknowledged to himself. Everything about her aroused him, and if she just happened to glance at the front of his pants, she would see the result of his sitting so close to her.

"Yes," he said, only because he sensed that was the answer she wanted to hear from him. "Just let me stretch out and get comfortable, then I'd like to hear anything you're willing to tell me."

Val immediately sank into the past and was barely aware of Reed moving the pillows from the other end of the blanket next to the ones she was using, and then lying down beside her. He lay on his side, facing her, and she was so engrossed in her own thoughts she didn't feel his eyes on her.

Reed waited for her to begin, and tortured himself by inhaling her scent and thinking erotic thoughts about the two of them. Then, too, there was this. He'd always liked women, and women liked him. He knew he had a reputation, but gossip had never bothered him or slowed him down an iota. If Val had had a long string of lovers in her "wild" youth, she would be no worse—or better—than him. So, no, he wasn't curious about her past. He frankly didn't care how many guys she'd slept with before him—if they ever got around to making love, that is.

But he would listen to her confession—that's what seemed to be going on—console her and then get back to the two of them. He would be patient if it killed him.

"No one ever cared what I did," Val began. "My parents were gone more than they were home, and even when they were there, I wasn't. They sent me to private schools, usually out-of-state schools. Jinni, too, but she was five years older, and I barely knew her. By the time I was old enough to want to know her, she'd gone off to college.

"I always had plenty of money to spend. I think Mother and Dad believed that an unending supply of money made up for their complete indifference to their daughters. Anyhow, I was running wild at fourteen. Even younger, in some things. But when I discovered boys life started to be fun. I brought them home and sneaked them past the servants. At first we played computer games or listened to music, but it wasn't long before we started fooling around. Experimenting with…sex."

Reed felt a sinking sensation. She had started her story way back when, and even he hadn't been experimenting with sex at fourteen. He'd been what? Sixteen or seventeen? Actually, he'd been several years behind many of his friends. The boys' locker room, where the football team suited up before games and showered afterward, had rung with brags and boasts of who was doing what with whom. He'd had nothing to brag about until after the Junior prom, but he, unlike most of the guys, said nothing about the girl or about losing his virginity that night. He'd figured it was no one else's business, and he wasn't going to trash the sweet, pretty girl he'd escorted to the prom by talking about what they'd done in his car after the dance.

Val's voice penetrated his fleeting memories of his own youthful indiscretions, and he heard her say, "After college I sort of…drifted. I didn't know what I wanted to do, and with so much money pouring into my personal bank account I really didn't have to do anything.

"But then one day I was with a friend, shopping, when

we spotted a new pet store. I never passed one up, and we went in. The first thing I saw was a large help-wanted sign. While we played with the adorable puppies and kittens they had for sale, I asked about the job. It didn't pay much, but the hours were flexible and it seemed like the perfect job for a person like me who had always loved animals. They hired me on the spot, and I began working there the following day.''

Val took a long, shaky breath. She knew what she was doing, opening that tightly locked door, freeing her secret demons, even *helping* them to escape. But it was as though the dam had sprung a leak and could no longer hold back the water. Something told her to lay it all at Reed's feet and then see his reaction. He would probably run so fast his heels would kick up dust…or snow.

In a way she felt as though she were talking to a therapist, but at the same time she knew she wasn't. The therapists she'd dealt with hadn't been real people to her, and Reed was. In fact, Reed was the most real person she'd ever known. Maybe she was baring her soul to him for a quite logical reason: if he decided to hang around and do nice things like sending her flowers after he knew her history, then she might be able to let herself really like him.

But she had reached the hard part of her story—although none of it had been easy—and she turned her face away from him toward the fire, symbolically separating them.

''I worked off and on at the pet shop for about a month and got along fine with my boss, who didn't mind if I came in late or called in sick when I wasn't. She said I was a natural with animals, and she liked me, I guess. Anyhow, I noticed a…a thirty-something man coming in quite often. At first just once in a while and then nearly every time I was there. He never bought anything, but he played with the puppies and wasn't unpleasant, although he rarely looked directly at me or said anything. I asked Dora, the owner, about him, and she didn't know who I was talking about, but he always made me…uncomfortable, and few people did.''

Reed felt tension developing in his system. He didn't like the direction that Val's story was taking. Something bad had happened to her, and she was leading up to it. He wanted to stop her from telling him about it, but how could he? She was finally talking to him, acknowledging his existence, treating him like a human being instead of some annoying entity she would prefer to have disappear.

And she had kissed him back...for a second time. Oh yes, that first kiss counted, the one he'd surprised her with the day he'd brought in the kittens for her inspection. She wasn't completely immune to him, though she would like him to believe she was. Until tonight. Actually, wasn't this storm a blessing in disguise?

"I...I was alone in the shop one day," Val said tremulously. "It was early...I had opened that morning. I was putting out food and water for the pets, and the bell on the door announced a customer. I turned to see who it was, to say good morning...and it was him...that guy who'd been making me feel so odd. He...he took a gun out of his jacket pocket and waved it in front of my face...." She began to sob quietly, little hiccups of anguish that nearly undid Reed.

He reached for her without hesitation and brought her head to his chest. "My God...my God," he whispered hoarsely. "I knew from what you were saying that something bad happened, but I never could have imagined something like that."

She wanted to snuggle into his arms, to accept his comfort and forget everything else. But he still hadn't heard it all, and he had to.

"He...he—" She tried to say it, but it was still so horrible when she let it come to the forefront of her mind that she just stammered.

"Val, say it." Reed was so choked up he could hardly speak himself. He was pretty sure of what she was having such trouble saying, but he couldn't put the words in her mouth. He gently stroked her hair and realized how close he was to bawling like a baby. "Say it, darlin', you can tell me anything," he whispered.

"He…beat me…and threatened worse."

Reed held her while she wept. Then, when she could talk again, he listened.

"He locked the door, then nailed it shut…and he kept me in the shop for sixteen hours. I learned later…much later…after it was all over and I was able to digest simple facts again…that Dora had come by, and when her key wouldn't open the door she called the police. I guess a small army of policemen was outside the place for most of the day before he…he finally gave himself up. They…took me to the hospital."

Reed pressed his lips to the top of her head. "My heart is broken," he whispered. "I'm broken. Val, I'm so sorry."

Val heard his words and realized how completely he understood what she'd told him. *Broken* was exactly what she'd been, and there would forever be a part of her that remained in shards.

But she hadn't expected him to grasp her agony so acutely.

"You mustn't dwell on it," she said huskily. "He's in prison and I went through years of therapy with excellent professionals. I…I'm fine now. I went back to school and became a veterinarian. I found Rumor and left New York, and I—I'm probably as happy as most people."

Most people didn't hide from the opposite sex, but Reed thought better of pointing that out. He nestled her more closely against him and gently rubbed her back.

"I care for you," he whispered softly. "You must know that."

"Even after hearing…my tale of woe?"

"Why would something from your past, an event that you had absolutely no control over, affect my feelings today? Yes, even after hearing the worst you could throw at me, I still care for you."

"But even before that one awful day I wasn't a very nice person."

"Because you were young and liked men? Hey, I was

young and liked women. Does that make either of us some kind of outcast? I don't think so, sweetheart.''

She turned to her side and lifted her arms to encircle his neck. "You're an unusual man," she whispered.

Her body was against his, her arms around his neck. He could hardly believe this was happening.

Reed had said all the right things during and after her story, and maybe that was why she was snuggled against him, all but inviting further intimacy.

A fleeting thought intruded on her rather luxurious mood. She had talked to professionals about that day, over and over, in fact, but never to an ordinary person. Maybe if she hadn't maintained complete silence on the subject, once out of therapy, but had talked openly about the horrors of victimization, she would have suffered much less than she had.

Was tonight going to change the guarded, wary woman she had become into someone like Jinni, who found joy in every day?

There was much to think about, Val realized, but did she have to ponder such weighty matters tonight? For the first time in a dozen or more years she was in a man's arms and feeling wonderful, and she knew in her soul that she wasn't going to say or do anything that would destroy the moment.

"Val," Reed whispered as he breathed in the delicious scent of her hair. "We're not drunk, are we?"

She laughed softly, the sound muffled by his shirt. "A bit tipsy, but not drunk. Nicely tipsy, to be honest. I feel as though I'm floating, but I'd rather blame it on your holding me than on the brandy.''

"Oh, babe, so would I, but I had to make sure this wasn't happening because of too much alcohol.'' He sought her lips for a kiss that became magical in seconds.

Val kissed him back, this time putting all those years of forgotten and buried passion into it. Her body caught fire and she knew he was feeling the same heat. Their kisses became wild, landing on noses, cheeks and mouths.

"Val...sweetheart." Reed slid his hand under her sweater. "Your skin is hot," he whispered.

"My skin is *tingling* and hot," she said breathlessly. "You've bewitched me."

"Other way around, babe. You've bewitched me."

"Maybe we're both a little witched," she whispered.

"A *lot* witched. Oh, my love...my darling." He took her mouth again, laying claim to it with a hard, passionate kiss that all but curled Val's toes.

She began unbuttoning his shirt, and with that one bold move let him know that undressing was the next step. Reed sat up and brought her with him. Together they got rid of their clothes. Val was so enraptured that she didn't think of the tiny scar on her breast when Reed removed her bra. He saw it and almost said something, but common sense prevailed. He gently kissed her breasts instead of talking about them.

She was a truly beautiful woman, he realized, slender, full-breasted and utterly enchanting. He felt enchanted, at any rate, being here with her on this stormy night. How had it all happened? And then he wondered again about the flowers she'd sent him and the note she'd written on the card and what it meant. She couldn't possibly have known he would come out here...or had she known in her soul what he would do?

The questions drifted away. Val, in all of her female glory, was completely naked, as he was. He left her briefly to do two things—feed the fire and put on a condom. Then he was back, kissing and caressing her, running his hands over the silky warmth of her skin, touching and holding her breasts.

Val's hands were as busy and curious as Reed's. He had a marvelous body; it was obvious that he took care of himself, and she approved.

Then, at almost the same moment, they said, "You're beautiful," which made them laugh, and added a joyous quality to their lovemaking.

Minutes later, after increasingly feverish kisses, Val still felt the joy but she also felt an urgency. She lay down and drew him on top of her. Before he could kiss her again she whispered, "I'm so ready, Reed. Please…do it. Make love to me."

He looked into her eyes and knew at that moment that he *did* love her. He'd wondered about his feelings for her, but now he knew who she was and why she had attracted him so strongly. He'd sensed her frailty and the fears behind her businesslike approach to every facet of her life. Since his childhood he'd never been able to turn away from someone in need of rescue. In Val's case his innate quality had turned to love without any prompting from his brain. He loved her, he was *in* love with her, and he wanted to tell her how he felt.

But before he could say another word, she pulled his head down for a hungry kiss, and he forgot about everything but doing as she had asked.

It was pure heaven.

For both of them.

Chapter Eleven

Sometime in the night they moved from the floor to the bed, and when Reed leaned over, kissed Val and said, "Wake up, sweetheart. Someone's coming," she was snuggled under a thick layer of blankets, their naked legs entwined, his warm body heating hers.

It took a second for her to come awake, but during that brief span she realized that it was morning, the storm had died down and every minute detail of the hours she'd spent in Reed Kingsley's arms were embarrassingly etched on her brain.

She almost *didn't* open her eyes. He'd kissed her and she didn't want to look at him. My God, how could she have behaved so...so shamelessly?

"Val, sweetheart, someone's coming. Sounds like a snowplow, but it's not alone."

Reed's message finally sank in, and yes, she could hear motors. She leaped out of bed and began scrambling for clothes. The cabin was cold as ice, and she hopped around on her bare feet until she found underwear and socks. Reed was doing the same, but he was laughing and she was not. She shot him a look that he didn't see, but it was obvious that he thought the situation funny. Someone was coming to the rescue. The storm was over and someone, probably Jinni, had called in the troops. The thought of facing family, friends or even strangers with Reed in the cabin and his crunched SUV outside making it evident that he had been there all night was a come-to-life nightmare.

"Start the fire," she snapped, "while I make the bed and put on some coffee."

"You don't mind if I finish dressing first, do you?" Reed said with a chuckle in his voice.

She faced him with her hands on her hips. "I would certainly like to know what's so damn funny! Everyone we know is going to hear about our spending last night together long before the sun sets tonight. I fail to see the humor in that, and if you had one ounce of good sense, you wouldn't be giggling like a schoolboy over something that's not remotely amusing!"

Working on the buttons of his shirt, Reed looked at her scowling face and realized how seriously she was taking this. "Hey, you're making too much of something neither of us could prevent."

"It would have been prevented if you had stayed in town, where you belonged!" Val spotted the blankets still on the floor in front of the fireplace and rushed over to them. Her heart was pounding, her stomach fluttering, and the vehicle or vehicles—it really sounded like more than one out there— were getting closer. Should she fold the blankets or leave them so anyone coming inside would think they had used two beds?

"Throw them on the sofa for now," Reed said. "And please step aside so I can build that fire you wanted."

"I'm freezing! I had to dress without a shower! I probably look like a…a slut and—"

"Oh, for hell's sake, stop beating yourself up over nothing.

Go put the coffee on and then fix your face, if you're so worried about looking like a woman this morning instead of a doctor in a white coat who wouldn't smile if her life depended on it.''

Val gaped at him, but he had immediately turned his back and started working on the fire. She finally shrieked, ''I knew the real Reed Kingsley would eventually show up! Well, thank you very much, you...you jerk!''

Reed shook his head, but there wasn't time for a completely unreasonable argument right now. As soon as the first flames appeared in the nest of paper and kindling he'd prepared, he got up, went to the front window and drew back the curtains. The bright sunlight nearly blinded him, but after a few moments he saw a large truck with a plow and two cars pulling to a stop directly in front of Val's driveway. One vehicle was his brother Tag's SUV and the other one was Jinni's. He had no idea who was driving the truck with the plow.

He couldn't help grinning. The whole thing *was* funny; Val simply had no sense of humor when it came to people knowing her business. And she could try to weasel out of the truth until hell froze over and Tag would still know what had taken place in this little cabin last night. Jinni Fairchild-Cantrell was nobody's fool, either, so Reed couldn't see Jinni letting her sister get away with a half-baked lie.

As for himself, he didn't care who found out about the greatest night of his life. He'd finally broken through Val's iron reserve, and once unleashed, she'd been as wildly responsive and passionate as a man could ever hope for from the woman of his dreams.

''They're getting out,'' he called to Val.

''Who's getting out?'' On the verge of outright panic, she rushed to the window. ''Oh, my God, it's Jinni and your brother and Jim!''

''Oh, yeah, you're right. It is Jim. I didn't recognize him at first, all bundled up like that.''

Val gritted her teeth. "I…I wish I had Guy Cantrell's formula for invisibility! I don't want to face any of them."

"Because you're such a terrible person, right? I mean, after all, lovemaking between two people who really care for each other is one of the worst crimes anyone could commit. We all know that, so should I start looking for a strong rope so we can hang ourselves from one of those big trees outside?"

Val glared at him. "You're not at all funny, so stop trying to be! Why did you come out here in the first place? I didn't need rescuing last night and if your stupid SUV wasn't parked behind mine with a tree holding it down, I wouldn't require anyone's interference this morning, either!"

"Do you always wake up this grouchy?"

"Do you always wake up grinning like an ape?"

"You didn't think I was an ape last night, sweetheart, but yes, now that you mention it, I *always* wake up in a good mood. You should try it sometime."

Val could see the three people standing near the plow talking and gesturing. The sight of the tree on top of Reed's SUV had obviously caused some discussion, and the fact that the snow was a good two feet deep between the road and the cabin also rated a few remarks, she was certain.

"Okay, it's time to come alive," Reed said. He took Val's arm and pulled her away from the window. "Look, I don't want this morning's surprise to ruin what we accomplished last night. Something very good grew between us, Val, and I don't want to lose it. I hope you feel the same. In fact, I'm counting on it." He saw the way she wouldn't quite meet his eyes, and felt a sinking sensation. "Val, you're not sorry about last night…about us, are you?"

"I'm sorrier than I can say," she said in a husky, misery-laden voice.

He put his hands on her upper arms and stepped closer to her. "Why, honey, why?"

"Don't pretend, Reed. You got what you wanted and…and that's the long and the short of it."

"I'm pretending nothing! You're talking about a one-night stand. Do you really believe that's all I wanted from you? Val, if you felt that way, why did you send those flowers? And write that card?"

She drew her eyebrows together in an expression of annoyed dismay. "What on earth are you babbling about?"

He stared at her. Was *she* pretending? Acting as though she knew nothing at all about that bouquet and romantically inviting note? But if she hadn't sent the flowers and written that note, who had?

No, Reed decided, she had done it and now didn't like admitting it, probably because of how far things had gone between them last night and the arrival of those people out there—her sister, his brother and a friend. As secretive as Val usually was, she probably felt sick at heart over the situation. Anyone coming upon the scene this morning would have at least a few questions about the events that occurred last night in this tiny cabin.

Reed wanted to hold Val and tell her not to worry. They were adults and what had developed between them was no one else's business. He *ached* to hold her, in fact, to gently wind his arms around her and bring her head to his chest.

But she had abruptly shaken off his hands and seemed to be running around the cabin like a chicken without a head. She looked frantic, picking up things and setting them down again, peering out the window, racing over to the bed to straighten the spread again, rushing to the fireplace to add more wood to the flames.

"Val, for heaven's sake!" he exclaimed. "Calm down."

She sent him a scathing look. "Keep your advice to yourself!"

"But you seem ready to explode. Look, I'm going outside. Jim and Tag are shoveling a path to the house and I should be out there helping. Where's your snow shovel?"

"I don't have one."

"But…everyone has a snow shovel."

"Not everyone," she snapped, and since the coffeepot had

finally stopped gurgling, she went for a mug and filled it. Reed, she saw, was getting into his heavy jacket. "As long as you're going out there anyway, would you mind telling Jinni to brave the drifts and come inside?"

He almost told her no. Her completely unreasonable attitude was getting on his nerves. But saying no to a simple request simply wasn't in him, although he wasn't above a little sarcasm. "I'll tell her, but since she's your sister, I'm sure she'll make up her own mind about it."

Val's glare landed on him again. "Do you consider independence to be a fatal flaw in everyone, or just in women?"

Reed threw up his hands. "There isn't time for another fight right now. Later, though, after we're back in town, we'll take up where we left off this morning and have a hell of a screaming match, if you'd like." Reed would rather kiss her than argue with her, but she barely gave him breathing room, let alone enough space to be himself and do something nice.

He strode to the door and pulled it open. Val went over to the fire with her mug of coffee and stared out the front window.

Everything outside was white and bright, and all three of the "rescuers" shouted hello at Reed. Jinni called, "Is Val all right?"

"Val couldn't possibly be any better. She's fine, Jinni."

"Go ahead and have your fun," Val mumbled when she heard that exchange, wincing when she thought of all the things Reed now knew about her. He had enough information to keep the gossips happy until spring…if he spread it around town.

Oh, he wouldn't do that, would he? Val felt tears stinging the backs of her eyes. What had come over her last night? Yes, she'd drunk some brandy, but a little alcohol shouldn't turn a naturally reticent person into a blabbermouth, should it?

Her sigh sounded sad and broken, even to herself. Something had definitely loosened her tongue last night, and if it wasn't the brandy, what was it?

And then there was the other thing…the lovemaking. Val squeezed her eyes tightly shut and suffered in darkness until she heard Jinni's voice getting closer to the cabin.

"Val? Open that door and let me see you!"

Val set her mug on the mantel and dragged her miserable body over to the door. She opened it and shaped a smile that was as phony as a three-dollar bill.

"Hi, Jinni. What's going on? How come you joined the rush to save me? Or did you instigate the whole thing? I'm perfectly all right, as you can see."

Jinni went in and stamped snow from her boots. "But none of us knew that, did we? That coffee smells wonderful. Got any left?"

"Of course." While Val filled another mug she was well aware of her sister looking around the cabin. Val felt like crying. She had loved this little hideout from the moment she'd set eyes on it, and any time spent here had been re-generative and energizing. After Reed's invasion last night and now this morning's fiasco, she wondered if she would ever feel the same about it again.

"Well, it ain't fancy but I like it," Jinni quipped.

Frowning slightly, Val handed the mug to her sister. "You're just saying you like it to be nice."

Jinni took the mug of steaming coffee. "Thanks. Listen, kiddo, I'm not feeling all that nice this morning. I worried about you and kept Max awake all night with my prowling. So, believe me, I'm really in no mood to schmooze with you about your affection for this rustic but quite homey place. Having said that and put it aside, I must admit that a different and much more interesting subject leaps to mind." She grinned teasingly at her sister.

Val felt her face turn pink. "I did not invite that man out here, Jinni."

"I believe you. Why wouldn't I? But that man, as you call him, has got it bad for you. I would have to describe Reed Kingsley as one of those rare males who believes that men should take care of the women they love."

"Oh, for pity's sake! He doesn't love me and…and I don't want him to!"

Jinni was wandering again, taking in the one bed and the pile of blankets on the sofa. "So, did he sleep on the couch? Or try to sleep? It's not nearly as long as he is. He's at least six feet tall, wouldn't you say?"

"I have no idea how tall he is, nor do I care to discuss his physical statistics."

"But you must admit that he has remarkable eyes. I really can't recall ever seeing such green eyes on another man. Can you?"

There were all sorts of things going on outside. Val could hear motors and shouts of the men, and she wasn't particularly keen on the discussion of Reed's green eyes going on *inside,* so she ignored Jinni's last question and hurried over to a window. "What on earth are they doing?"

"Probably getting that tree off of Reed's vehicle." Jinni went to the window and stood next to her sister. "Jim said he'd be able to move the tree with the winch on his truck." She grinned. "Isn't this fun? I didn't even know what a winch was before today."

"A condition that was hardly life-threatening," Val drawled. "Sometimes ignorance is bliss."

Jinni turned her head to look at her sister. "You're not happy this morning. Did Reed put you on the spot last night?"

"Jinni, please, I don't want to talk about him…. Oh, my gosh, they moved the tree!"

Jinni looked out the window again. "So they did. Now they'll be able to move the wreckage of Reed's SUV out of the way so you can get yours back on the road. The wind was horrible in town, but apparently it was worse out here. Val, do you realize that if Reed hadn't parked exactly where he had the top of that tree would have hit the cabin?"

Val was so distraught over everything that had happened since Reed showed up last night that she wished everyone would go back to town and leave her alone. They wouldn't, she knew, and she had tons of food to load into her vehicle, and the water pipes to drain, and the electricity to turn off, and…damn! Her whole weekend had been blown to hell by that high-velocity blizzard!

Jinni left the window to get more coffee and noticed the cell phone on the counter. "It didn't work out here, just as you said. I had hoped it would, and I tried to get you at least a dozen times after the storm broke."

Val hated the resentment she felt toward everyone for being such busybodies, but she especially hated feeling that way toward Jinni, who had gone so far out of her way to nurse Val during her cancer scare. But she was far, far from being a child, and it was really no one else's business if she visited her cabin without alerting the entire population of Rumor. And yes, that fallen tree could have knocked a hole in her cabin, but maybe it wouldn't have. Who really knew which way a tree would fall in a high wind?

"So, what happened?" Jinni asked after a sip of her fresh coffee. "Reed just knocked on the door, or what? You must have been thrown for a loop, but was it a nice surprise?"

"I would hardly call Reed Kingsley's unwanted and completely unnecessary concern for my safety a nice surprise," Val said sharply. Then something inside her wilted. She was taking the anger she felt for her own disgusting behavior out on Jinni. How could she?

"Jinni, I'm sorry," she said in a quieter vein. "I'm upset, but nothing that happened was your doing. Sometimes I'm such an ingrate I can hardly believe myself. After all you did for me during the past couple of months, I should be kissing your feet, not yelling at you."

Jinni cocked her eyebrow. "Neither you nor I are the kind of people to kiss other people's feet, so forget that notion. And you haven't been yelling. Besides, I sort of understand why you're upset this morning." Jinni's blue eyes contained a diamondlike twinkle when she turned them on Val. "Maybe *upset* isn't the best word for the shock of discovering that you're still full of vim and vigor toward the opposite sex, given the right setting and opportunity, but it will do for the moment.''

Val was staring at her sister with her mouth open. Closing it, she cleared her throat and asked, ''What on earth are you, uh, inferring?''

''Inferring? I'm saying it straight out, sweetie. It's completely obvious what took place in this cozy cabin last night, and I couldn't be happier about it. Now, show us a smile and stop acting as though you committed some unpardonable sin.''

Val's eyes burned and she feared a sudden deluge of tears, but then the door opened and the three men came in. She said hello to Tag and Jim, then retreated to the fireplace while Reed gave them coffee. Jinni followed her to the fire and whispered, ''He's very handsome, Val, and he's especially nice. I would love to see you and Reed become a committed couple.''

Val made no response. She couldn't.

In all honesty she wasn't sure if she would *ever* be able to discuss last night with her inquisitive and well-meaning sister.

It took almost two hours to load Val's SUV with everything she'd brought with her and then winterize the cabin. Everyone helped, and Val saw some of Reed's things being stuffed into the back of her vehicle, when his belongings should have been stowed in Tag's.

But she wasn't doing much talking, and decided to let it go. Certainly she felt none of the merriment the rest of the group seemed to be enjoying. The men, especially, were so jovial about carrying boxes and suitcases out to the vehicles that she wondered if Reed had told them how easily he had scored last night. The thought made her wince, and she realized she might be doing a lot of that in the coming days.

Reed wasn't feeling nearly as cheerful as he let on. Val was withdrawn again, barely speaking, and she worried him. For one thing, he couldn't catch her eye, even when he spoke directly to her. And when she was forced to reply to him, she made it short and quick.

Val's resentment grew with every trip out to her SUV. She wished everyone, even Jinni, would climb back into his or her own vehicle—taking Reed along, of course—and go back to town. She was being forced to leave, and she couldn't be happy and smile about it to save her soul.

Finally, everything was ready. The water pipes had been drained, the electricity turned off, and Val waited for everyone else to leave so she could lock up. Jim went out first, then Tag Kingsley.

Jinni said, "Val, do you want to drive in front of me or behind me?"

"Behind. You go along. I'll be out as soon as I lock up." Jim had asked for the keys to her SUV, and it was idling and warming up out in the road.

Jinni began walking out. "I won't start driving until you're behind the wheel," she said as she went through the door. She sent Reed a little smile, which Val didn't miss.

Reed was the last one inside. "May I ride with you?" he asked.

"Uh...I need to, uh, do some thinking." Val looked at everything but him. "I'd like to be alone."

"Jinni would like to see us together. I would like to see us together. In fact, I doubt that there's a soul anywhere who *wouldn't* like to see us together."

"You're very sure of yourself. Maybe a little too sure."

"That's not true. Not this morning, anyhow. Val, we need to talk, and the trip to town would be the perfect opportunity to do so. I don't know what changed with the light of day, but something did and I'm scared to death to give it a name. We need to talk about it."

"I...can't. Please, everyone's waiting. We have to go. You first, so I can check everything one last time, then lock up."

"Why won't you look at me?" She stood there gazing through the front window, and he took a long, troubled breath and gave up. "Okay, fine. I'll see you in town." He went to the door and left.

Val wanted to throw herself on the bed and cry. She did *not* love Reed Kingsley, she told herself. She didn't even like him...much. Jinni might think his good looks mattered, but they didn't matter to Val. Neither did that sanctimonious air of rushing to everyone's rescue that he wore like a banner. Who in hell did he think he was? She hadn't needed rescue! And he'd saved her from nothing twice now!

Gritting her teeth, Val wrapped her long red scarf around her neck until it covered the lower portion of her face. Slapping dark sunglasses on her eyes, she went outside, pulled the door shut behind her and put the key in the lock.

The drive to town was pure agony. She stayed about four car lengths behind Jinni's vehicle and hated that Tag and Reed were right behind her. Jim and his big truck led the parade, and the whole thing frustrated Val so much that she couldn't hold back tears no matter how hard she tried.

About halfway to Rumor she began thinking about the passion between her and Reed and more tears fell. She knew she'd been much too hard on him this morning, blaming him for her fall from grace, or whatever one called what she'd done after so many years of contented celibacy.

But that was what made her so angry. She *had* been content, and Reed had taken that away from her. Why shouldn't she hate him?

She didn't hate him, though, and admitting that was probably the most disturbing element of the entire debacle that had taken place last night and this morning.

She probably would never really enjoy going to her cabin again, she thought with a fresh burst of tears. "Damn him," she whispered.

And there was one more side to this whole degrading affair, one she hadn't let herself think about until now. Even if she had developed serious feelings for Reed last night, which she hadn't, she would never let herself become a burden to a man. And in spite of the doctors' optimism, she worried the cancer could come back.

So Reed had no chance at all of becoming important to her.

She simply would not allow it.

And maybe someday he would thank her for it.

Chapter Twelve

The closer the four-vehicle cavalcade got to Rumor, the less snow was on the ground. At the edge of town Val saw about three inches of the white stuff and nary a fallen tree. She viewed the calm wintry day of bright sunshine and clear blue sky with a rather cynical eye. Obviously the storm had been much less severe at Rumor's elevation than in the mountains, which was three thousand feet higher.

Val saw Jim turn off and figured he was taking his big truck home and would return in his pickup. Next she saw Tag make a turn, which made sense, as Reed would want to get his mangled SUV back to town—or to some mechanic— and that required a tow truck. Maybe the Kingsleys owned one and the brothers were headed to the Kingsley Ranch, she mused.

But at least Reed wasn't following her home. In fact, no one was following her; Jinni was still in the lead, and it was soon apparent that she intended to hold that position all the way to Val's house.

Val suddenly felt like the most ungrateful person alive. Did she even deserve a sister as wonderful as Jinni? When she'd been scared to death about the cancer diagnosis, and Jinni had rushed to her side, she'd been more than grateful, but she had changed since then. And it didn't appear that she'd changed for the better.

"I'm still grateful for Jinni," she whispered brokenly. "I just wanted a weekend alone at the cabin."

It made sense, of course. She was thirty-five years old and, according to her doctors, cancer-free and healthy. Jinni, apparently, couldn't quite let go of her role as caregiver and morale booster. In short, she still worried about Val, and maybe she always would.

Sighing again, Val pulled into her driveway. Jinni had parked to the side to give Val plenty of room to drive into her garage. Instead, Val parked next to her sister's car. The two of them were getting out of their vehicles when Estelle, wearing a wool cardigan, came outside.

"I'm so glad you're home, safe and sound," the older woman exclaimed. Val couldn't muster a real smile to save her soul, but Estelle didn't notice, immediately turning to Jinni.

"Max phoned about an hour ago. He asked that you call his cell phone the minute you got back."

"He did?" Jinni looked first surprised, then concerned. "Something must be wrong." She ran ahead to the house. "I'll call him right away."

"Would you like some help unloading your things?" Estelle asked Val.

"I'm going to leave everything right where it is for now. Maybe Jim will unload for me when he gets here. He turned off and I figured he was taking his big truck home."

"Sounds right to me. He'll probably be along in the pickup any minute. Well, let's go in. The sun is brighter than a new penny but it's not throwing a whole lot of heat." They walked together and Estelle asked, "Are you feeling all right, honey? You look a little peaked."

Val flushed. She'd gotten precious little sleep last night, but there was no way she could explain that to anyone. A painful twinge hit her. She had actually told Reed about her past, including that one terrible day, the memory of which still disrupted her sleep far too often. What in God's name had come over her?

"I'm fine, Estelle," she said, and marveled that she could speak so evenly when her emotions were in shambles and running wild throughout her system. She had worked so hard in Rumor to lead a private life, and in one fell swoop, in one ridiculous night, she had destroyed her squeaky clean reputation, opened her legs to a man she wasn't even sure she liked and then, this morning, been rude to her sister. Val wished she could go to bed and hide under the covers for a month. Maybe by then things would be back to bearable.

Jinni was still on the phone, standing in the kitchen when they went in, and Estelle whispered to Val, "Would you like some nice hot tea, honey?"

"Estelle, a cup of hot tea just might cure me."

"Of what, hon?"

"You'd never believe it," Val mumbled. "I might be coming down with a bug or something," she added quickly, when she saw Estelle's bright eyes scrutinizing her.

Her friend nodded. "You look it."

I look exactly like the fool I am. "I'm going to take a shower and put on some clean clothes, Estelle, so give me about ten minutes on that tea, okay?"

"Of course."

Jinni said into the phone, "I'll see you then, Max," and she hung up. "Well," she exclaimed with her gaze shifting from Val to Estelle and back again. "Seems we have a mystery on our hands."

"What kind of mystery?" Val asked.

"An elderly man was found wandering the streets during the worst of the blizzard…around three in the morning, Max said. He was half-frozen and terribly disoriented. A deputy took him to the clinic and Max said he was examined and put to bed. They are trying to find out who he is, because he keeps mumbling things about the fire.''

"The fire! Well, my word, surely he hasn't been wandering the streets since then!'' Estelle exclaimed.

"One would think not, but no one seems to know his identity, least of all him.''

"He has amnesia?''

"That's still undetermined. But since he keeps mentioning the fire, the sheriff called Max, thinking, I suppose, that if anyone should hear anything new about the day it started— if the old guy knows anything new, of course—it would be the Cantrells. Anyhow, the doctors at the clinic said the old guy isn't dangerously ill or anything, so they're not planning to have him transported to one of the area's hospitals. Max said it's still a possibility, though, and everyone involved, especially Guy's defense lawyers, are shaken up and demanding to talk to the man before he's moved anywhere.''

"Max said no one recognizes him?'' Estelle was frowning.

"That's what he said, yes. Apparently the old guy has a long beard and hair, and his clothes were pretty much worn out. Plus they weren't nearly heavy enough to keep him warm in a blizzard.''

"And there's no sign of a strange car parked somewhere in town? I mean, how'd he get to Rumor?''

"I suppose he could have hitched a ride with someone.''

"There weren't very many 'someones' out driving around last night,'' Estelle said dryly.

Jinni nodded. "I know. So does Max…and the sheriff. They're both at the clinic, incidentally, waiting for whatever happens next, I guess. Anyhow, like I said, Rumor has a mystery on its hands.'' She looked at Val. "Are you going to faint?''

Val blinked. "Of course not. Why would you ask me that?''

"Probably because you're white as a sheet. Estelle, is she pale or is my imagination running amok?''

"I already told her she looked peaked,'' Estelle said.

Val threw up her hands. "I'm hitting the shower. You two figure out who that poor old man is while I'm under water so hot that I'll come out of it looking pink as a boiled lobster. Maybe then you'll stop discussing the color of my skin."

"Ha-ha," Jinni said drolly. Val vanished and Jinni turned to Estelle. "I'm going to leave and check on Michael. Max said he talked about visiting his uncle Guy today, which is fine, but Max has been tied up with the lawyers and hasn't seen his son since early this morning. Anyhow, I told him I'd make sure Michael was all right."

"I never would have figured Max Cantrell for a worry-wart," Estelle said.

"And you probably would have been right, but he told me himself that he and Michael are much closer than they used to be. I love both of them, and they love each other. That makes me very happy, Estelle."

"Oh, Jinni." Estelle put her arms around her and hugged her. "I'm so glad you found what every good woman deserves—a loving husband."

"Me, too, Estelle." Smiling, she started for the door. Before going through it, though, she looked at Estelle one more time. "My situation is just about perfect, but Val's isn't. I wish she had what I do."

"A loving husband," Estelle murmured. "I don't think she wants what you have, Jinni."

"Yes, she does. She just doesn't know it yet. Tell her I'll be back later."

"Will do."

Jinni hurried out.

Val began trembling when she undressed. She couldn't stop thinking about last night, with the biggest, most disturbing, most frightening question being why she'd told Reed about the day that had come very close to destroying her. For years and years, ever since it had happened, she'd not talked about it to anyone other than professionals.

But she had also told Reed about her promiscuity. *Did you*

think hearing what a naughty girl you'd been would turn him off?

In truth, all the sordid facts of her past had seemed to make him like her more. What kind of man was he that he could learn such disgusting things about a woman and still like her? Still want her?

Val knew how deeply shaken she was over this. She could feel it in her stomach and see the proof of it in her unsteady hands. Last night had been a serious jolt that she might never get over. The rhythmic jabs of pain that came with remembering that Reed Kingsley now knew all of her secrets was close to unbearable.

No, not all, she thought sadly. There was still one buried in the deepest recess of her psyche. She'd blurted everything else last night—why not that as well? Anguish struck again when she thought that she had not only forced Reed to listen to her story, she'd then made love with him! What must he think of her?

Val got into the shower, where her tears mingled with the water, cleansing her skin. Nothing could cleanse her soul, though; she knew she was never going to be the same.

Even though, damn him, it was all Reed's fault! Why had he fed her brandy last night, if not to loosen her inhibitions?

But that was the bind, wasn't it? He'd supplied the brandy, but he hadn't forced her to drink it. And had she really drunk enough to completely forget the strict standards by which she had lived since her move to Rumor?

Neither had he forced her to make love, to kiss him and hold him and touch him as though she would never get enough of him. Oh, the things she'd done with him. The things he'd done to her…again and again. And she had loved every moment of it, with her last clear memory before falling asleep being snuggling her backside into the curve of his warm, manly body.

"Damn…damn," she whispered, while tears streamed down her face.

Drying off a short time later, she frowned and pondered

Reed's remarks about flowers and a card. He had to have meant the bouquet and card he'd brought to her, even though he'd said that she had sent *him* flowers. His tongue—or brain—must have gotten twisted, or some darn thing, because if he had actually received flowers from a woman, they hadn't come from her.

Of course, there was probably more than one woman hot on his trail!

Physically refreshed from her shower, and knowing that nothing would ever heal the emotional bruising she herself had caused last night, Val decided to put the whole thing from her mind and attempt to accomplish something productive today. Yes, she would still like to hide in bed for a few months—even a few days would be good—but it was a ludicrous wish and impossible.

She got dressed.

Tag drove Reed home so he could get his pickup. Reed also had a snappy little sports car in his garage, but it wasn't sports car weather. No telling where the day might take him, and the pickup had four-wheel drive.

During the drive from the cabin the two brothers had talked about the storm. Then Tag had mentioned Reed's crunched vehicle.

"That tree falling exactly where it did was really something, Reed. The wind must have been two or three times more powerful out there than it was in town."

"That tree was destined to topple," Reed said. "It was just a matter of time."

"Why do you think that?"

"When the people who built Val's cabin cut through that hill to make the driveway, they damaged the roots of that tree. I checked it out, Tag, and the roots—those I could see—were black and soggy, obviously long dead. That pine was still standing by the grace of God, and when a gust of wind hit it, it went over."

"You know, Jim, Jinni and I were looking over the mess

of the accident before you came outside and it appeared to us as though the tree would have hit the cabin if your rig hadn't been parked where it was.''

"Yes," Reed said quietly. "I'm sure you're right."

"Darn good thing you weren't still behind the wheel." Tag sent his brother a glance. "You could have been as mangled as your SUV."

"Timing is everything, isn't it?"

"It sure counts for a lot. So, how'd you and Dr. Fairchild get along?"

Reed delayed answering, but finally said in a quiet voice, "I don't want to talk about Val, Tag."

His brother nodded. "You never have talked about your women. What made me think you'd start now?"

Reed made no reply. He wished he could think of Val as "his woman," and during the night she had been. For a while, anyhow. This morning he didn't know what to think. She had awakened angry and resentful, and he didn't understand that.

He sighed inwardly. Maybe he never would understand Val…even though he was nuts about her. And maybe he should hike his butt to a shrink and get professional help. Why in hell would he fall for a woman with more problems than anyone else he'd ever known?

Was that Val's drawing power? God help him if his life-long penchant for helping the underdog was now choosing him a mate that any sane man would run from with the speed of a lightning bolt.

Jinni spotted Michael's bicycle at the sheriff's office. He'd been easy enough to find, but she decided to talk to him so she could tell Max that she'd seen him with her own eyes and he was fine. She walked into the building and smiled at the deputy on duty.

"Hello," she said. "I don't think I've seen you before. I'm Jinni Cantrell. I've been here with my husband a few times, but today I'm here alone. Is Michael Cantrell visiting his uncle?''

"Yes, ma'am, he is.''

"Well, would you mind asking him to come out here and talk to me for a minute?''

The deputy said, "Wouldn't mind a bit,'' and got up from his desk. He disappeared through the door that Jinni knew led to the cells and the visitor's room. In a minute Michael came through the same door, with the deputy right behind him.

"Thank you,'' Jinni said to the deputy, then turned and said to her stepson, "Hi, Michael. Can we talk a little?''

"Uh, guess so. What about?''

"Let's go outside.''

Michael followed her out. "Jinni, is something wrong? With Dad, I mean?''

"No, no, nothing like that. It's just that your dad is very busy today and he asked me to…to…'' Jinni hesitated. Michael was an adorable, almost-sixteen-year-old boy with an overload of confidence that might or might not be pure bluff. Jinni adored him, and she was getting to know him a little better each day. She knew that he would not take kindly to her checking up on him, which was what she'd been about to tell him she was doing, at his father's request.

She switched gears. "Your dad asked me to let you know that I got back from the mountains safe and sound…with my sister, also safe and sound.''

"Really?''

Jinni smiled in an attempt to allay his obvious skepticism. "I think he thought you might be worrying about me. Anyhow, I'm back in town and now I can tell him that all three of the Cantrells are just fine.''

"Uncle Guy's not fine. Jinni, if they convict him and he has to spend the rest of his life in jail for something he didn't do, I think he'll just give up and…and die.''

Jinni's heart ached for the boy. "Your dad is doing everything he can to see that doesn't happen, Michael. In fact, he's following a rather murky but sort of interesting lead right now that might unearth some information about the day the fire got started.''

Michael's downcast expression vanished. "What lead? Tell me what's going on, Jinni. Please!"

Jinni became concerned that she had given the boy false hope. She tried to backtrack. "It...it's so iffy, Michael. I really shouldn't have mentioned it."

But Michael wouldn't let her get away with that. "I have a right to know if there's even a sliver of a chance of getting Uncle Guy out of this mess. Tell me what Dad's working on, Jinni."

She studied the very adult expression in Michael's vivid blue eyes. He had outgrown childhood recently—since his uncle had been arrested, to be completely accurate. He was a handsome, smart and sometimes sweet young man. Right now he looked far more determined than sweet, but he was the child Jinni had never had and she loved him, whatever his mood.

"All right," she said huskily. "Briefly, it's this. An elderly man was discovered wandering around in the storm. A deputy took him to the clinic. He's disoriented. Doesn't even seem to know his own name. But he keeps mumbling things about the fire. His clothes weren't adequate for winter weather and—"

"Jinni! He's Old Man Jackson! The people who knew him wondered what had happened to him when the fire destroyed Logan's Hill. He had a house up there in the woods, and it was burned to the ground. But no one ever found his body. It's him, I know it is!"

"But, honey, if his house was gone, how did he survive all that time? What did he eat, where did he sleep?"

"He knows things we don't, Jinni. I used to ride my bike on some of the trails on Logan's Hill, and I ran into him a couple of times. He was leery of people coming around, but we talked. I would bet anything it's him, and what if he saw what really happened that day? Jinni, I gotta go to the clinic and see that old guy for myself.''

Jinni's heart sank. Her big mouth had gotten her in trouble more times than she cared to remember, and it seemed that she still didn't know when to shut up. Now Michael was all worked up over something that could be nothing but wishful thinking. No one could survive for months and months on nothing, in an environment that could be as cruel as it was beautiful. Especially not an elderly person.

''Are…are you going to tell your uncle about the man at the clinic?'' she asked, hoping she didn't look as worried as she felt.

Michael hesitated a moment. Then he shook his head. ''I don't think so. Not yet. I'll see how it turns out first.''

Jinni breathed a quiet sigh of relief. She was so proud of Michael. The sensibility and maturity of his decision far exceeded what most people expected from a boy his age.

But he *was* anxious. ''Are you going to the clinic, Jinni?'' he asked. ''I'll ride with you, if you are, but I can take my bike if there's something else you have to do.'' He went over to the deputy. ''I have to leave. Would you tell my uncle I said goodbye and that I'll be back later on?''

Still regretting the small but powerful uproar she'd inadvertently caused by once again speaking out of turn, Jinni listened to the deputy agreeing to Michael's request. Then the boy flew to the door, proving his intent to get to the clinic as fast as was physically possible.

Jinni followed him out. ''Leave your bike here,'' she said. ''I'll drive.''

Jim and Estelle left for the day around two. Jim had been staying abreast of the weather forecasts and told Val that the area was in for more bad weather. ''There's a whole series of storm systems rolling in from Canada and the Pacific Northwest,'' he said. ''Forecasters are predicting another blizzard within ten to twelve hours.''

For the first time since the first snowflake fell, Val was

glad she was back in town instead of at the cabin. She wasn't happy that her weekend had been ruined, and she wasn't enough of a hypocrite to pretend that she was, but it was only sensible to feel some relief over not being stranded in ten feet of snow.

After the Worths had gone, Val puttered in the Animal Hospital, checking on the pets in the Dog House and the Cat House and generally staying busy with small jobs that Jim wouldn't even notice. He was great with the bigger chores and willing to do anything Val asked, and she appreciated both him and Estelle more than she could say. In fact, now that she was so used to having them around, the mere thought of them deciding to retire again—this time from her employ—gave her an awfully empty feeling. She decided that she really must let them know more often how much she cared for them as friends, not just as employees.

But keeping her feelings locked and sealed was a habit hard to break. She'd gone a little crazy last night with Reed, and for the life of her she couldn't figure out what had caused her to throw caution to the winds and talk and talk and...talk. And after that....

"Dear God," she whispered as she walked from the Cat House to her office. The things she'd done with that man! In truth, she didn't know what hurt her most today—the fact that she had bared most of her secrets or that she'd bared her body so wantonly!

She forced herself to do some paperwork, then felt her eyes getting heavy. She hadn't slept enough last night and it was catching up with her. Moving from her desk chair to the small sofa she'd had installed specifically for catnaps, she actually groaned at the pleasure lying down and shutting her eyes gave her. She knew she would worry again when she woke up, but for now, she had to indulge in some blessed sleep.

She heard nothing and was aware of nothing for over two hours. She didn't dream, she barely breathed, and when she finally opened her eyes twilight had settled in. The room was gray and shadowy, and at first she didn't realize that she wasn't alone.

She stretched, yawned and sat up. It was then, at that precise moment, that she saw Reed Kingsley. He was seated in one of the chairs she kept near her desk for visitors, only he had moved it closer to the sofa. Had he been watching her sleep?

Her face burned. Had he no scruples, no respect for a woman's privacy?

"How long have you been here?" she asked in a cold, harsh voice.

"About an hour," Reed said with slightly upturned lips. It was more of a hint of a smile than the real thing, because he knew now that he could never count on Val's mood. She had looked like an angel in sleep, but the present gleam in her eyes could hardly be described as angelic.

"You sat there and watched me sleep for an hour? There is something seriously wrong with you!" Val got to her feet. "It's almost dark. Why didn't you turn on a light?"

"And wake you? Why would I be that unkind?" Reed, too, stood. "You were tired and needed to rest."

Val sniffed. "I'm going to lock up and go to the house. Do you mind leaving now?"

"Yes, as a matter of fact, I do. May I go to the house with you? Val, we really need to talk about last night. Our attitudes are miles apart and unnecessarily conflicting. Honey, I don't want any conflict between us. I want—"

She stopped him with an abrupt movement of her hand. "I don't want to hear it!"

"Val, please don't do this. Don't you have a glimmer of understanding for what we could have together? Please let me go home with you. I promise to do nothing that offends you. I only want to talk this thing through."

She stood still and studied the sincerity in his eyes, in his stance. He *couldn't* be in love with her, he just couldn't! She wasn't ready for love; she might never be ready!

She had to bring this whole disturbing affair to a screeching halt, and it wasn't going to happen if she kept refusing to talk to him.

"All right, fine," she said flatly. "You can come to the house. But the only thing we're going to do is talk, do you understand?"

"Perfectly."

Chapter Thirteen

"You go on to the house," Val told Reed. "The back door isn't locked, and I have a couple of things to do here before I can leave."

"I could wait."

"No!" She took a sharp breath and then spoke more calmly. "Please, go over there now. I'll only be a few minutes."

"Is Estelle at the house?"

"She and Jim went home several hours ago."

Reed came close to smiling, even though he had absolutely no faith in Val appreciating the effort. "Then no one will bring out the shotgun if I just walk in."

"I don't even own a shotgun."

"Or a sense of humor," Reed added. But he was still nearly smiling, and anyone seeing his face would have known he was teasing.

Anyone but Val, that is. She figured he was trying to get a smile out of *her*. "If you're planning on talking utter nonsense during our discussion, we might as well forget the whole thing.''

In truth, she wished with heart and soul that he would flippantly say, ''You're absolutely right,'' and walk out laughing...or even angry. The only subject he could possibly want to talk about was their atrocious behavior last night, and thinking about it made her feel ill. What would verbalizing her overwhelming deluge of self-disgust do to her poor, already roiling stomach?

But she had danced to the music last night, and the piper *always* had to be paid, in one way or another. She would take her lumps and convince this man that however inane and inappropriate her conduct last night, it had been an aberration and would never be repeated. Deep down she feared that he was really back for a repeat performance of amorous activities, and it was not going to happen.

Val didn't breathe normally until Reed accepted her preference of finishing up at the hospital by herself, and left her alone. Then, experiencing enormous relief, she leaned weakly against a wall and sucked in huge gulps of air, attempting to put herself back on an even keel.

Not that she'd been all that ''even'' *before* Reed's arrival...or, rather, before she'd passed out on the sofa. She had messed up big time last night and she was going to pay for it, make no mistake. The knowledge burned like a small flame in every cell of her body. One *always* paid; the only unknown in that harsh fact of life was the type of payment fate would demand.

It took Val almost twenty minutes to pull herself together enough to face Reed. Locking up took about three minutes, brushing her hair and grimacing at her pale reflection in the bathroom mirror took another five minutes. The rest of the time was spent pacing.

She suffered the agonies of hell while working up the courage to get this unholy meeting over with, and finally, *finally,* she was able to force herself through the door, make sure it was locked behind her and take the steps that brought her to her own back door.

Sucking in air as though she had to stock up because there was none in the house, she turned the knob and stepped inside.

"Michael, are you positive? Son, I mean *really* positive."

"He looks a lot different, Dad. He's so thin and his hair and beard are a foot longer."

"A foot longer?"

"Well, maybe not a foot, but he's a lot hairier than when I last saw him."

Jinni had been listening to the conversation between Max and Michael. They were both so hopeful that the poor old mystery guy at the Family Clinic might be Mr. Jackson, a hermit or recluse who people believed must have died in the Logan's Hill fire, even though no unidentified human remains had been found.

If possible, Max was even more hopeful than his son. For one thing, he had never set eyes on Old Man Jackson. Sheriff Tanner, who also maintained that he'd never come face-to-face with Mr. Jackson before the fire, was hot on that trail now, as were the lawyers working on Guy Cantrell's defense strategies. Jinni thought it odd that an old man had lived so close to town and no one had really known him. But then, she realized, she'd never known a hermit herself.

The problem that had everyone running in circles, of course, was that the elderly man wasn't quite conscious, nor was he coherent when he was awake. Everyone kept talking about moving him, by ambulance, to the hospital in Whitehorn, where the medical staff might be able to bring him around.

The doctors at the clinic said he was malnourished and ill from exposure. They could find no broken bones, and his vital signs did not indicate an emergency situation. But if the sheriff wanted him taken to Whitehorn, they would sign the release forms.

The sheriff, it seemed, was in a bit of a quandary.

"I don't think they should move him," Jinni said quietly, speaking for the first time in at least thirty minutes. She hadn't wanted to intrude on the extremely serious discussion between her husband and stepson, but they had reached somewhat of an impasse, mostly caused by Michael's honest admission of not being a hundred percent positive that the man was Mr. Jackson.

"The doctors at the clinic have said clearly that they're doing the same things for him that physicians in Whitehorn would do. He's not really ill, Max, not physically ill. He's old and he's hungry and exhausted, and they found him half-frozen. The poor old fellow probably needs exactly what he's getting—warmth, fluids and food. I have faith in the doctors at the clinic, don't you?"

"Well, sure," Max agreed enthusiastically. "And I'd like him to stay right where he is until his memory returns. What if he saw everything, Jinni? Guy told quite a story about the day the fire got started, and what if Old Man Jackson can verify everything he said?" Max's exuberance collapsed then and he sat back with a sigh. "*If* he's Old Man Jackson."

"I think he is, Dad," Michael said. "I just can't prove it."

"And you're not a hundred percent positive," Max added quietly.

Michael hesitated, then said, almost under his breath, "No sir, I'm not."

It occurred to Jinni then that when the elderly man at the clinic did come around, maybe the story he had to tell about that day—if he had one—would be in direct opposition to the one Guy Cantrell had related. Her heart pounded as she pondered the possibility and how it would affect the family. Max, his mother and Michael were so certain of Guy's innocence. Jinni couldn't agree or disagree based on personal experience, as she'd never met Guy until after his arrest. But he seemed like such a nice man, and she had a hard time picturing him as a killer.

Still, other than Guy himself, no one knew what had taken place that day. At least until now. Small wonder Max was so wound up about the old man in bed at the clinic.

Val walked into her house, immediately spotted Reed's jacket draped over the back of a kitchen chair and his hat on the table, and inhaled nervously.

She went to the living room and there he was, seated on the sofa. He was on his feet the second he saw her.

"No need for that," she said, and sank into the nearest chair.

Reed sat again and smiled at her. "You're through working for the day, right?"

"I…suppose so. Unless an emergency comes up. Why?"

"I was thinking that we might drive to Billings and have dinner in a nice restaurant."

The time had come to say her piece. She'd known it would happen shortly after they began talking, but she wasn't prepared for the discomfort of looking him in the eye and telling him to stay away from her.

She cleared her throat. "I don't think so."

"All right," Reed said quietly. "Dinner in Rumor then?"

"No."

"You have other plans."

"Of course I don't have other plans! I'm not even supposed to be here! If you would bother to think about it, you would recall that I had planned to spend the weekend at my cabin."

Reed drew his eyebrows together in a frown of confusion. "Why are you so angry with me? You were angry with me when you didn't even know me. I thought that last night would change things between us, but it didn't, and I'd like to know why it didn't. You were soft and sweet and loving last night, and—"

"I was drunk last night!"

"You were *not* drunk! Relaxed, yes. A whole lot less tense

than normal, but not drunk. Hell, do you think I would ply a woman with liquor to get her to say yes?''

"Seems to me it sort of turned out that way."

Reed was thunderstruck. He fell back against the sofa and studied this woman who had the power to crush his spirit, his ego and his confidence with a few words.

Val knew that she had struck an almost fatal blow, and the regret she felt over wounding him so terribly was like a stab in her own heart.

"I'm sorry," she said stiffly, remaining standoffish and guarded despite the remorse in her soul. "You didn't force me to do anything, least of all drink a little more than I should have. But nothing we did...nothing *I* did...means anything today. It's important to me that you understand that."

"I don't, and I never will. How can you sit there and say something like that? You don't sleep with every guy who comes along, so why wouldn't I think that last night meant something to you? It sure as hell meant something to me."

Val got up, walked in a circle, then stopped and faced him. "Don't you realize that the cancer could come back?"

"What?" Reed stared in utter dismay for a moment, then got to his feet. "Would you mind telling me what that has to do with the feelings we showed each other last night?"

"It has everything to do with everything! My God, you're not a stupid man, Reed. Step into my shoes for a minute and tell me you wouldn't worry about a recurrence if you were me."

"It's over with. It's done. It's in the past! Val, you're not going to let it ruin the rest of your life...your *healthy* life, are you? That makes no sense."

"It makes perfect sense. Maybe you are stupid."

He moved quickly, closing the gap between them, and grasped her arm. "I'm not stupid and neither are you, so please tell me you're not backing off from a relationship with me because you might become ill again. Val, you can't live your life that way."

She looked into the dark green depths of his eyes and saw anguish. She was still hurting him, still delivering almost fatal blows, and that hadn't been her intention. All she'd wanted to do was to make him understand that she—that she...

God, what *had* she wanted him to understand? That she was afraid of a relationship? Afraid of commitment? Afraid of trusting a man?

She'd said none of those things, although what she had said was true. She would rather die than become a burden to a man of his stature. He wasn't your everyday Joe, he was somebody, and she couldn't see him holding her head while she bent over the toilet after a chemo treatment!

Still looking at him, her eyes became watery. He was so beautifully handsome, so breathtakingly masculine, so real and alive.

And he didn't deserve a woman with her past. Hadn't he heard her last night when she'd bared her soul?

"Tell me one thing," she said in a husky, emotion-laden voice. "Why in God's name do you want anything to do with me?"

The question nearly floored Reed. His mind spun with confusion as he looked into her teary eyes. "Why in God's name *don't* you want anything to do with me? You're not immune to the chemistry between us. You proved that last night."

"Chemistry? Like that's really important! Try again."

He knew she meant that he should give her a better answer to her question, but he didn't have a better answer. Feelings of every description were involved, he knew that much, but nothing else was clear.

Except for the chemistry. That was so clear and overwhelming he was nearly swallowed up by it. He stopped thinking—and worrying—and acted, pulling her forward at the same time he stepped toward her. She was suddenly against him, in his arms.

A squeak of protest came from her lips, but even that was silenced when he pressed his mouth to hers. He kissed her until her lips softened under his, until they parted and he felt her tongue.

Until he heard the sob that welled in her throat. Taken aback, he raised his head and looked at the tears spilling from her eyes.

"You're not just fighting me, you're fighting yourself. Why, Val? Why are you fighting either of us?"

"B-because the cancer could—could come back," she stammered brokenly.

He broke away from her and practically shouted an obscenity. "Stop saying that! Serious relationships are for better or worse. What do you think I would do if you happened to get ill again—leave you flat? Ask yourself if that's what you would do if the man you loved became ill. Damn, Val, it happens every day. Do you think people like Jim and Estelle Worth would—"

"Just stop it!" she shouted. "You haven't ever *been* ill! You don't know what it's like, so don't act all noble and giving and…and pretentious about something that's horrid and humiliating and destroys every vestige of human dignity."

"You don't need to yell at me."

"Oh, for God's sake! You yelled first, but then it's all right for you to do anything you please because you're a Kingsley!"

"Now you're sniping at my family? Come on, Val. I don't deserve that and neither do they."

She could not have felt more miserable than she did at that moment. "You're right," she said wearily. "This is ridiculous, and it's not going to get any better. Please go."

"Not until you tell me what changed between the middle of last night and this morning."

"You irritating man, I wasn't drunk this morning!"

"That's an excuse, not an explanation!"

"Reed, I told you all about myself last night. I hit the highlights…or, rather, the low points…and after hearing my perfectly dreadful life story, why in hell do you still want to know me?'' She had started that little speech in an almost normal voice, but she was shouting again by the time she got to the final word.

"Because I live in the present, not the past! I hope to hell you're not determined to punish yourself for ancient events that were beyond your control, even when they took place."

"Punish myself?" she whispered, struck hard by those two words. Years ago her therapist had worked diligently to make her believe she deserved no punishment for anything she'd done during her short lifetime, and certainly not for being the victim of a deranged rapist. Maybe the therapist hadn't worked quite diligently enough.

Still, she hadn't believed that her lifestyle of closely guarded privacy and very little social interaction with men was a form of self-punishment.

Nor did she believe it now! She lifted her chin. "I don't need or want your psychoanalysis. You're not qualified for the job, believe me. I would like you to leave now and not bother me again. I do ask one thing of you, however. I have no idea why I told you so many sordid details of my past, but I did, and if you spread what I said around town, I wouldn't be able to look anyone in the eye again. So I'm asking—"

Wounded to his core that she would even think such a thing about him, Reed broke in. "You don't know me at all." His lips curled in an unnatural sneer. "Let me put this as crudely as you seem to prefer conversations between us to be. I *never* talk about the women I sleep with. So long, babe, see you around."

Val watched him walk out of her living room, her mouth open, her eyes wide and startled. He could be cruel, after all. That was the one thing that had never entered her mind; she had never pictured him as a hard, cruel human being.

Maybe she should have.

Sick to his stomach, Reed drove home. It was over between Val and him, and it had barely gotten started. Maybe last night had been a dream and hadn't really happened at all. Thinking of it that way somehow made it a little more bearable.

Still, when he got to his house, he went inside and locked the door behind him. Almost praying that no one would call or come by, he ran a tub of water, got undressed and climbed into the bath. Leaning his head back against the lip of the tub, he released the tight hold he'd had on his emotions, and when a few tears dribbled down his temples, he didn't wipe them away.

What difference did a few tears make? His heart was broken, and the worst of it was he didn't know why he felt so shattered. Last night Val had been all woman in his arms. Today she couldn't stand the sight of him. Why, for God's sake. Why?

Would he ever know?

Jinni walked into Val's house via the kitchen door around seven that evening and found her sister sitting in the dark in the living room.

"For Pete's sake!" Jinni exclaimed. "What's going on? What happened to the lights?"

"I didn't turn them on, and believe me, nothing is going on."

Jinni snapped on a lamp and immediately took a long look at her sister. "You're down in the dumps. How come? Aren't you feeling well?"

"Jinni, I am feeling as well as you are. Honestly, why does everyone constantly question my health?"

Frowning a bit, Jinni sank into a chair. "Probably because you've been wearing a last-rose-of-summer face for a good two weeks now. Is there something you're not telling me? Have you been talking to your Billings doctors?"

"I haven't been near Billings for at least a month."

"Well, you've been acting awfully down in the mouth, kiddo, so something's going on." Jinni paused a moment. "Does your blue mood have something to do with Reed Kingsley?" she asked quietly.

Val gave it all away by sucking in a sharp breath. Just hearing his name had stolen her breath, and her unexpected reaction was as much a shock to her as it was to Jinni.

"This *is* about Reed! Val, I swear that if he's done something to break your heart, I'll find him and give him the dressing down of his life!"

Val gasped. "You will do nothing of the kind! There is nothing between Reed and me, nor will there be in the future. I set him straight on that today."

"Today? This morning before we all left the cabin?"

"No, this afternoon."

"He came by this afternoon? And you set him straight. As in what?"

"As in I don't want him hanging around."

Jinni's jaw dropped. "You told him that? Val, what do you want to do, live alone for the rest of your life?"

"Yes," she said dully. "Change the subject, Jinni. You must have come over here for a reason. Isn't Max at home?"

"Max is home, but he's holed up in the study with his lawyers. I ran over for a minute to tell you what's happening. Everyone at my house is practically drooling because of the elderly man at the clinic. If he's the Logan's Hill hermit, then he might have seen what took place the day the fire started. Michael thinks he is Mr. Jackson, but the poor old guy is so emaciated and weather-beaten that he can't be sure. The sheriff is trying to find someone in the area that knows Jackson better than Michael does, someone who can identify him unequivocally."

"I see," Val murmured, truly unable to work up any enthusiasm for this latest chapter in the life and adventures of the Cantrell family. She felt guilty about it, but only because of Jinni's connection. Not that she wanted an innocent man to be convicted of murder, but her brain was already so overcrowded with her own problems it was hard to find space for Guy Cantrell's.

Jinni was worried about her sister, and even the drama

playing out in her own house couldn't quell the concern she felt for Val.

"I…wish you would give Reed a chance," she said softly, although if she had stood up and shouted the words they would not have had a greater impact on Val.

"And I wish people would let me decide for myself who I should or should not like!"

"Are you telling me to mind my own business? Val, you *are* my business."

Val choked on a sob. She'd been crying on and off since Reed walked out, and trying not to show it since Jinni walked in. Leaning forward now, Val covered her face with her hands.

"Please, Jinni, let me figure this one out for myself," she whispered. This was one thing Jinni couldn't do for her.

Jinni jumped up and hurried over to kneel by her sister. "You're in such terrible pain. Sweetie, if you like Reed so much, why are you shutting him out?"

Val touched her sister's beautiful face with gentle fingertips and winced when she saw the mist in Jinni's big blue eyes.

"I've been leaning on you far too much, Jinni. I want you to believe what I'm going to say about Reed. He and I are fine. We will never be more than friends, but I think he's accepted that, as I have. I also apologize for not being more sympathetic to your problems. I've become so obsessed with my own that I've forgotten how to be nice to you. Can you forgive me?"

Jinni threw her arms around Val and hugged her. "Of course I forgive you." She leaned back and grinned then, and Val saw a devilish twinkle in her eyes. "But I still wish you would give Reed a chance."

Chapter Fourteen

Even through her restless dreams, Val heard the wind. She opened her eyes and listened to the unmistakable sounds of another winter storm. Getting out of bed, she padded barefoot to a window at the front of her house. She moved the drape aside to look out, and saw snowflakes dancing in the glowing balls of light surrounding every streetlight. A car slowly passed by—a sheriff's car. It turned south on Logan Street and parked near the building housing the sheriff's office.

Val's gaze moved from that building to the one directly on the corner of Logan and Main—the volunteer fire station. She could make out one lighted window on the second floor and wondered if someone was there. Reed, maybe? Did he sometimes spend a night at the station? She thought it odd that she had never noticed how clearly—even during a snowstorm—she could see the place from her house.

Sighing heavily, she dropped the drape and returned to her bed. Almost constantly thinking about Reed, in one context or another, was terribly disturbing, but she didn't seem able to break the pattern. It was, in fact, becoming a troubling habit.

But she had only herself to blame. True, he should not have rushed to her rescue every time he'd imagined her *needing* rescue, but something told her that a sensible reason for shooting off her mouth at the cabin and then compounding that self-degradation by sleeping with him would forever elude her.

Then, of course, she'd tried to turn back the clock by being mean and nasty to him, and it hadn't worked. Despising herself hadn't worked, either. She had attempted to despise Reed, but whenever she concentrated on that effort, her foolish brain dredged up memories of the other night—his tender but passionate lovemaking, his eyes looking at her with exquisite adoration, his scent, the distinctive quality of his voice.

In a sudden burst of anger, Val pounded her pillow. She had *not* been longing for a man! She hadn't even thought about sex—not in a good way, not in a yearning way—in years, so why now? Why had she been so damn easy?

It was a long time before she fell asleep again.

Val was outside when the phone rang. She left the snow shovel leaning against the house and hurried inside to answer.

"Hello, this is Dr. Fairchild."

"Val, it's Jim. Are you snowed in, honey?"

"I was…sort of. But I've been outside shoveling the walks."

"Now you should have known I'd be happy to drive to town and clear those walks."

"I did know it, Jim, but I wanted to get my blood pumping this morning, and I couldn't resist doing it myself. I'm almost finished, and you are not to worry about me. And please don't get Estelle all upset because I actually got off my butt for an hour or so to get a little exercise."

Jim laughed. "You're mighty hard on yourself, Doc."

"I should be, and so should you and Estelle. I've leaned

on you two far too much. Before I got sick I did everything around here, Jim, and it didn't hurt me in the least.''

''I know, but you've gone through quite an ordeal and—''

''And I had you and Estelle and Jinni to help me through it. Jim, dear friend, I appreciate your concern, but I'm fine and you and Estelle are to stay home and enjoy your Sunday, all right?''

''Well...if you're sure. Oh, the forecast is for more snow, in case you haven't heard.''

''I hadn't, but when I'm done outside I'm going in for some breakfast and the morning newspaper. I'm sure the *Rumor Mill* has the weather forecast for the coming week.''

''Yes, it does. Well, if you're sure you don't need us today, Estelle and I will see you tomorrow.''

''' 'Bye, Jim.''

Val went back outside and finished clearing her sidewalks. It was a bright and shining morning. Cold, yes, but she was warmly dressed and not at all uncomfortable. The sun was out, making the snow gleam, and the sky was so blue it hurt her eyes to look at it. Montana was rarely gloomy, even during winter months.

After putting away the snow shovel, Val went inside, got out of her heavy clothes, washed up and then made some coffee, scrambled eggs and toast. She sat at the kitchen table with her breakfast and the Sunday paper. For the first time since her misadventures at the cabin, she wasn't thinking about Reed or suffering over her wanton and bordering-on-asinine behavior.

Spreading the paper out to read the front page while eating, she saw a headline: Identification Unknown!

Val read the article below it:

An elderly man was brought to the Family Clinic by a deputy early Saturday morning during the worst of Rumor's first blizzard of the season. The man carried no identification and, according to doctors at the clinic, is unable to identify himself. His age is estimated at seventy to eighty years, he has long gray hair and a beard, and his height is approximately six feet.

The sheriff's department is eagerly seeking anyone who might have knowledge about this man. It has been suggested that he could be Robert Jackson, the man who lived on Logan's Hill prior to the fire. If his description is familiar, please contact either the sheriff's department or the Family Clinic.

Val's phone rang just as she got to the end of the article. It was Jinni.

"Did you read the paper yet?" her sister asked.

"I'm in the process, but I saw the front page article."

"Well, we're all hoping someone knows Mr. Jackson well enough to identify him. Plus, Max has been in contact with several specialists in the field of geriatrics. He's trying to arrange for one or more of them to come to Rumor and examine our mystery man, so now everyone has stopped talking about moving him from the clinic to Whitehorn, or somewhere else." Jinni paused, then asked, "Are you eating?"

Val had been nibbling on a bite of scrambled egg. "It's okay. I can eat and talk at the same time."

"I just wanted to keep you updated."

"I'm glad you called."

"You sound a little more upbeat today. Are you?"

"I don't know. Maybe. I shoveled the sidewalks this morning."

"You did? Isn't that too strenuous for you?"

"Not according to my doctors. They released me without any activity restrictions. Besides, I can tell for myself that I'm doing well."

"Val, I get all weepy when you say something as wonderful as that."

"That's 'cause you're a softy with a heart the size of Chicago. Jinni, sometimes I'm so thoughtless and rude I hate myself afterward. I apologize for being such a shrew to you and everyone else."

"You've got good reason, sweetie. A whole list of good reasons, actually. So, what're you going to do today?"

"Putter around. Nothing earthshaking. Why? What are *you* doing today?"

"A lot of praying, I think. The Cantrells are so certain of Guy's innocence that I've started believing in it, too. Max is tied up with the lawyers again, and Michael is hanging around the fringes of their conversations, so I've been thinking of attending church this morning. Why don't you come with me? I could pick you up and we could ride together."

"What time is it?" Val twisted around to see the digital clock on the microwave. "I haven't showered, but I think I could make it. Yes, I'd love to attend church service with you."

"I'll be there in about forty-five minutes."

"Great. See you then."

Val gulped down the rest of her eggs, set the dishes in the dishwasher and then hurried down the hall to her bathroom. She showered while looking forward to a pleasant hour in the community church with her sister.

She could putter later.

Reed had morning coffee with his folks, answered their questions on how his SUV had gotten smashed, and then listened to them discussing the article in the newspaper about the mystery man at the clinic.

"Someone must know Mr. Jackson well enough to identify him," Carolyn mused. "Stratton, did you ever meet him?"

"Not that I can recall," he replied.

"He's no youngster," Carolyn said thoughtfully, "so some of our older citizens might know him. I wonder how long he lived on Logan's Hill before the fire. Reed, do you know how long he lived out there all by himself?"

"Afraid not," Reed answered.

"And where on earth did he live after his house was burned to the ground?" his mother continued. "This is very strange."

Reed finished off his second cup of coffee and got to his feet. "I have to leave. Thanks for the coffee and the company, as usual."

"Goodness, you're running off so soon?" Carolyn said, showing her surprise.

"I have things to do, Mom. Talk to you later, Dad." He smiled at his parents and left the breakfast room. Before he reached the front door his smile had vanished. He felt sympathy for the Cantrell family and understood how important learning the identity of the mystery man could be to them, but he had a mystery of his own to deal with and its name was Valerie Fairchild.

He'd put in a lousy night, tossing and turning, and battling nightmares when he did manage to fall asleep, and then staring at the shadowy ceiling when he woke up again. Debates and arguments and piles of advice had whirled in his brain for hours. Now, as he drove home, the same arguments played out in his beleaguered brain.

Get over it! Get over her!

No, wait, she's afraid of something. She came out of hiding, revealed her true self at the cabin, then resented it in the morning.

Well, she sure can't still be afraid of the insane jerk that held her hostage for sixteen hours, can she?

Maybe not him, exactly, but what about men in general, because of him?

Reed sat up straighter. Was that it? Was she afraid of men, leery of *him,* because of that one long-ago incident? Yes, it must have been sheer terror for her, a horrifying experience no woman would ever forget. But she was letting it ruin any real chance of happiness she might have with a man who truly loved her. Happiness with him! Reed knew in his soul that he could make her happy, if she would just let him try.

He was suddenly alive and humming again. He'd figured out Val, he was positive of it. She had kept to herself and shut out men for years and years because of that one awful experience.

But he *knew* she had feelings for him, in spite of her determination to keep him at arm's length. She *had* sent the flowers, along with that very special card. She had invited him to her home—possibly in a moment of weakness that she regretted afterward, which could be the reason she had gone off to the mountains. But for a few minutes, at least, she had cared enough about him to let him know it.

He sucked in a breath and felt emotion stinging the backs of his eyes. He would not desert her. He had to help her get over the past. If ever a woman needed rescuing, possibly from life itself, it was Val, and he loved her and would do just about anything to put a genuinely warm smile on her beautiful face.

When he walked into his house he went directly to the telephone and called his friend Derek Moore in New York City. Knowing Derek as he did, Reed was counting on receiving some good advice from his attorney pal. Fortunately, Derek was at home and answered on the third ring.

He sounded surprised—and pleased—to hear from Reed. "So, how are you?" Derek asked.

"Fine…to a point. Derek, I need some information. I have a friend. I believe I mentioned her when you were in Billings a few weeks back. About ten years ago she was held at gunpoint by some bonehead for sixteen hours, I think it was. It happened in a pet store in New York City. Her name is Valerie Fairchild, but that's about the only inarguable fact I have on the incident. I desperately need to know more. In particular, I need to find out if that jerk is still in prison."

"Then there was a trial and a sentence," Derek said. "That makes researching the case a little easier. Reed, I'll do what I can and let you know what I find out."

"I know you have friends in the police department, Derek."

"Some very good friends. Don't worry, I'll dig out any available information on the case. Give me a day or two, though, all right?"

"Absolutely all right, and send me a bill for your time."

Derek laughed. "Hey, I can do an old friend a favor without billing him, okay?"

"Well, I'd be happy to pay the price, Derek, and you know I can afford it."

"That's not the point, old sod. Now, tell me, what else is going on in Montana?"

During an especially moving prayer, delivered by Pastor Rayburn, Val reached for her sister's hand and held it. It was an emotional moment and Val thanked God for the closeness she and Jinni now enjoyed. In all her life—before the past few months—Val had never felt close to a living soul—not her parents, not Jinni, not any so-called friends. How wonderful that Jinni had found Max. This magical sensation of truly loving and knowing and trusting a person through and through must be similar to what Jinni felt for her husband, Val thought.

She wasn't positive of that conclusion, however, and during the drive from church after the service was over, she brought it up. "Jinni, tell me if I'm being too nosy, but what's it like to fall in love…and actually *know* it's love?"

"Could you possibly be feeling some unusual symptoms and wondering if the disease might be love?" Jinni teased.

"Absolutely not!" Val said quickly, flushing to the roots of her hair.

Her sister laughed. "You know what they say about people who protest too adamantly."

"Jinni, I am not falling in love! I only had a special feeling of closeness to you during that final prayer, and it started me thinking about what you must feel for Max."

"All right, sorry I teased you. When I first started feeling giddy around Max, I wondered if it was more than chemistry and would last. Sexual attraction seems to be the first symptom of love, and we certainly had that. I recognized it right off, but I'm not sure Max did. Anyhow, we laughed together, too. Not at first. Actually, at first *I* laughed a lot and I think Max thought I was sort of nutty. Which I am, poor guy. He'd never met anyone like me before, and he didn't immediately succumb to my charms. But gradually—or maybe not so gradually, now that I think about it—we both realized what it meant.''

"Gradually but not so gradually. That's a pretty confusing description, Jinni.''

Her unique laugh rang out again. "It is, isn't it? I'm sorry, Val, it's just hard to put feelings into words.''

"Yes, it is,'' she murmured.

Jinni turned into Val's driveway and left the engine idling while she turned in the seat to look at her sister. "Something happened between you and Reed at the cabin, didn't it? Something more than sex?''

"A *lot* happened,'' Val said, almost sadly. "None of which I understand.''

"He likes you, Val. Why else would he risk his own neck to make sure you survived a blizzard?''

"Possibly because that's what he does? Just for the hell of it? You said you were sort of nutty. Well, so is he. Everyone is in their own way, I suppose, but he's a little weirder than most.'' Val frowned, bit down on her lower lip and looked out the side window of the car, then said in a husky, uneasy voice, "I don't know what to make of him.''

Jinni reached out and laid her hand on her sister's arm. "Sweetie, I think it would be more accurate to say that you don't know what to make of feelings that you haven't allowed to see the light of day for far too many years. Dare I say something like that? You know I want only the best for you.''

"I do know that,'' Val whispered. She forced a smile and looked at her sister. "Don't worry, I'll work it all out.''

"Of course you will. It's not easy for anyone, you know. Falling in love can be darn scary.''

"Jinni, I am *not* falling in love!'' Val opened the door and got out. "Thanks for inviting me along. I enjoyed the service. And please call me if anything breaks on the mystery man at the clinic.''

"Will do. See you later.''

*   *   *

Sunday dragged for Val. By the middle of the afternoon she had done all the puttering around the house that she could stand. Pulling on a jacket, she walked over to the Animal Hospital to check on the dogs and cats in the kennels.

The dogs barked joyously when they heard her footsteps, and she spent some time with each one, petting and talking to them. Some were recovering from treatment, some were boarded while their master or mistress was away from the area, but all of them were lonely, and if there was one thing Val understood, it was loneliness.

After the dogs, she went to the Cat House and played with the cats. Cats and dogs were so different from each other, she thought. Every single one of the dogs had begged for attention, but only a couple of the cats welcomed her touch. *A lot like people. Certainly men and women are vastly different. Reed is like a big, friendly dog and I'm the cat, squeezing into myself, trying not to show interest in anything around me.* Feeling rather silly about comparing people to pets, Val thought of the role animals had played in her life.

She loved all animals, and one of the saddest events of her teen years had been a trip to the circus. She had been so excited about it, so brimming with anticipation, so looking forward to seeing the elephants doing their tricks. But she had sat and cried because those beautiful elephants had the saddest eyes she had ever seen. They were miserably unhappy in captivity, forced to do ridiculous tricks for ridiculous people, and Val had wanted to stand up and scream at the crowd, "Doesn't anyone else see the pain and anguish of these animals?"

She had never gone to another circus, and during high school and college she had become very active in animal rights groups.

About an hour later Val walked back to the house. The sun was gone and a light sprinkling of snow had begun to fall. She felt as lonely as the pets in her kennels, and blamed

Reed for that, as well. Oh, she'd been lonely many times during her years in Rumor, but she had never dwelled on the feeling. She had, in fact, believed that she was as content as she would ever be—*could* ever be—and now she feared that *contentment* was just another word. Reed, with his passionate eyes and kisses, had caused that. She had let him know from the very beginning that she wasn't interested and never would be, and he had refused to leave her alone. Now she was paying for his stubbornness, when *he* was the one who should be doing the paying.

Suddenly, a frighteningly familiar wave of weakness struck her. She lost all the strength in her legs and sank to the sidewalk, on her knees. Tears sprang to her eyes. She'd thought she was over these spells; the last one had been that day in MonMart, sometime ago. Obviously she couldn't count on good health, and she recalled—with a painful wince—boasting to Jinni about feeling so well that morning. Bragging a bit to Jim on the phone, as well. Surely exerting herself a bit by shoveling snow hadn't brought this on?

Val stayed down until the worst of the weakness had passed, then she cautiously got to her feet. Weaving slightly, she slowly made her way to the house.

Inside, she went to the bedroom, took off her jacket and stretched out on the bed. Her heart ached, for those few minutes outside on her knees had brought back every dreadful second of her fight with cancer. *It could come back, don't ever think it couldn't. Maybe it already has!*

She could think of nothing else, and after a while she wondered if she would ever be healthy again, if she dared to put her trust in feeling well. She could hope, but that was about all she could do, she decided, as tears sprang forth again. Dear God, she thought in a sudden spasm of agony, she didn't want to burden Jinni again! Jinni or anyone else!

She was still lying on her bed thirty minutes later when her doorbell rang. Sitting up, she realized that remnants of her debilitating weak spell were still with her. Sighing because life or fate or some damn thing had delivered another blow, she pushed herself up and off the bed.

The day had darkened considerably, and she switched on some lights as she went from her bedroom to the front door. She had no idea who had come calling, but it never entered her mind that the person outside on her stoop might be Reed. But when she opened the door, there he was, carrying a big box and smiling tentatively.

She gaped at him, too stunned to even say a civil hello.

Since she seemed to be speechless, Reed took the initiative. "I hope I'm not interrupting anything, but these are yours. They were put in Tag's rig by someone on Saturday morning, and I thought you should have them."

Val went weak again, but it was a completely different feeling than what she'd experienced outside. This was an emotional weakness, and possibly more difficult to deal with. It didn't seem to matter what she said to Reed, or how she said it, he kept coming back. How did a woman get through to a man like him?

Then she noticed the handkerchief—with a few drops of blood—wrapped around his right hand. She stood there looking at it and told herself to ignore it because she would be sorry if she gave Reed even one tiny opening.

In the end she had to know. "Did you cut yourself?" she asked, trying to sound as though she was only curious because, after all, they were both human beings.

"I tangled with a roll of barbed wire in the back of my pickup just now, while I was getting this box."

Val's eyebrow shot up. "Old, previously used wire?"

"No, brand-new wire."

"Then there's probably no reason for you to get a tetanus shot. How badly were you cut?" She swung the door open so he could step inside.

"Where do you want me to put this box?"

"Right where you are. I've got a few things of yours that I'll get after I take a look at that cut. Come with me to my bathroom. I have a good first aid kit in there.'' Val waited while he set down the box, then led the way.

Reed hadn't expected anything from her—except for maybe a resentful thank-you for his delivery of her things— but he instantly warmed toward her when she expressed concern for his injury.

''I realize a hand isn't a paw,'' she said dryly as they entered her large bathroom and she switched on the overhead lights, ''but I believe I'm qualified to judge whether or not you might need some stitches.''

Reed grinned. ''Would you sew me up, Doc?''

''Of course not. Someone else would have to do that. I'm not licensed to treat two-legged creatures, as you well know. Sit on the commode and let me take a look.''

Still grinning, Reed sat down and held up his wounded hand. He watched her face as she removed the handkerchief, and kept watching while she peered closely at the cut.

She felt his eyes on her and was shocked at their impact— *his* impact—the almost smothering sensation caused by his nearness.

She put on her most professional face, even though she was having some trouble with regular breathing. It was surprising and discomfiting and embarrassing, and she wished she had taken that damn box, given him his, said a quick thanks and let him leave.

But she hadn't, and now she had to make the best of a completely unnecessary situation. She spoke rather stiffly. ''I believe you can get by without stitches, but the cut needs dressing. I can apply an antibiotic cream and a bandage, but if you'd rather have an M.D. take a look at it, then you should go to the Family Clinic.''

''I trust you implicitly,'' Reed said, ''and would appreciate your medical attention.''

Val opened a cupboard to take out her first aid kit. The movement put her back to Reed, and she realized in that instant that her heart was beating abnormally fast. He affected her…she liked him…all her denials had been in vain. It came rushing at her with such force that breathing evenly was impossible. She'd asked Jinni about falling in love, and now this was happening to her—this powerful reaction she couldn't control.

But she couldn't be in love. She just couldn't!

"I don't think I would need a tetanus shot even if the wire had been used. I had one last summer," Reed said.

With the kit in hand, Val turned around. "In that case you should be, uh, safe." She didn't like the husky quality of her voice or the quickened beat of her heart. In fact, she couldn't force herself to look at his eyes, and prayed that he wouldn't catch on to the astonishing discomfort she was feeling because of him.

Her prayer was destined to go unanswered, as Reed had *already* caught on. He could hardly believe that she was having a hard time with this perfectly innocuous encounter, but he wasn't above pressing the issue and worming his way a little further into her heart.

She busied herself with the kit, taking out a medicated swab to clean around the wound. "It's more of a tear than a cut," she murmured. "Hold on to something. I'm going to douse it with antiseptic and it's going to sting."

"No problem... Hey, that hurts like hell!"

"Told you it would sting. Sit still. As soon as that dries I'll apply the antibiotic cream and put on a butterfly bandage. You'll have to remove the dressing and check the wound before you retire tonight, and then do it again in the morning. If you see the slightest sign of infection—reddened skin around the cut, maybe a bit of fever—you are to immediately have an M.D. look at it."

"Yes, ma'am," he said with a devilish twinkle in his ocean-green eyes.

Ignoring the twinkle, trying to ignore everything else about him, she set to work dressing the cut, and when she was through she put a small tube of antibiotic cream and some bandages in a plastic bag and held it out to Reed.

''Take these with you.'' She realized that her hand wasn't altogether steady.

He stood and reached for the bag, but instead of taking it, he walked his fingers up her arm and around her neck. Then he gently urged her forward and into his arms.

She knew he was going to kiss her, and she knew she should stop him.

But she didn't.

She couldn't.

Chapter Fifteen

Reed's kiss was soft and sweet. Val felt herself sinking into it, body and soul, even though the fierce guard at the gate to her emotions was ringing warning bells like crazy. *I should stop this now! Why did I let him come in? What's happening to me?*

The questions raced through her brain, barely making an impression, as something Val had never believed could come to pass took control of her senses. She had fought Reed's attentions tooth and nail, using every weapon she could dream up, and all along she had been falling in love with him. *It can't be true...can it?* Unlike the previous questions, this nearly frantic attempt at self-analysis made an indelible impression, one that she suspected would stay with her for a very long time.

She tipped her head back, breaking the kiss, and whispered in abject misery, "I wish I were someone else."

Reed wrinkled his forehead, searched her misty eyes and tried to make sense of what she'd just said. "Why would you want to be someone else?'' he finally asked, barely able to speak above an emotional whisper. It was amazing to him that she had let him kiss her—even now wasn't pushing him away—and yet couldn't hide how unhappy he made her.

"Haven't you figured me out yet? From everything I told you about myself, you should have,'' she said huskily, her voice sounding as teary as her eyes looked.

"I don't care about your past, Val, and neither should you.'' He *did* care, but only because she couldn't seem to put old events in some sort of logical perspective. He had called Derek for information on the single incident that might fall into the unforgettable category, but even a fright as serious as that one had been shouldn't still be steering Val's ship ten years later.

Val sucked in a quick breath that Reed interpreted as a startled reaction to his attitude. He wasn't being cavalier about her pain, he told himself, and he hoped he hadn't come across as uncaring. But he couldn't lie about this. He had no trouble at all facing her past, and she should get over it. It was how he felt, and he would do anything in his power to help her clear that hurdle.

"Did you even hear me the other night?'' she asked, referring to the story of her life she never should have blabbed to anyone.

"Of course I heard you. But it was all so long ago. It's only meaningful today if you let it be.'' He lowered his head, putting his lips very close to hers. "Nothing you told me can compare in importance with what came afterward. I've hardly thought of anything but our night together,'' he whispered. "Tell me you haven't forgotten it.''

"There's nothing wrong with my memory.'' Her mind was suddenly bombarded by erotic images of them making love in that chilly cabin, doing things under the covers that she'd forgotten existed. Apparently that night had been a milestone, a breakthrough, the end of her total disregard, dislike and distrust of men and the beginning of feelings she didn't deserve. She couldn't thank Reed for something that never should have happened.

More to the point, she couldn't thank him for making her fall in love with him! My God, her recent health problems were worse than her youthful indiscretions and that one terrible day that had changed her life so drastically. For her, the word *cancer* was more frightening than any other in the dictionary. And those moments of weakness again today— only a short time ago, in fact—were a reminder of how helpless one became at the onslaught of serious illness. She could never put Reed through that.

She tried to step back from him. They were in her bathroom, after all, hardly the place for conversation *or* for soft, tender kisses. Well, there wasn't going to be any more kissing and certainly no sex in here! Not anywhere in her house, for that matter. She should not have let him come in! But she'd gotten concerned over a little blood on the handkerchief wrapped around his hand. There had to be something seriously wrong with her to be so easily led astray by this man.

There is something serious going on, old girl. It's called love!

Whatever it was hurt like hell, and she blamed her pain on Reed. Why hadn't he let her be? She had never encouraged him!

Instead of the kiss Reed craved so desperately, he got a look from his beloved that was anything but promising. His heart skipped a beat when she eluded his embrace, spun away from him and left the bathroom.

He stood there a moment, feeling as though he had egg on his face. She kissed and backed off; it was her pattern. He knew it well, so why did it never fail to take him by surprise?

Sighing, he stuffed the plastic bag she'd given him into his jacket pocket and walked from the bathroom into her bedroom. She wasn't waiting for him with open arms, which was something he would have given almost anything to see. But it had been a foolish hope, and admitting once again that he was never going to get through to the woman he loved—

in spite of her occasionally warm receptions—he strode through the bedroom and down the hall.

She was waiting in the front foyer holding a large plastic bag. "Thank you for bringing those things," she said, nodding at the box he'd delivered. "These are yours."

"Thank you for dressing my wound," he said, taking the bag from her. He didn't immediately open the door, but rather stood there looking at her. "Why, Val?"

"Why what?"

"You like me and then you don't. You confuse me." He raised one hand to touch her but she took a quick step back and put space between them. He tried to smile and failed miserably. "I've wondered from the first how you got under my skin so fast, and why I couldn't stop thinking about you when you made it so clear again and again that you would rather I disappear. There's really only one answer that makes any sense, and I guess I've known it all along. Maybe it's time you knew it, too. I've heard, and read, that very few people have control over who they fall in love with. In other words, conscious choice plays a very small role in the process."

Val was so stunned she couldn't open her mouth to respond. She had watched the incredible green color of his eyes growing darker as he shocked her to speechlessness, and knew he meant every word he said.

"I guess what I'm getting at is that I didn't ask to fall for you, and apparently the powerful and mysterious emotional affliction that struck me missed you completely. Love is probably our most complex emotion. It is mentally and physically demanding, causing joyous euphoria if returned and almost unbearable pain if it isn't. I…wish it had never happened, Val. My feelings for you have made you unhappy, and they sure as hell haven't done much more than that for me, either."

He put his hand on the doorknob. "If anything changes your mind about me, about us, I'd be pleased to hear it. You know how to find me."

And he was gone.

Val felt glued to the floor. She stared at the closed door, felt the wintry chill that had entered the foyer as Reed left, and realized that he had told her he was in love with her.

She began trembling, and when she could finally move she returned to her bedroom and lay on the bed. It was too early to call it a day, but she had nothing better to do than to lie there and remember every moment she and Reed had ever shared, whether accidentally or deliberately.

For years she had believed she had endured almost every misery known to mankind, but now she knew differently.

Reed was right. Unless love was shared, it was the most painful of all emotions.

How sad that he loved her and she loved him and yet they could never be together.

But life would be much sadder for both of them later on if they got together now and she became ill again.

She had done the right thing to let him leave believing she cared nothing for him.

Monday dawned clear and cold. The people of Rumor awoke to six inches of new snow on the ground and a weak but very welcome sun in a cloudless sky. The town came alive early. Thanksgiving was only ten days away and the businesses of Rumor were in a holiday spirit, with decorated windows depicting Pilgrims, turkeys and pumpkins.

Reed had taken it upon himself to distribute the flyers announcing the Name the Park Contest, and since they were finally perfected and ready to go, he made the rounds of Rumor's business establishments on this bright November morning. Everyone he talked to thought the contest was a great idea, though if the truth were known, Reed wasn't nearly as enthusiastic about it as he had been. Feeling like a lost child was completely foreign to him; he'd always been totally content with his place in the world.

But he put up a good front, and no one could guess how badly he was hurting inside.

The Max Cantrell household was a beehive of activity. Jinni poured coffee for the group of men seated in the study with her husband. Michael had left for school at an early hour, Max and Jinni had eaten a quick breakfast together, and then the professionals arrived.

Jinni sat with her own coffee and listened. At the moment, Max had the floor. "A lady by the name of Dee Dee Reingard dropped in at the Family Clinic yesterday afternoon," he said. "Her house is close to Logan's Hill, and was decimated by a fire last summer. Folks rallied and built her another, but my point is, she said yesterday that through the years she's seen Mr. Jackson on occasion. Before the fire, that is. Prior to that she sometimes brought food to him and occasionally Jackson would get close enough to say a few words. She's seen nothing of him since the fire, and she, like so many of the people in the area, assumed the man had died in the flames.

"I escorted her to his room, thinking she might be able to identify him, but all she said was, 'It could be him, but I just can't say for sure. Let me think on it and come back tomorrow.' Gentlemen, I promised to pick her up at her home and drive her to the clinic at ten this morning. I believe she is still our best....''

Jinni tuned out the conversation. Max had already told her everything he was now relating to his hired professionals, both legal and medical. Jinni knew that the geriatric specialists had thoroughly examined Mr. Jackson, if that was his name, and had said the old man was in reasonably good health, considering his age and exposure to the elements. Expectations were that he would recover.

Jinni quietly rose and went to another room, sat at a beautiful antique desk and dialed her sister's number. Estelle answered. "Val's still in her bedroom, Jinni. I'll go and let her know you're on the phone."

Jinni's heart skipped a beat. "She's not ill, is she?"

"I only talked to her through the door, but she didn't say anything about not feeling well."

"This is much later than she usually gets started in the morning, isn't it?"

"Yes," Estelle said softly. "Hold on, honey, I'll go knock on her door."

Val was showered and ready to get dressed. Wearing a bathrobe, she'd *been* ready to get dressed for more than an hour. Instead she had dawdled, procrastinated, put off facing the day. It was about as unhealthy an attitude as a person could have, she knew. The message had been pounded into her head by well-meaning therapists: avoiding life's realities was dangerous to anyone's mental health.

But maybe she didn't give a damn anymore, she thought dismally. Life had always been hard for her, even in her glory days when she had partied big time with a long string of boyfriends whose names and faces had faded to oblivion.

Sighing, she went to her closet and stared at her clothing. Everything looked stale and uninteresting. Jinni was right, she thought; she needed to go shopping.

But even the prospect of a new wardrobe didn't perk up Val's spirit. Clothes were clothes. What did it matter if they were old or new, too big or a perfect fit? Tears stung her eyes. Was it even possible to be more unhappy?

Estelle rapped at the door. "Val, honey, Jinni's on the phone. Do you want to take it in there?"

Val went to the door and opened it. She couldn't take her misery out on Estelle. "Thank you," she said quietly. "I'll pick up in here."

Estelle looked worried. "Are you all right, Val?"

"I'm not ill." She could tell that she hadn't appeased Estelle's concern with that brief reply, but what else could she say? Certainly not the truth—that she was heartbroken and lovesick and deeply immersed in self-pity. This time, in the face of this most current body slam, she simply could not keep self-pity out of the picture. Life hadn't been kind to Valerie Fairchild, and she would like to know why. Her own sister, Jinni, with the same parents, the same upbringing, had grown up golden, while she had hit every pothole in every road she had ever traveled.

Still, she adored Jinni, and she walked over to the phone on the bedstand and picked it up. Out of the corner of her eye she saw Estelle pull the door closed.

"Hi, Jinni," she said, trying very hard to sound normal.

"Are you still in bed?"

"Of course not. I'm just moving slowly this morning." Val heard the kitchen extension being hung up and she sank down on the edge of the bed to converse with her sister in comfort. "And to answer your next question, no, I'm not ill."

"Well, something's wrong. I can hear it in your voice."

"Your imagination has run amok this morning. There is nothing wrong with my voice."

"Not *with* your voice, *in* your voice. I can read you like a book, little sister."

"Oh, you cannot!"

"Now you're angry? Don't try to convince me everything is peaches and cream, sweetie pie, I know you far too well to be put off the scent with a quite laughable show of anger."

"You are absolutely incorrigible."

"Agreed. Now, what's really going on over there?"

"I…I can't figure out what to wear today. I hate my clothes. They're either outdated or so big they practically fall off."

Jinni took a moment, then said, "You're obsessing over clothes this morning? Val, I'm serious now. Is that your only reason for still being in your bedroom at this late hour?"

"When can we go shopping?" Val asked, deliberately dodging her sister's curiosity.

"Well…not this week. Max is determined to get to the truth of the fire so Guy can be exonerated, and I really should stick close to home, at least close to Rumor, in case he needs me for something. But let's shoot for next week, okay?"

"Has anyone identified the old man at the clinic?"

"Not yet." Jinni related everything going on with the old

fellow in bed at the Family Clinic. "Maybe Dee Dee will be a little more helpful today. We're all hoping, even though I feel certain she did her best yesterday. Mr. Jackson, if that's who he is, must have changed drastically in appearance since she last saw him. The specialists Max brought in said he is terribly undernourished, and of course he's quite old. Poor man. Val, do you think it's possible that he eluded the fire and has been living out there in the wilds ever since?"

Val heaved a sigh. "Jinni, life has taught me anything is possible."

"That's true," her sister said slowly, her voice laden with suspicion again. "What is it you're keeping from me, Val? Don't you know you can tell me anything?"

Tears filled Val's eyes. "Jinni—"

But Jinni broke in. "What in the world? Oh, it's Michael! He just ran past this room with the speed of a tornado. I've got to go and see what's happening. Call you later."

Val put down the phone, then sat there staring at nothing. Her eyes dried of their own accord, and she wished listlessly that she had the energy and desire to face the day.

She expelled a long, dejected sigh and made another wish: that she could crawl back in bed and sleep away the day.

But Jim and Estelle were already at work for her, and Jinni was already worried about her. She *had* to pull herself together and get dressed.

There was chaos in the Cantrell mansion. Michael was at the epicenter of the storm.

"I didn't remember it until a little while ago, Dad. I left school and rode my bike home as fast as I could. There's a lot of ice out there, but I've got those good tires on my bike, and I made real good time. Anyhow, I remembered seeing that red thing on Mr. Jackson's neck when he bent over one day. I asked him if he'd gotten burned or something and he laughed and said it was a birthmark. He said, 'It's my raspberry, Michael. I was born with it.'"

Everyone began talking. The doctors had seen the birthmark, and it was solid proof that the man at the clinic was Robert Jackson.

Now all they had to do was wait until he regained consciousness, which the physicians were positive could happen at any time.

Max took his wife's hand in one of his and Michael's in the other. They stood as a family for several moments, each of them thinking the same thing. Maybe Mr. Jackson had seen the murders and maybe he hadn't. But if he'd been a witness to the crime, then whatever his story of that dark and horrible day turned out to be, it could mean the difference between freedom or a life in prison for Guy Cantrell.

Somehow that deeply felt, shared concern for a loved one brought the three of them closer together.

Reed spent Monday afternoon plowing snow at all three of the homes on the Kingsley Ranch, his folks', Russell's and his own. There were hired men perfectly willing and able to do the job, but Reed needed hard work to get his mind off Val.

Besides, he loved working outdoors in weather like this—crisply cold and so bright from the sun's rays reflected off snow crystals that he had to wear his darkest glasses. Dressed warmly, he worked for hours, and by dinnertime, with the sun going down and a decided drop in temperature promising a freezing night, he was ready to quit plowing and take a long soak in a tub of steaming hot water.

Satisfied because all of the access roads and driveways at the ranch were cleared and passable, Reed went into his house, took off his winter outerwear and walked in stocking feet to the telephone to check for messages.

He listened to them and jotted down a couple of names and phone numbers, but he felt a yawning disappointment because none were from Val. Why he'd even hoped she'd call escaped him.

He muttered a curse. He could work himself to death trying not to think of her, and still suffer. Why even try? he asked

himself with a sullen, half-angry twist to his lips. The anger
was aimed mostly at himself for being such a damn fool, but
there was plenty left over for Val. She was completely unreasonable, and she wasn't very honest about life, either. Did
she care how badly she hurt other people, him in particular?
No, she did not, and that didn't put her on any pedestal he'd
ever heard about.

Yet he loved her.

Growling because he couldn't seem to do anything about
his own damn feelings, he went to the kitchen for a bottle of
red wine and a glass, then took his bounty to the master suite.
He turned on the flow of water to fill the large tub in his
bathroom, undressed and dropped his dirty clothes in the
hamper.

He stepped into the tub, sat down, leaned back and absorbed the luxurious sensation of hot water warming his
body. He closed his eyes and sat that way until the water
level reached his chest, then he flicked off the faucet and
reached for the wine bottle. He yanked the cork—he'd
opened the bottle a few days back and it was about half-
full—and filled the glass. Then he sat back again, drank his
wine and told himself that a man couldn't have it any better
than this. A day of work, a tub of hot water and some ex-
ceptional wine. He had it good, no doubt about it. Hell, Valerie Fairchild should have it so good.

He looked at the bandage on his hand and felt a suspicious
stinging at the backs of his eyes. His emotions were in shambles, and it angered him. He told himself that everything had
gone his way for so long that he couldn't take rejection like
a man. He told himself to stop behaving like a spoiled boy
instead of a grown-up. There were hordes of available
women in the world. Hell, he could go down to Joe's Bar
this very night and find all the female companionship he
could handle. Val wasn't the only fish in the sea.

But a momentary release of sexual pressure wasn't what
he wanted so badly he could taste it; he wanted Val.

And then Reed tortured himself by thinking of their night

together in her cabin. He shut his eyes and relived those hours, minute by minute. With her inhibitions—or whatever it was that hid her emotions—weakened by brandy, she had become hot as a pistol in his arms. They hadn't slept. The passion between them had been truly incredible; he couldn't imagine a more sensual experience.

Groaning, he tried to rid his brain of those burning memories with physical activity. Grabbing soap and a washcloth, he bathed and then climbed from the tub. Drying off, he decided to eat whatever was on hand for his dinner. He wasn't fit to sit at his parents' table, or at Russell's, Maura's or Tag's, though any one of them would welcome him should he drop in at mealtime. If all he could find in his refrigerator was the makings of a cold cheese sandwich, so be it. He was home for the night, and as if to prove it to himself, he donned a shapeless sweatsuit and house slippers.

At some point of the evening, possibly while eating a dry and unappetizing sandwich, he faced facts. Val wanted nothing to do with him. He had to get on with his life without her. This moping around, feeling sorry for himself, had to stop.

It felt like a decision, but when he went to bed later he felt a lot more like bawling than sleeping.

He didn't like that feeling one little bit. He wasn't a maudlin crybaby, damn it; he was a Kingsley, and he could take whatever life handed him.

Or didn't hand him.

Chapter Sixteen

The talk of the town on Tuesday was the *Rumor Mill*'s first installment of "...the complete story of the Logan's Hill murders."

Tuesday's publication began with the fire, and included before-and-after photos of Logan's Hill that clearly depicted the ravages of the forest fire that had occurred so close to home. A chronicle of events, based on interviews with citizens, law enforcement personnel and firefighters, brought readers through the first day of the fire.

Everyone who read it could hardly wait for the next installment, and the town was practically jumping with excitement. Interviewees were identified by the paper, and some of them were "doggone proud to be part of the hottest news story ever published by the *Rumor Mill*."

Reed read it and smiled faintly. He'd been interviewed several weeks ago and had all but forgotten it.

Val read it, then reread the paragraph citing the interview with Reed Kingsley, Rumor's fire chief, in which he explained the first day's attack on the fire by the courageous local citizenry. The reporter then switched gears and praised Reed highly, as his quick thinking had clearly played a major role in saving the town from the fire's voracious appetite.

It was a lengthy article, full of drama, but it was drama as real as the morning sun and it had happened to all of them, to every resident, and more than a few folks shed tears while reading it.

Jinni read it with her heart in her throat, then slid the newspaper across the breakfast table to Max, who had just sat down. She got up for the coffeepot and brought him a cup. Quietly she asked, "Would you like some eggs, darling?"

He was already absorbed in the article. "Not now, thanks."

She resumed her seat and waited for him to finish reading. When he did, he raised his eyes and looked at her. The sadness in his tore at her heartstrings. She knew he had complete faith in his brother's innocence and he was doing everything possible to prove it. The last thing he needed was a reporter writing about Guy's arrest and incarceration for two murders he hadn't committed.

"When the series reaches Guy's role in the whole awful episode, the newspaper cannot say he's guilty, Max," Jinni said softly. "And everyone already knows he's in jail, awaiting trial. In fact, the newspaper has nothing to publish that hasn't circulated around town at least a dozen times. They're only trying to sell papers."

Max folded the newspaper and picked up his cup of coffee. "Which they have every right to do. In fact, Jinni, if I were running the *Rumor Mill,* I wouldn't let this story slip by unnoticed, either. We've had murder investigations and trials before, but Guy's invisibility formula adds something to the story that no other ever had. Believe me, this series *will* sell papers."

Thinking about Max's theory, Jinni fell silent. Guy's story of invisibility had affected people in a dozen different ways. A lot of townsfolk couldn't quite believe it and laughed whenever it was mentioned. With her own ears Jinni had heard remarks such as, "I don't believe in little green men, either. Invisibility? Give me a break."

But not everyone knew or understood Guy's genius. Jinni had pondered the subject quite a few times since her brother-in-law's arrest, and while she, too, didn't completely comprehend his scientific mind, she wanted to believe in him as much as Max did.

The compact cellular telephone attached to her husband's belt rang and he quickly reached for it. "Hello," he said almost sharply. "Holt, good morning."

Jinni sat up and took notice. Sheriff Holt Tanner phoning at any hour was meaningful; his calling at this time of day put Jinni—and Max, she could tell—on alert.

"Thanks, Holt. I'll be there in ten minutes." Max flipped the phone closed and got to his feet while reattaching it to his belt. "Jackson is finally awake and talking. He knows who he is and the doctors are optimistic about his memory. No one has asked him any questions about the fire. Holt said the attorneys are gathering in the waiting room and getting antsy, but the doctors are refusing any visitors until Mr. Jackson is examined again and resting comfortably. Holt thought I would want to be there, which I do."

He looked at his wife, and Jinni saw great concern in his beautiful blue eyes. "Would you like to come to the clinic with me?" he asked.

"Do you want me there, Max?"

"Jin, it's up to you."

Should she be there? she asked herself. In the middle of a swarm of anxious lawyers, along with doctors that cared— or should care—about the health of the old man more than the answers to the questions raising the attorneys' blood pressures? The sheriff would be there, and only God knew how many others. A journalist from the *Rumor Mill,* maybe? A photographer?

"You go on," she said, rising to kiss him goodbye. "I'll go in my own car. And don't worry if you don't see me. I have visions of chaos at the clinic this morning, and while I've never been one to shy from crowds, I see no reason to get in the way by barging into the eye of that particular storm.''

Max put his arms around her and gave her a warm kiss. "You will never be in the way as far as I'm concerned, so barge if you feel like it.''

She smiled and ran her hands over the unique softness of his cashmere sweater. She loved touching him, with or without clothes, loved looking at him and hearing his voice. Could any woman be more fortunate than she?

"I usually do, darling,'' she said with just the right mixture of female smugness because she'd gotten her man, and pride because *her* man was such a rare breed. "Oh,'' she added on an afterthought, "do you want your mother there? It wouldn't be a bit of trouble for me to pick her up and drive her to the clinic, if you'd like.''

Max hesitated, then shook his head. "No, I'll fill her in later on…whichever way this thing goes. Let's not raise her hopes or upset her until we know, okay? See you later, honey.''

He slipped away and in a few minutes left the house. Jinni resumed her seat at the table, pulled the paper over and laid it flat to read the story again, this time more thoroughly. She wondered if she'd been hiding her head in the sand about the true and extremely serious nature of the Cantrell family's worry about Guy.

In the next instant, though, she realized that she was being unduly hard on herself. She was on Max's team and would do anything to help him get through this, and in her heart she believed he knew it. She also believed—with every fiber of her being—that she had magically attained today's most precious and elusive commodity, a happy marriage. She and Max would weather the storms of life and grow old together. It was a beautiful thought, one that touched her soul.

If only Val had what she did, Jinni thought. Then everything would be perfect!

Val was at the Animal Hospital tending to the kenneled dogs and cats, checking on those that were in treatment or recovering from a surgical procedure. She'd been busy for several hours, her mind wandering from this to that, when the actual time dawned on her. It was ten o'clock and Jim and Estelle hadn't arrived!

Instantly concerned—they always showed up before eight—Val went to the phone and dialed their home number. For one thing it was snowing again, and it wasn't just a flurry. The falling snow was heavy and dense, and it was piling up fast. Perhaps the storm had interfered with their usual routine, Val reasoned.

But no one answered at the Worth home, and Val's initial concern turned to heart-thumping dread. Had they been in a road accident? Navigating in such a heavy snowfall was treacherous for anyone, even for a good driver like Jim.

Val checked her appointment book and saw two clients scheduled for the day. She phoned each of them and rescheduled for another time. Neither objected and in fact seemed relieved. No one looked forward to driving in weather like this.

Val wasn't looking forward to it, either, but Jim and Estelle might be stuck in a drift between their house and town, and she couldn't stand around and do nothing. She was bundled up and on her way to the door when the phone rang.

She rushed back to her office to answer it. "Animal Hospital," she said breathlessly.

"Val, it's Jim. Listen, I'm calling from the Whitehorn Hospital. Estelle was sick all night. Doctors here say it's a bad case of the flu and they want to keep her here for the day at the very least. I have to stay with her. Are you all right?"

Relief of enormous proportions flooded Val's system. She loosened her jacket and sat in the chair at her desk. "I am *perfectly* all right, and you are not to worry about me for one more second. But call me later in the day and let me know how Estelle is doing, would you?"

"Sure will. Is it snowing there? It's a whiteout here, Val, bad as I've ever seen."

"It hasn't reached that stage here yet, but it's really coming down, make no mistake. If this keeps up, we'll have a foot of new snow by nightfall. Jim, thanks for calling. I was…getting worried.''

''I'll call again this afternoon. 'Bye for now.''

''Goodbye, Jim.'' Val put down the phone and sat there thinking of Estelle in the hospital and Jim remaining by her side through thick and thin. After forty years of marriage their love and respect for each other was so obvious that it was almost a tangible thing. How lucky they were.

And how unlucky I am.

The heavy snowfall was definitely impeding business. MonMart, normally so busy that the checkout stands were continuously in use, had only a handful of customers wandering the aisles. Reed watched the first floor from an upstairs window for a while, then decided to go to the fire station. He went to his office to get into his down-filled jacket, his hat and gloves.

Russell stuck his head in. ''I'm thinking of leaving, too. Might as well spend the day with my family. There's sure not much going on around here.''

''My sentiments exactly. Say hello to Susannah for me.''

''There's always paperwork,'' Russell said, frowning slightly. ''But it's a great day to build a snowman. Little Mei would like that.''

Reed grinned. ''And so would Suzy and Russell. Have fun, bro. See you later.''

Jinni was already driving in the rapidly deepening snow, which didn't scare her in the least. She was a good driver— at least she'd always believed she was—and she'd grown up in New York, so she'd cut her teeth driving in weather like this. To be honest, she saw the falling snow as beautiful and felt that it made Rumor look like one of those adorable towns in the Swiss Alps, which she had visited on four different occasions. Someday, when all this business with Guy was behind them, she hoped to entice her wonderful, sexy, handsome husband into doing some traveling.

She also had a party to plan, she recalled with a rise of excitement as she stopped at the corner of Main and Logan Streets—her and Max's wedding shindig, which they had agreed to put off until after Guy's trial. Jinni wanted something extra special for that particular party, and she had made numerous lists of favorite caterers, menus, dress and accessory designers and possible places in which to hold a knock-'em-dead celebration for several hundred people.

A car was slowly slipping and sliding on Main from the east, and Jinni waited for it to finally reach Logan and go on past her so she could make a right and drive to the Family Clinic. Instead, it turned—or tried to turn—onto Logan, and plowed straight into the back half of her SUV!

"You moron!" she shrieked while climbing out.

But then an elderly man stumbled from his car and Jinni's temper cooled so fast she felt more dizzy than furious.

"Are you hurt?" she asked with genuine concern.

"No, ma'am, but your car sure is. Are you all right?"

And so it went until Reed, who had seen the accident while pulling into the fire department's parking lot, jumped out of his rig to run across the intersection.

"Jinni, hello. And Mr. Hodges. Either one of you injured?"

"I'm right as rain, not even a bruise. It was all my fault, Reed," Mr. Hodges said forlornly. "There's ice under all that snow and I shouldn't have been driving today."

"I'm fine, too," Jinni said. "It wasn't a serious bang because I was stopped and Mr. Hodges here was barely moving. His car sort of slid into mine. Should we call the sheriff?"

"I don't think so. Not for a fender bender with no injuries. We can deal with it ourselves." Reed got the whole thing organized, with the names of insurance companies exchanged, and the three of them were about to go their separate ways when Jinni glanced across the street to her sister's place.

"What in the world is she doing outside shoveling snow again? It's too much for her!" she exclaimed.

Reed turned in time to catch a glimpse of Val and a snow shovel disappearing around the north corner of her building.

"Where's Jim?" Jinni demanded of no one in particular. "He should be doing that shoveling, not her."

Reed wanted to cross over to Val's place and offer assistance so badly that he had to force himself to mind his own business.

But then Jinni asked, "Reed, are you terribly busy right now?"

"Not especially. Why?"

"Well, I'm on my way to the clinic." She explained in brief terms what was happening there. "So, even with a dent in the back door of my rig, I'd really like to be on my way. What I was wondering is this— If you're really not busy, would you please go over to Val's and find out why she's shoveling snow again? She has Jim Worth working for her, and why isn't he outside doing that hard work instead of her?" Jinni frowned and added, "Oh, maybe I should just go over there myself."

"Jinni, you've got a particularly heavy load today and I'm free as the breeze. You go to the clinic, and I'll walk over to Val's and find out what's going on."

"Are you sure you don't mind?"

"I'm sure."

"Well, if you're absolutely positive. I hate burdening someone else with my responsibilities, but I do seem especially overloaded today. Not that Val would appreciate my considering her a responsibility, but if sisters and brothers don't watch out for each other, who will?"

"You couldn't be more right." Reed watched Mr. Hodges drive away, then looked back at Jinni Fairchild-Cantrell, who positively glowed in a faux fur, leopard-print jacket, matching boots and hat, and chocolate-brown slacks. A stunning woman with more style than anyone else in Rumor—with the possible exception of his own mother—Jinni had a vivacious personality and a smile that could melt the polar cap.

She was perfect for Max Cantrell, Reed thought, and then depressed himself by thinking that Jinni's sister, Val, might not be quite the clotheshorse her sister was, but she was perfect for *him*.

He looked away, squinting through the dense snowfall. He wouldn't be breaking his mind-his-own-business vow by seeing Val, because he was really only helping out Jinni.

And so he turned back to Val's sister once more and this time smiled at her. "You skedaddle—cautiously, of course— and I'll check on Val. It would be my pleasure, and please don't think of it as an imposition. Say hello to Max for me and give him my best. He already knows I'm rooting for the Cantrell family, but if events permit, tell him again, all right?"

"I'll do that, Reed, and thank you." Jinni climbed into her SUV and drove away. When she was positive that Reed could no longer see her face, she smiled and said, "Thank you, Mr. Hodges. I never would have thought of inciting a car accident to get Reed and Val together one more time, but what took place couldn't have been more perfect. After all, what's a little dent compared to Val's happiness?"

Reed trudged through the snow to Val's corner. Thinking of coming face-to-face with her in a minute or two quickened his heartbeat. He could stack vows to stay away from her from the earth to the clouds and still get giddy as a schoolboy when an opportunity to actually talk to her presented itself. He could tell himself a million times that he had to cut her out of his life, and then get all overheated from envisioning himself standing before her.

He swore softly, cursing his weakness for someone who didn't give a damn about him, as he managed to find the curb, completely concealed under a small mountain of snow. The town was inundated; Reed could hear the plows at work somewhere off in the distance. But when snow fell in this quantity, Rumor's two snowplows had an uphill battle to keep even the main streets open for traffic.

He finally reached the driveway and parking strip at the

side of the Animal Hospital and swore again when he saw it had recently been shoveled clean. It was a large area and Jinni was right, he thought. Where was Jim Worth on a day like today?

Reed tried the side door of the building, which was locked, then pushed the button that announced callers to whoever might be inside. There was no response, and he decided Val was either shoveling on the *other* side of the building or she had called it a day and gone to her house.

He followed the sidewalk around the corner, glared at the snow-free walk between the Animal Hospital and Val's house, then trudged on. Knowing Val, she might slam the door in his face. Knowing her, she might not even open the door to begin with.

Still, even while knowing he was asking for another icy shoulder from the woman who would cause him restless nights for a long time to come, when he reached the back door of Val's house, he knocked smartly, as though he had every right to be there.

Val was standing under a hot shower. She'd not only exhausted herself with all that snow shoveling, she had practically frozen off her fanny. It hadn't seemed that cold when she first went outside, and she had actually enjoyed the sensation and sight of snow falling on her and everything around her.

She shouldn't have forced herself to finish the job, she knew now. She'd overdone it, overtaxed her strength, abused and overused her bank of energy, which *still* wasn't back to the level she had enjoyed before her chemo treatments.

At least she was warming up. All she'd been able to think about during the final few minutes of the task she'd set for herself this morning was a hot shower, and it was indeed working the exact magic her icy body needed.

Finally warmed clear through, she flipped off the shower lever, stepped out onto a bath mat and wrapped a big soft towel around herself. Her hair was dripping and she used a smaller towel to fashion a turban around it. With a third towel she patted her face, arms and legs dry, then began applying the moisturizers she always used after a bath or shower.

Reed had knocked three times and then he tried the doorknob. Surprised to find the door unlocked, he'd stuck his head in and called, "Val? Val, are you home?"

She had to be inside, he told himself, then, in the next heartbeat, scared the tar out of himself by wondering if something was wrong. Had she collapsed? That question destroyed any concern connected with trespassing, or going where he wasn't wanted, and he stepped in and shut the door behind him.

Val wasn't in the kitchen, he soon discovered, nor the living room. He had started down the hall leading to the bedrooms and bathrooms when he heard a shower running.

Of course! Reed gave a massive sigh of relief. She'd come in cold and was warming up in the shower. Very sensible.

For a moment he stood there and pondered his next move. Should he leave quietly? She would never know he'd been there, would she?

That idea didn't set right. Maybe something perverse in his system needed another putdown, or maybe he needed to see her rosy and dewy from her shower.

An idea struck him, and without pausing to think it over, he headed for the kitchen and put a teakettle of water on the stove. Smiling a bit, thinking she might appreciate a cup of hot tea, even if it did come from him, he took off his heavy outdoor clothes—including his boots, which left him puttering around in his woolen socks—and hung everything in the laundry room.

Val, not hurrying with the application of her array of moisturizers, suddenly stopped. Her heart was in her throat. She'd heard something, a noise, a sound that shouldn't be in her house! It wasn't Estelle or Jim, but it could be Jinni. They were the only people who had keys, but if Jinni had let herself in she would have searched the house until she found Val, even if she'd still been in the shower. Jinni wasn't a bit bashful, and whoever was making noises at the other end of the house wasn't her!

"Oh God," Val whispered, almost too terrified to breathe. She always kept her doors locked, and surely she'd thrown the dead bolt when she came inside a short time ago.

Or had she? She couldn't remember for certain, and it sent her into a tailspin. Someone was in the house! There! Another noise!

She was wearing towels! Oh, my God, she thought wildly, and forced herself from the bathroom to her bedroom, where she grabbed clothes and then, nearly dizzy from fear, decided that she didn't have time to get dressed and opted for a pink knit bathrobe instead. Tossing the towels into the bathroom, not caring where they landed, she stuck her feet into a pair of slippers, nervously pushed her wet hair back from her face and tiptoed to the telephone. She had almost finished dialing the sheriff's number when she wondered again if Jinni was her unannounced visitor. She didn't want the sheriff to come roaring to the rescue if this was a false alarm.

The sounds were coming from the kitchen, Val finally realized, and whoever was in there wasn't doing anything to conceal his or her presence. It *had* to be Jinni.

Feeling somewhat relieved, Val left her bedroom and walked through the house toward the kitchen. At practically the same moment that she reached the doorway, Reed walked past it.

The only thing Val saw was a man, and she screeched loudly enough to wake the dead. Reed jumped a foot and let out a yell because he hadn't expected anyone to shriek at him, and the last thing he saw was Val making tracks, running toward her bedroom as fast as her legs would carry her.

He got his bearings in record time and ran after her, shouting, "Val! Val, calm down, it's only me, Reed!"

Chapter Seventeen

Val trembled so severely that her legs gave out and she started sinking. Reed managed to scoop her into his arms before she hit the floor. Holding her, he moved to the bed, but instead of laying her on it, he sat down and cradled her on his lap.

"I'm sorry. I'm sorry," he repeated hoarsely. Never in a million years would he intentionally frighten anyone, and to think he'd caused Val such anguish nearly killed him.

A sense of safety overrode the objections that would ordinarily have driven Val to anger over his audacity. She didn't even need to ask questions to know what had happened. Obviously he'd come to her door. He'd probably knocked and she hadn't heard him because of the shower. Then he'd tried the door and found it unlocked. He'd known—or guessed correctly—that she was inside, and knowing his penchant for taking care of the weak-minded—one of which she definitely had become—he had walked in to once again save her from herself.

Then, of course, he'd caught on that she was in the shower and had instead veered to the kitchen to do something superhuman to save mankind in there.

Okay, so you have him figured out. What about you? How about working on Val Fairchild now? You're sitting on his lap and his arms are around you, in case you haven't noticed.

She'd noticed. She'd noticed plenty. His warmth saturated her flesh; his strength made hers unnecessary, and since she had so little at the moment, she gladly relied on his. And then there were all the little prickles and tingles of awareness here and there in her body that were easily recognizable and should be eradicated at once.

Only she didn't want to annihilate the best feelings she'd had since the night at the cabin. In truth, the emotions she'd devised on her own lately were very poor substitutes for those flaring within her at the moment, even though she knew in her soul how combustible the situation really was.

She glanced up and realized how intently Reed was gazing at her. And could she possibly look worse? Her damp, uncombed hair was probably sticking up in twenty different directions. Her face was completely devoid of makeup. Her ancient old pink robe was at least two sizes too big.

And still she saw his incredible green eyes as pools of adoration and desire. How could he want a woman who looked like this?

"Are you feeling better?" he asked, his voice deep and gravelly.

"I'm not frightened now, if that's what you mean."

"I walked in. I shouldn't have."

"Please stop apologizing." Without intent or design she snuggled closer to his wide, warm chest. It felt so good. *He* felt so good. And she felt safe.

Reed's heart nearly stopped. This was amazing. He truly hadn't anticipated anything this wonderful occurring when he'd agreed to check on Val.

His arms tightened around the woman he loved. He dipped

his head and pressed his lips to her forehead just as the kettle in the kitchen let out an ear-piercing whistle.

"I forgot the tea." He was so unnerved that he cursed himself for a half-wit. She was on his lap, in his arms, right where he wanted her, and a stupid interruption like this one could ruin everything.

Val crawled from his lap to the bed. "Would you mind turning off the burner?"

Reed got up and ran from one end of the house to the other. He switched off the burner, moved the teakettle and ran back to Val's bedroom. She had succeeded in surprising him again, he saw at once, as she had gotten under the covers and was now lying with one arm crooked over her eyes.

Wondering how best to get her communicating again, he approached the bed and gingerly sat on it. She could, after all, rise up without warning and blast him to kingdom come. He wanted desperately to have her back where she'd been before the interruption.

"Are you all right?" he asked quietly. When she neither moved or answered, he added, "You didn't know it was me in the house, did you?"

"No," she whispered.

He could see her mouth below her arm, and he watched it while he said, "I've never seen anyone so frightened before, Val. How can I undo the damage?"

Her lips didn't move for the longest time, but finally Reed saw and heard her whisper, "You didn't do the damage. Someone else did that."

He knew then that the fright he'd caused her today was somehow connected to the incident she'd told him about. He felt terrible for causing her such distress.

"I'm so sorry," he said, his misery apparent. "Can you ever forgive me?" He was surprised to see her move her arm from her face and look at him. He tried to smile and knew it was a weak effort, but how could he pretend nothing was wrong and give her a big grin at a time like this? Emotions, both his and hers, were running on high, and if she told him she would forgive him for everything he'd ever done to annoy or disturb her, if he ran naked in the snow from one end of Main to the other, he would do it.

But she made no such silly requests. Instead, she folded back the blankets and invited him into her bed without saying a word.

He was stunned and could only stare at those turned-down blankets. His mind raced. Was this truth or dare time? What was she thinking? Was he forgiven? Had she decided to like him? Maybe love him?

"You can't get in bed with so many clothes on," she whispered huskily. She couldn't help herself. She loved him. Yes, regret would torment her to tears later on, but right now she needed his love, his arms around her.

Reed was astonished. This was incredible, unimaginable. He got off the bed and began undressing, fumbling with ordinary buttons in his haste. His fingers felt thick and awkward. Taking off one's clothes was as natural as breathing; a man shouldn't have to think about it.

Actually, he *wasn't* thinking about it. His thoughts, every one of them, were on Val, warmly sensual and inviting, lying there with her gorgeous aqua-blue eyes never straying from him. This was a miracle, he decided, and maybe it was a *permanent* miracle. Dare he hope for so much?

By the time his clothes had been transferred from his body to the floor, he was completely aroused. And when she moved the blankets another few inches so he could get into bed, he saw that she had done something with her robe and was naked. His entire system burst into flames.

Slipping into bed beside her, he hungrily kissed her face, her forehead, eyelids, cheeks, her lips, and his desire grew so fast and with such force that he could barely maintain control. He tried to keep it slow and easy, but that was a lost cause, and before he knew it he was on top of her.

She was a willing participant, kissing him back or instigating her own kisses, touching him in all the right places, holding and stroking his manhood, driving him further and further toward the edge of the cliff.

He couldn't hold back any longer and he slid into her, groaning with the intensity of the pleasure rippling throughout his body. He'd been suffering, make no mistake, putting in nightmarish nights and nerve-shattering days, remembering the night at her cabin much too often and too clearly, remembering the following morning with more pain than any man deserved just for loving a woman.

He began moving, his hips rising and falling with hot and almost fierce thrusts. Val whimpered almost at once, but he didn't ask if he was hurting her because he knew the difference between whimpers of pain and passion. She was as feverishly ready for this as he was, and they rode the wave locked together, in perfect harmony.

Val was a mirror image of Reed's passion, and her mind had totally deserted her. It didn't matter. She wasn't lonely or frightened or hiding; she was in the open and free and soaring to long-forgotten heights.

They rushed to the finish line, neither holding anything back. They cried out together, more than once, writhed as one entity and shared a final kiss that started out greedily and ended with unmistakable tenderness. Then it was over. The room was silent; the bed no longer rocked with unleashed passions. They both lay where they had fallen, Val with her eyes closed, Reed on top of her with his face all but buried in the pillow next to her head.

Minutes passed with neither moving so much as an eyelash. Reality returned slowly for each of them, but Val knew that Reed's reality was vastly different than hers. Her first sound was a sigh she tried to suppress, but knew the second it happened that Reed had heard her.

He raised his head and smiled. She saw his expression as one of happiness and supreme satisfaction. Everything was perfect in his world. He was a man accustomed to getting what he wanted, and he'd wanted her. No one had forced her into bed with him; quite the contrary, which should have made this easier and didn't. Unlike Reed, who seemed abnormally blessed with a doting family and an enviable self-confidence, she had struggled through every day of her complicated and difficult life. It wasn't Reed's fault. It really wasn't even *her* fault. That was just the way it was, and she had long ago stopped trying to turn herself into a member of one of those sappy, happy TV sitcom families that anyone with a lick of sense knew was pure fiction.

Except maybe the Kingsleys came close to that dream. Certainly Reed fit the mold.

Val sighed again and Reed's smile faded. "That sounded ominous," he said. "Tell me I'm imagining things."

She couldn't hide from the piercing energy of his eyes, so she bolstered her courage and looked directly into them.

"You're not imagining anything. Let me be blunt. You unlocked a door that never should have been opened. Please go."

He was thunderstruck. "Go? As in get out of this bed and out of your life? You're not talking about the door to this house, are you?"

"You know I'm not," she whispered. "Please. I...I'm asking nicely."

Reed stared at her until emotion caused his eyes to burn. She wasn't going to change her mind, he realized, and though he was full of questions, he was also hurt and angry.

"Fine," he said gruffly. He moved away from her and got off the bed. He was dressed in minutes, finally standing at the foot of the bed and willing her to look at him, which she avoided by again covering her face with her arm. "This is great, Val," he said harshly. "A real kick in the teeth. Well, lady, next time you have an itch that needs scratching, send for some other sap. Frankly, you are driving me over the hill, and that's something I've never said to another human being!"

He walked out.

On Wednesday morning the Rumor Family Clinic was buzzing with whispered conversations about the doings in

Robert Jackson's room. It had taken some serious maneu-
vering; organizing an event such as this one on short notice
was usually impossible, but Jackson's room was filled to ca-
pacity with chairs, tables and people. Mr. Jackson's bed took
up the lion's share of space, so everything else, including
furniture, Judge Fred Liggitt, Prosecutor Anthony Morrow,
Sheriff Holt Tanner, Max and Jinni Cantrell and Guy's defense team were crowded in elbow-to-elbow. There was also
a reporter from the *Rumor Mill* in the group surrounding the
old man's bed, and one other person, a surprise witness, a
Mrs. Bridget Plum—Birdie to her friends, she explained after
being sworn in.

They had effectively turned the hospital room into a court-
room, although the judge, speaking in somber tones, had
made it very clear that this was not a trial. "This is, ladies
and gentlemen, an informal hearing to get at the truth. Yesterday, according to Mr. Morrow, Mr. Jackson related certain
events pertinent to the serious charges pending against Guy
Cantrell. That testimony must be verified and put on record
before Mr. Cantrell's trial can proceed."

Mrs. Plum was speaking. "Bobby and I grew up together.
Our parents were friends, Bobby and I were friends, as far
back as my own memory takes me. No one has yet informed
me of what he told you yesterday, but I know this much. If
Bobby Jackson said it, then it's true."

"You know Mr. Jackson well enough to vouch for his
veracity when he's lived as a hermit for at least ten years?
That's difficult to believe, Mrs. Plum," the prosecutor said.

"Objection," a defense attorney said. "Badgering the witness."

The judge intervened. "Mr. Morrow, personal opinion is
not allowed in this hearing. Confine your remarks to questions."

"Thank you," Mrs. Plum said to Judge Liggitt, while
looking disapprovingly at the prosecutor who had dared to
doubt her word. "Allow me to say this," she said pertly.

"Just because Bobby preferred a solitary lifestyle after he lost his dear wife, Hannah, didn't mean that his true friends forgot him. I saw him quite often, actually. You see, my home lies only a few miles on the other side of Logan's Hill, and he hiked down to see me or I hiked the hill to see him. I lost five hundred acres of forest in the fire, but I've thanked the good Lord many times for sparing my house and grounds. Considering that the Plum Ranch consists of five thousand meandering acres, my loss was minimal."

Jinni sat very close to Max, with her hand tucked in his arm. She felt him tense up suddenly and she whispered, "What?"

"I know who she is," Max whispered back. "So will everyone else very soon now. You'll see."

"May we all hear what took a good friend such as yourself so long to come forward in this case?"

"You may. I've been in Scottsdale, Arizona, since October. I have excellent people running the ranch and have been wintering in Arizona for quite a few years now. I believed Bobby died in the fire, as everyone else around here did. I still don't know why he didn't come to me instead of living in that cave under the waterfall all summer. Then, the other day, there it was, the whole story, or rather, as much of it as was known at the time, on a national news program. I immediately booked a flight for Montana."

The head defense attorney spoke. "Are we doubting Mrs. Plum's probity? She does not claim to know anything about the homicides, her testimony is strictly limited to Mr. Jackson's character. I suggest we move on."

"Not quite yet," the prosecutor said. "Yesterday Mr. Jackson related a strange tale indeed. The only person who could identify him, until today, was a Cantrell—Michael Cantrell, a young man of fifteen years. Both Michael and Mr. Jackson claim some sort of bond that I find unusual, or perhaps I should use the word *convenient*. After all, Guy Cantrell is Michael's uncle, and with Mr. Jackson having so few allies, it's not completely out of the question that he might stretch the truth to help his one friend.''

''That's utterly ridiculous,'' Mrs. Plum said with a derisive snort. ''For one thing, Bobby Jackson has more than one friend. In the second place he wouldn't lie to save his own soul. You, sir, are the one stretching the truth, twisting it around, in fact, to fit a scenario better to your liking.''

''And you, ma'am, a complete stranger to everyone in this room, expect the members of this panel to accept your opinion of Jackson's character when the story *he* wants us to believe sounds more like a fairy tale than reality. How did he live on the hill all summer? The fire must have decimated berry bushes and…and… Well, whatever it was he was eating before the fire.''

''Bobby grew a large garden every summer. Last year's crop was destroyed, but he had a root cellar full of vegetables and canned goods that the fire passed over with very little damage,'' Bridget Plum replied. ''And I usually gave him any supplies he needed beyond that. I *was* concerned about the inevitable winter months and had asked him to stay with me during bad weather. Bobby's a sweet man, but he can also be stubborn as an old mule. He's like most men in that respect.''

The prosecutor looked disgruntled for a moment, then changed tactics. ''I think everyone would agree that since you are vouching for Mr. Jackson's honesty, we should learn a bit more about yours.''

''No one has *ever* doubted my word,'' Bridget said icily.

The prosecutor smiled. ''Of course, we only have your word on that, don't we?''

''I am not amused, Mr. Morrow,'' Bridget snapped. ''I was raised in a Christian home, and I do not lie.''

''Let's learn a little more about your background, Mrs. Plum. That Christian home you speak of was on the same land you now call the Plum Ranch?''

''No, it was not. I married Harold Plum over forty years ago.''

"And prior to your marriage you lived with your parents?"

"Of course."

"Their names, please?"

"Winslow and Harriet Kingsley," Mrs. Plum said.

A hush fell over the entire gathering. Anthony Morrow gaped at the woman. Jinni Cantrell felt as though a bolt of electricity had somehow entered the room and was still bouncing from person to person. She heard Max chuckle quietly, deep in his throat, and she marveled that the Kingsley name could produce such astonishing results.

Morrow cleared his throat. "You're a Kingsley."

"My daddy and Stratton Kingsley's daddy were twins. Everyone always said they came out fighting at birth and never stopped until they completely cut ties with each other and went their separate ways. The two sides of the family have never gotten together. It's entirely possible that the Kingsleys on this side of the hill don't even know I own the Plum Ranch only a few miles away on the other side of Logan's Hill." She smiled. "That information took a bit of starch out of your collar, didn't it, young man?"

The weather had been typical for Montana—a blizzard one day and bright sunshine and melting snow the next. When Val saw the incredibly beautiful morning, she decided that she had to get away and do something to get her mind off of yesterday and Reed, if only for a few hours. Jim and Estelle were at their home instead of at the Whitehorn Hospital—Jim had phoned—but Estelle had to take it easy for a few days. Val told him to stay home with his wife and not to worry about coming to work, that she was doing just fine.

It wasn't true. She wasn't fine at all. But she didn't give a whit about her business or anything else. After feeding and caring for the animals in her kennels, she got ready and drove to Billings, where she shopped until she was ready to drop. She drove back to Rumor late in the afternoon with her SUV full of new clothes and a who-gives-a-damn-about-clothes sensation in the pit of her stomach.

She hadn't finished unloading her new things when Jinni's rig pulled into her driveway. Her sister jumped out. "Where in heck have you been all day?"

"Shopping," Val said dryly, because with her arms full of packages her day's activities had to be perfectly obvious.

"I wanted to go with you!"

"You've been busy, Jin, and I needed something to do today."

Jinni peered into the back of Val's SUV. "I'll get the rest of these things. Wait until I tell you what happened today."

They trudged into Val's house and deposited their parcels with those Val had already brought in. "Looks like you had fun," Jinni said. "Can I see?"

"Later. I'm going to make some tea."

"Whoa, girl, today is not a tea day. Today is a champagne day!"

"Oh, really? Well, sorry, but I'm fresh out of champagne."

"Wine will do. I know you have wine."

"Help yourself. I'm going to haul this stuff to my bedroom."

Ten minutes later they were settled on the sofa, one curled up at each end, sipping some very good red merlot. "You're bursting at the seams," Val said. "So, what was so great about today?"

"Guy has been freed."

Val stared a moment. "Jin, that's wonderful! Max must be doing handsprings."

"Just about. Actually, when I said Guy was freed, I meant that he's *going* to be free by tonight. Seems that even though everyone now believes he didn't do it, there are oodles of loose ends of legal mumbo-jumbo to tie up."

"I'm not doubting your enthusiasm, but what made everyone—I assume you're speaking of the law—start believing in Guy's innocence? Something must have happened."

"Indeed it did, and therein lies my story. Here goes. The Logan's Hill fire was deliberately set. Not to burn down the whole country, but it was started to promote a romantic little setting for Wanda Cantrell and Morris Templeton, who, dear sister, were having an affair. Mr. Jackson told the whole story. He saw everything, and I do mean everything. He said that he'd seen Wanda and Morris on the hill together several times before that fatal day…doing it.'' Jinni couldn't help smiling. "That was the way he described what he saw. 'They were up there, doing it.' He's a funny old guy, Val, and he saw Guy show up that day and catch his wife and that gas station attendant in the throes of passion. A fight ensued, the campfire got scattered and everything started to burn. Jackson said it spread so fast there was nothing he could do to stop it. Anyhow, Guy was knocked out, but get this, he suddenly disappeared. Right before the old man's eyes, Guy disappeared.

"Jackson said that he yelled and shouted for Wanda and Morris to get out of there, but it was too late. The fire had gone wild in seconds and he knew it was going to spread. He ran full tilt to his cabin, grabbed a few blankets and some food and then ran farther up the hill to a cave behind the Logan's Hill waterfall. He stayed in there until the fire passed, then tried to leave. There were so many hot spots that he had to stay in the cave for another day. When he could finally leave, he found his house burned to the ground, but his root cellar was relatively undamaged and it was full of vegetables, fruit and canned goods. That's what he's been living on, along with some bounty from a lady friend by the name of Bridget Kingsley-Plum. Citizens of Rumor thought he was dead, and all this time he was living in that cave. Isn't that something? He'd still be there if we hadn't had that fierce blizzard. Anyhow, he saw the whole thing, and he swore that Guy did not kill Wanda and Morris. In fact, Guy wasn't even there when they died. He had disappeared. Val, Guy's story at MonMart that day was true. He actually invented something that makes a person disappear. Isn't that something?''

Val had been listening intently, but hearing the Kingsley name so unexpectedly made her choke on a swallow of wine. ''Wait a sec. Back up a bit. There's another Kingsley? I never heard of a Bridget Kingsley.''

''She's Bridget Plum now—for many years, to be accurate—but her maiden name was Kingsley. She talked about a split in the family between her father and Stratton—who were twins, incidentally. But she's lived in the area all her life. Imagine that.''

''Yes,'' Val murmured. ''Imagine that.'' What Jinni had said about Guy's invisibility, which Val had considered more myth than fact since the day she'd heard about it, entered her mind again. Was the whole town crazy? Maybe she wasn't the only kook living in Rumor. Wouldn't it be a hoot if the town she had chosen out of many, in which to live quietly and heal her wounds, had been chock-full of loose screws all along?

Chapter Eighteen

Reed sat in the dark. At 6:00 p.m. his living room wasn't completely black, but it was close, as the outside pole lights provided very little illumination inside, and they were the only ones burning anywhere on his property.

The day had been a total bust. He had awakened with a throbbing headache, not surprising considering the lousy night he'd put in. Instead of bounding out of bed full of energy and eager for the new day, as he normally did, he had dragged his weary bones to the bathroom, taken a couple of headache pills and then stumbled back to bed. He could not remember the last time he'd spent a self-pitying day in bed, or if he'd ever done something so out of character.

Around eight that morning he'd heard his phone ring four times and then his mother's voice when the answering machine switched on. "Reed, dear, you haven't missed morning coffee with us for so long, we've become a bit worried. Well, apparently you're not there, so something must have come up to take you away from home. Call when you can."

He had pulled the pillow over his head. There'd been a few other calls, a few other messages, and he'd ignored them, too.

Now, dressed in old sweats and staring dully into the darkness that felt so much better to his wounded pride and shattered ego than the bright light of day, he knew he had to pull himself together. He wasn't the first man to be used and abused by a woman, and he wouldn't be the last. So what if every cell in his body was crying out in agony? So what if he couldn't stop loving Val, even while telling himself that he never wanted to set eyes on her again?

A few minutes later the phone rang once more, four times. The answering machine switched on and Reed heard Derek Moore's voice. "Reed, sorry I missed you. I have the information you wanted and—"

Reed told himself he didn't give a damn now about Val's past, but still he leaped from his chair and made a dive for the telephone. "Derek, I'm here. What did you find out?"

"Reed, you said Valerie Fairchild was the name of your lady? The one you told me meant so much to you when we had dinner together in Billings?"

The strained note in Derek's voice caused Reed's stomach to lurch. Of course, he hadn't eaten anything all day, which could account for the discomfort, but instinct told him otherwise.

"Yes, that's her name," he said, speaking quietly, as though he was in full command of his faculties, when it wasn't true. He hadn't commanded anything all day and projecting strength he didn't feel was hard to do. "What's wrong, Derek?"

"How did you find out about Jay Johnson?"

"Never heard the name before. Who is he?"

"The man who raped your lady." Reed froze. Derek went on speaking. "He'll never get out of prison, Reed. Serial rapists are…"

Reed's own thoughts were suddenly louder than Derek's voice. Val had been raped the day that bastard had kept her in the pet shop with a gun in her face for sixteen hours? She hadn't even hinted at rape when she'd talked about the incident at her cabin on Friday night. Had she intended to and faltered because of something he'd said? Or hadn't said? Maybe he hadn't been supportive enough, and maybe support and encouragement were what she'd been seeking.

Oh, God. A shudder racked his body. Sex wasn't what she'd needed that night, and he'd let her down by behaving like a horny kid.

Derek's voice came through again. "Anyhow, you can see why I hesitated in telling you about it...unless you already knew, of course. Did you?"

"Uh, yes. She told me, Derek. What I didn't know was whether the...the, uh, guy was still incarcerated."

"He is and always will be. He's not in an ordinary prison, Reed. He's in a state institution for the criminally insane. The people I talked to said he would never be released. His brain is mush. From drugs."

When the call was over and Reed was back in his chair, once again staring into the darkness of his own living room, tears spilled from his eyes and rolled down his cheeks.

He no longer felt sorry for himself. All of his feelings were for Val...and so were the tears.

An hour later he decided to drive to town and get something to eat that he wouldn't have to fix himself. He could get that at his folks' place, but he didn't consider himself fit company for anyone, least of all his parents. His mother had a way of knowing with one look whether or not something was bothering him.

And yes, something was bothering him, something serious and painful that felt frighteningly permanent. In truth, he felt as though some alien creature was digging holes in his gut, and he suspected he would never be free of that particular pestilence for the rest of his life.

He did not foresee great happiness in his future and drove the familiar road to town with tightly drawn lips and a sorrowful heart. It was a cold, dark night and the asphalt was snow-free but icy in spots. He was almost in sight of Rumor when his emergency radio beeped loudly. He recognized the voice. "All volunteers report to the station at once. We have a fire."

Reed pushed the gas pedal a little harder.

Val was abnormally restless. She had felt anxious and nervous since Jinni went home, even during her trip to the kennels to make sure the thermostats were set correctly for the cold night ahead.

She hadn't shown Jinni the things she'd purchased in Billings's best shops. Once they had started talking about Guy's upcoming release from jail and what had brought it about, there'd been so much to say and think about that the rather trivial subject of new clothes had slipped by the wayside. Jinni was so relieved for Max, Michael, her mother-in-law, and, of course, Guy, although she barely knew him, that she had gone on and on about the Cantrells. Val had understood Jinni's bubbling happiness for her husband and in-laws, but there was no question that it had underscored Val's own flat and emotionless life.

Then Jinni'd left, and shortly afterward Val had suffered the strangest sensation, as if her own house were closing in on her. She'd told herself to stop imagining such ridiculous things, but found it nearly impossible.

By the time darkness had fallen Val was so unnerved she couldn't sit still. When she remembered the bags and packages in her bedroom she rushed through the house with a sense of relief; at least putting away her new clothes was something to do.

But when she turned on the ceiling light and looked at the pile of decorated sacks in all shapes and sizes, and the many garments in plastic bags that covered the bed, her relief turned to aversion. She had needed a few new things, but she'd gone way overboard.

"What does it matter?" she mumbled as she removed garments from wrappings and hung them in her closet or folded them into dresser drawers. Most of her purchases, she realized unhappily, were things she would probably never wear. Her style had become ultraconservative lately, and a switch to brightly colored, dramatically designed clothing would probably shock the town.

On the other hand, did people in this town notice Dr. Fairchild enough to see what she wore?

She sat on the bed, then fell back with her eyes closed and her heart thumping in her chest. She had hoped very much to fit in with the people of Rumor, but she never had, had she?

Her business was successful because she was a good vet, but she was a square peg in a round hole and couldn't seem to get beyond the most casual of friendships with any of the townsfolk she met. She had never blamed anyone else for her inability to draw warmth from others; it was a quality she'd once admired about herself and then lost on that dreadful day in the pet shop.

Val shuddered and sat up. She never let herself dwell on the awful details of that day. Not that she hadn't talked about them in the past. A number of therapists and psychologists had brought her face-to-face with every segment of that day, and she had gotten very good at rattling off disgusting facts with little emotion.

That was how she had lived ever since, she thought now, and no one had noticed or cared that she was an emotionless woman. In Rumor she'd been accepted as a capable vet, and possibly, at first, people had discussed her and wondered about her solitary lifestyle and somber demeanor. But the local gossips had become bored with Dr. Fairchild very fast. That, too, might be nothing but a figment of her imagination, Val knew. It was likely that no one in Rumor had *ever* wondered about her lack of a love life.

Then she'd come face-to-face with Reed Kingsley and he'd caused the first crack in her self-protective armor. It was just a small crack and she'd told herself to ignore it. It meant nothing as long as she didn't let it have meaning. That had worked…for a while…and it may have worked forever if she hadn't found that lump in her breast. That had set off a chain of events she hadn't been able to control with home-made remedies.

Was it weird of her to acknowledge that if she hadn't contracted cancer she would never have really known her sister? That assumption hinted at joy over a disease that could weaken the strongest person, and God knew she truly felt nothing remotely joyful about her ordeal.

But she had a sister now, and before Jinni had come flying to the rescue, all Val had had was a handful of memories.

She trembled and felt as though an earthquake was gathering force for a huge explosion within her. She would have to be completely numb not to realize that something odd was happening to her. She wasn't herself anymore, not the "emotionless self" she'd been since her final therapy session many years ago, at any rate.

She wasn't emotionless now, she realized between gasping breaths. Her emotions were shaking her soul, causing a flood of tears, stealing her breath and scaring the daylights out of her. What was going on?

She couldn't fight it, whatever it was, and she toppled over on the bed and cried until there were no more tears left in her. She lost track of time, but she finally felt calmer and got off the bed to wash her face. Her eyes were pink and puffy, she saw in the mirror, and she asked her reflection, "Were you crying over Jinni because you have her now or over Reed because you will never have him?"

Her mirror gave her no answer, nor was there an answer within her heart. Feeling saddened by it all, she went to the dresser and found the card Reed had tucked into the flowers he'd brought her. She read his message about wanting to sweet-talk her, read it again and decided the words didn't coincide with the man she'd come to know. He was far more intelligent than this silly message implied, so had she confused him so much that he'd been willing to try anything to gain her attention?

An unusual panic seized her, and she stumbled to the bedroom's one chair and sank onto it. Her heart was in her throat and she was breathing as though she had run a mile. Her eyes were huge and darting, as though she was seeking relief for the turmoil within herself from some inanimate object in her bedroom.

And then the truth of her feelings rose up and nearly choked her. *I ruined everything. Me. I did it all. I destroyed the one chance for everlasting happiness that fate practically hand-delivered to my front door. For the first time in all my years I am sincerely, genuinely in love, and I chased him off. Poor Reed.*

The telephone rang, jarring Val from the depths of hell that she had driven herself to. She stared at the phone on the bedstand, then sighed and forced herself to her feet.

"Hello," she said, sounding every bit as forlorn as she felt.

But Jinni didn't notice. "Val, come on over. We're celebrating Guy's release and we'd all love to have you here."

Val could barely hear her sister. Music and laughter, the sounds of a merry crowd, nearly drowned out Jinni's voice. "Hmm...I don't know, Jin. I'm really not in a party mood."

"If you were here, you would be. You wouldn't be able to stop yourself from joining in the fun. Come on, Val. Throw on something pretty and... Say, did you happen to buy something pretty today? I didn't get to see your new clothes."

"I...guess so."

"Well, get yourself all dolled up and come over! One of these lawyers having a fine old time with us is single!"

Val saw Reed's image in her mind's eye. As if she would flirt and act silly with a stranger when she was in love with a man of Reed Kingsley's caliber, she thought with a touch of pathos. Truth was, though, she didn't have Reed and never *would*.

"Val, you get yourself fancied up this very minute and come over here!" Jinni demanded teasingly.

Why not? Anything is better than sitting here and crying because your life is such an abominable, pathetic mess.

"All right. I'll be there in about twenty minutes," she said.

"Great! I'll be watching for you."

Val put down the telephone and went to the closet to decide on something to wear. Her heart wasn't into a party; the very idea turned her off. But so did sitting around this silent house, dissecting herself and wallowing in self-pity. She pulled out a velveteen dress in a luscious shade of blue-green that was very close to the color of her eyes. She had tried it on at the store and knew it fit like a dream. She had high-heel shoes to match, but she would wear her snow boots to get to the Cantrell mansion, and change shoes when she got there.

Her eyes were still a bit puffy, but she ignored that and quickly put on some makeup. She vigorously brushed her hair into place, fluffing it a bit more than usual, and finished off her outfit with small gold hoops in her ears and a light touch of cologne at her throat and wrists.

She was getting into her heavy black overcoat when she heard the sound. Her heart jumped into her throat with immediate dread. When the siren on the roof of the fire station called in the volunteers, there was a blaze somewhere in Rumor.

Val raced to a window at the front of the house. She could see the fire station, and it had come alive. Vehicles were arriving in droves. Drivers and passengers jumped out and hurried into the building.

And then Val saw the pickup truck Reed had been driving since his SUV got crumpled in the mountains. It skidded around the corner, fishtailed for a moment, then straightened out and finally turned into the parking area of the fire station. He got out and ran to the door of the building.

Val couldn't breathe. Just seeing him made her heart beat faster. Whatever it was that had been tearing her apart felt as though it had succeeded. She'd been split into two different women—Dr. Fairchild, who rarely smiled, and Valerie, a woman aching with love for the man across the intersection.

Val ran from the window to her front door and went outside. A fine snow was falling again, she noticed, but she didn't give a damn. Turning in a circle, she searched the horizon until she saw the reddish glow in the sky—the fire!

"Oh, no," she whispered. The glow was directly over a residential area.

The huge door of the fire station went up and out came the fire truck, its siren screaming, its numerous red lights flashing.

Val didn't stop to think. She ran back inside for her car keys, then raced through the back door to the garage. In seconds she was driving down the icy street, following the fire truck.

She parked in an out-of-the-way spot. People were gathering. The volunteers all wearing bright yellow jackets, were running, shouting, getting the hose unwound and working. Val knew a family lived in that house, the Stowes, and there were at least four young children to worry about.

"They're out!" someone shouted, and Val saw a woman, a man and the kids running from their burning home. Seconds later, however, the woman shrieked, "Where's Shannon? She isn't outside! Shannon! Shannon!" Mrs. Stowe began running back toward the house.

Her husband caught her and Val saw Reed run over to the couple. He said something to them, grabbed a blanket from someone's hands and headed for the house himself. Val's heart nearly stopped. One second his form was silhouetted in stark relief against the flames and the next he was gone, a part of the fire itself.

"Please God," she whispered over and over. The crowd had grown larger, and Val could hear everyone talking about Reed and little Shannon, who was only three years old.

The scene had a surreal quality for Val—the fairy-dust snow falling on her face, the brilliant colors of the fire, the families huddled together, the worried crowd conveying so much hope for the life of a child and a man with unlimited courage.

And then, without any fanfare whatsoever, Val felt a hundred pounds lighter, as though a crushing burden had flown from her shoulders. "My God," she whispered, stunned even while recognizing what had taken place. The side of her that had been fighting for dominance all day had overcome the staid, determined-to-be-unhappy personality she had permitted to direct her life for more than ten years.

Instantly, she knew she wanted what Jinni had—a man who loved her and a happy marriage—and what Mrs. Stowe had—a family. *And if you should succeed and the cancer comes back?* Val sucked in a breath as her heart skipped a beat. Would Reed love her unconditionally?

Her mind began racing. Did Reed love her now? He had loved her, or at least he had tried in numerous ways to make her believe that his feelings for her went deeper than sexual attraction. She sighed soulfully and noticed a dull ache in her chest that had to be caused by her heart breaking. Yes, it was all her fault, but she knew now that she had the courage to be honest with Reed. It would, of course, be up to him after that.

Her brutal self-analysis vanished when Reed reappeared. He had the blanket-wrapped child in his arms, and Val walked toward the Stowes, watching closely to see if the little girl was all right. Reed handed her to her sobbing mother.

"She's fine, Mrs. Stowe," he said. "She's just scared. I found her under the table in the laundry room."

"Oh, my baby!" Shannon peeked from under the blanket, looked at everyone staring at her, and then smiled. The relief of the crowd was almost tangible, and Val saw tears on more than one face.

Reed glanced in Val's direction, and he couldn't seem to stop looking. Nor could he prevent his legs from taking him toward her. She, too, began walking…toward him! He could barely swallow the massive lump in his throat. What was she doing here? Why was she looking at him with…dare he call her soft and womanly expression *affection?*

"Reed," she said after hiccuping away a sob.

"Val," he breathed huskily. "Do you know this family?"

"I…think so. But I'm here because of you. You're the most courageous person, the most wonderful man I've ever known and…and I'm in love with you."

He couldn't speak. His heart was pounding so loudly he could barely hear. He wanted to take her by the arm and lead her away from the fire, away from the crowd, but instead he said quietly, "I can't do this now. Go home. I'll come by."

The ache in Val's chest hung on, but something told her there was relief in sight. "Don't worry about the time," she said a bit raggedly, looking directly into his glorious green eyes. "I'll be waiting." She watched him hurry off. He had a fire to extinguish, a job to do, and she loved him for being the kind of man who cared so much for other people that he was forever rescuing someone from something.

Even from themselves, she thought as she returned to her car. If anyone had ever needed assistance in figuring out who she was, it was Dr. Valerie Fairchild. Without Reed, would it have ever happened?

She drove by the Cantrell mansion, congratulated Guy and the rest of the family, said hello to the punch-drunk lawyers—more like *champagne*-drunk lawyers, she thought drolly—then pulled Jinni into another room and explained why she wasn't staying.

"Reed's at the fire. Did you hear the sirens? Anyhow, he's coming by my place when it's out. I…I told him I'm in love with him," she said softly.

Jinni looked at her sister for a moment, got tears in her eyes and threw her arms around Val. "I'm so happy…so happy."

Val wasn't sure what she was. Scared, yes. Nervous, definitely. After all, just because she had finally faced her feelings for Reed didn't guarantee he still wanted her. She'd been terribly mean to him, and not all men could forgive the kind of treatment he'd received. The waiting was going to be terrible, but maybe she deserved to suffer for a few more hours.

It was close to midnight when Reed rang Val's doorbell. He was on an adrenaline high; she was in love with him. She had said it right to his face, and he believed her.

The door opened, he stepped inside, pulled her into his arms almost before she could say hi, and kicked the door shut with his foot. A second before his lips covered hers, he whispered, "I love you, too. How did this miracle happen?"

She didn't get to answer. One kiss followed another and then, as if by magic, they were in her bedroom. Earlier she had put on one of her luscious new nightgowns—one of the things she'd bought and then decided that she would probably never wear—a dark red satin gown with skinny straps. It was sexier than anything she'd worn for more years than she cared to admit.

Reed pushed the straps from her shoulders and watched the red satin slither down her body to the carpet. "You're so beautiful you take my breath away," he told her.

This time she believed his compliment was heartfelt and she brought him to her bed. "You set me free," she whispered between kisses.

He raised his head to look into her eyes. Recalling what Derek had told him, he made a decision. He would never talk about what he knew of that terrible day unless Val did first. He'd fallen hard for her the first time he'd set eyes on her, and maybe it was because he'd known instinctively that she had needed him…or someone like him.

No, definitely not someone *like* him. Only him, just him. She had needed Reed Kingsley and now she had him, just as he had needed her and now he had her.

He would ask her to marry him before morning. And if she dared to wriggle around a straightforward "Yes" by talking about the possibility of her becoming ill again, he would kiss her until she gave in. Marriage was for better or worse, in sickness and in health, and it was time she understood that he took those vows seriously.

Of course, there were a few questions for which he'd like answers, such as the reason she'd invited him over on that fateful Friday night and then taken off for her mountain cabin.

Whatever answers he unearthed, there was no question in his mind about his life taking a major upswing tonight.

As for Val, if she had been any more ebullient she might have sailed away to never-never land. She giggled at the thought, then snuggled closer to her beloved. They would talk; she had so many things to say to him, but that could wait until later.

After all, they had the rest of their lives to talk.

Within days, Rumor, Montana, was in the news—big time. The media—representatives of major newspapers and television networks—descended upon the small town, and everywhere one looked there were TV trucks and vehicles with out-of-state license plates. Journalists, photographers and technical people crowded the town's few restaurants, and the reporters interviewed anyone who would talk to them.

Guy Cantrell couldn't stick his nose out of his own house without being accosted. "Mr. Cantrell, did you really invent an invisibility formula?"

"What are you going to do with it?"

"Have you been offered enormous sums of money?"

The questions were endless, and finally Guy asked Max to arrange a press conference so he could say his piece. He hoped that would be the end of it.

It was held in the high school gymnasium, and what space wasn't taken up by news people was used by the locals.

Guy walked to the podium. The flashbulbs and lights nearly blinded him. He put one hand on each side of the stand and blinked at the crowd. When the noise subsided, he cleared his throat and spoke.

"I'm a science teacher and amateur inventor. I was working on a formula for the quick healing of burns when I accidentally discovered the side effect of...of invisibility.'' Dozens of shouted questions suddenly echoed in the gym. Guy held up his hand. ''Please, let me finish. While I believe my invention could be of great benefit in the healing process of severe burns, it is also very dangerous, and I will not release the formula to the world until I have figured out what part of it causes the invisibility. That's all I have to say on the subject. Good day.'' He left the podium and began leaving the stage.

''Hey, wait a minute,'' someone yelled. ''We heard you were offered millions from a bunch of pharmaceutical companies for that formula. Did you turn all of them down?''

Guy stopped and faced the audience again. ''Yes, and I will continue to do so. Please inform the public that this formula is not safe, nor is it for sale. I am not sure how it works, and until I am it will not be passed on to anybody.''

''That could be dangerous in itself, Mr. Cantrell,'' a female voice called. ''Don't you understand that unscrupulous people might stop at nothing to get their hands on a magic potion that causes invisibility?''

Guy frowned, giving everyone the impression that no, he had not even thought of such a thing. ''I pray that doesn't happen,'' he finally said, and disappeared behind the curtain.

''Is that man living in the dark ages?'' one reporter asked another.

''Nope. He's living in Rumor, Montana,'' the second man quipped.

They walked out laughing.

* * * * *

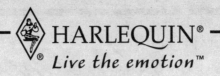

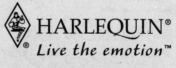

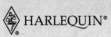

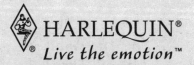

HARLEQUIN®
INTRIGUE®

BREATHTAKING ROMANTIC SUSPENSE

Shared dangers and passions lead to electrifying
romance and heart-stopping suspense!

Every month, you'll meet six new heroes
who are guaranteed to make your spine tingle
and your pulse pound. With them you'll enter
into the exciting world of Harlequin Intrigue—
where your life is on the line
and so is your heart!

THAT'S INTRIGUE—
ROMANTIC SUSPENSE
AT ITS BEST!

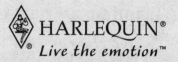

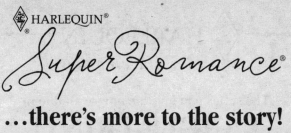

HARLEQUIN®

Super Romance®

...there's more to the story!

Superromance.
A *big* satisfying read about unforgettable
characters. Each month we offer *six* very different
stories that range from family drama to adventure
and mystery, from highly emotional stories to
romantic comedies—and much more! Stories
about people you'll believe in and care about.
Stories too compelling to put down....

Our authors are among today's *best* romance
writers. You'll find familiar names and talented
newcomers. Many of them are award winners—
and you'll see why!

If you want the biggest and best
in romance fiction, you'll get it
from Superromance!

Exciting, Emotional, Unexpected...

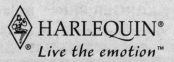

HARLEQUIN®

Live the emotion™

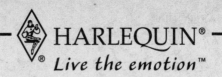

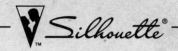

SPECIAL EDITION™

Emotional, compelling stories that capture the intensity of living, loving and creating a family in today's world.

Desire

Modern, passionate reads that are powerful and provocative.

nocturne

Dramatic and sensual tales of paranormal romance.

Romantic SUSPENSE

Romances that are sparked by danger and fueled by passion.

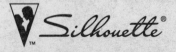